*She gazed up at him,
so breathtakingly handsome,
so clever and well spoken.*

It wasn't just the moonlight and the strange spell he seemed to cast over her. Moonlight, daylight, gaslight, or morning light, wherever she saw him, she liked the look of him. She loved the sound of his voice, his mouth tasted wonderful to her, he even smelled good to her.

So what if she didn't know him better? She was levelheaded, never one to leap into anything, no matter what the lure. And she knew there'd be time enough during their engagement for her to find out more about him.

One thing she knew above all. She dared not let him go. Where on earth would she ever meet his like again?

"Come, Eve," he whispered. "Let go of harsh reality. Life's an adventure. Step into one, with me."

Other **AVON ROMANCES**

A Dangerous Beauty *by Sophia Nash*
The Highlander's Bride *by Donna Fletcher*
The Templar's Seduction *by Mary Reed McCall*
Tempted at Every Turn *by Robyn DeHart*
Too Scandalous to Wed *by Alexandra Benedict*
A Warrior's Taking *by Margo Maguire*
What Isabella Desires *by Anne Mallory*

Coming Soon

Seduction Is Forever *by Jenna Petersen*
Sin and Scandal in England *by Melody Thomas*

And Don't Miss These
ROMANTIC TREASURES
from Avon Books

Bewitching the Highlander *by Lois Greiman*
How to Engage an Earl *by Kathryn Caskie*
Just Wicked Enough *by Lorraine Heath*

EDITH LAYTON

BRIDE ENCHANTED

AVON

An Imprint of HarperCollinsPublishers

AVON BOOKS
An Imprint of HarperCollins*Publishers*
10 East 53rd Street
New York, New York 10022-5299

Copyright © 2007 by Edith Felber
ISBN: 978-0-06-125362-1
ISBN-10: 0-06-125362-6
www.avonromance.com

First Avon Books paperback printing: September 2007

Avon Trademark Reg. U.S. Pat. Off. and in Other Countries, Marca Registrada, Hecho en U.S.A.
HarperCollins® is a registered trademark of HarperCollins Publishers.

Printed in the U.S.A.

10 9 8 7 6 5 4 3 2 1

To brand-new Hugo Norbert Holland,
my brand-new hero.

Acknowledgments

To Gillian Roginsky, whose delicious tales of her youth in England always inspire me.

BRIDE ENCHANTED

Chapter 1

Good lord, but he was beautiful. Not the right word for such a masculine man. Not exactly the wrong one either. He moved like a freshening breeze through a field of ripened grain as he crossed the crowded ballroom. Bodies shifted to form a path, voices murmuring in his wake. Bright as the sun and cool as deep water. He was, Eve thought, surely the most handsome man she'd ever clapped eyes on. But what was odd was that his brilliant dark brown gaze seemed fixed only upon her.

Eve turned her head to see whom he was staring at as he approached. The sea of transfixed females standing behind and beside her on the fringes of the dance floor didn't offer a clue. Dewy miss to dowager, they were all staring at him. So she turned back to get a closer look at the newcomer, the fascinating Aubrey Ashford, before he passed her by.

He was everything they said, but much more so: tall, lithe, and graceful. Well dressed, of course, in immaculate linen, a high neckcloth, a dark tightly fitted jacket stretched over his wide shoulders, and formal breeches and stockings that showed off straight, strong legs. But it was his face that stopped her breath. He had thin dark brows arched over watchful eyes. His complexion was smooth, his dark hair slightly overlong, his cheekbones high, his mouth classical. A pronounced chin was the only thing that gave that glorious countenance a slight imperfection, making it seem a bit more human than a face seen in marble in a museum. And so, far more accessible.

He stopped, directly in front of her.

Eve was caught in his steady gaze. She wondered vaguely if she should move aside. She was too enthralled, head back, staring at him, to think clearly. She tried to shake herself to action so she could step away. She was many things, but not a ninny.

She was Eve Faraday, a woman of three and twenty, and no fool. She was a bit too short for fashion, though a little too tall to be called a "pocket Venus." She was wearing a charming gown tonight, in green, her favorite color. Her figure was slender, with just enough bosom to do justice to the low neckline, but she knew it wasn't spectacular. Her short wavy curls were brown. Her eyes were brown. She'd been called an "imp" by her father and a "pixie" when she grew older. She'd had beaux and never propped up the walls at a ball.

But she knew very well she wasn't a raving beauty or in fashion. She wasn't a swan-necked beauty like Miss Simpson, standing nearby. Or a classic English lovely like blond, pink-cheeked Miss Lord, or dark-haired and exotic like Miss Lake, the current rage of the Season.

Although her family was well to do, she wasn't fabulously rich or titled. And everyone in the *ton* knew this gentleman before her was from an old family, and said to be incredibly wealthy. Mr. Aubrey Ashford didn't need her family's money. So there was absolutely no reason for him to be standing still, looking down at her, and smiling. He'd recently returned to Town after a long absence. Maybe he mistook her for someone else?

"Miss Faraday?" he said in a soft, melodious voice.

She nodded, unable to speak.

"I couldn't wait to find someone to introduce us. I am Ashford. May I have this dance?"

She blinked. "Why?" she blurted.

He smiled. "Because I wish to dance with you."

"Oh," she said.

He offered her his arm.

She took it, and dazed, stepped into the dance with him.

They were playing a waltz. She was glad for two reasons. One, that she was old enough to have permission to dance it with him. And two, if she was not many things, she was, at least, a good dancer.

But while she was good, he was sublime. They moved around the floor as though dancing on air. Yet she didn't forget they were on earth. She couldn't, not in his arms. He was cool and yet warm, distant, and yet somehow he made her feel as though he was concentrating on her alone. He wore gloves, as was proper, but the touch of his hand on hers and the feeling of his other hand at her waist made her whole body tingle.

She caught a sudden scent, leaned closer, and inhaled. Yes, the glorious fragrance of sweet grasses and deep woods emanated from him. Most men wore lavender or sandalwood, if they wore any scent at all. He smelled of the whole spring earth. He smiled to see her nostrils widen. She opened her eyes, saw his expression, and embarrassed, moved away as much as the dance allowed.

All the while they danced he smiled down at her. She avoided his gaze because she didn't know how to respond. So she let herself move with him and the music and found herself feeling treasured and excited, anxious and yet thrilled by how well they moved together. She wished she were the swan-necked Miss Simpson or the exotic Miss Lake. But she was who she was, and so resolved to enjoy the dance until she had to stop and face reality again.

She was both glad and sad when the music ended. He walked her to the sidelines, but didn't leave her side.

"They're playing a country dance now," he remarked. "I think I'll wait until the next waltz before we dance again."

"You're going to ask me again?" she managed to say.

"Of course."

Now, suddenly, she once again became aware of herself and her surroundings. She gathered her wits. She had to know. "Why me?" she asked, tilting her head to the side. "I'm flattered, of course. But also puzzled. We're in a room filled with beautiful, rich, and educated females just perishing to be asked by you. Now, what's the jest, please?" Her tilted brows came down as a thought occurred to her. "Oh. I think I see. Was it a friend of the family? No!" she gasped, aghast. "Was it my brother? Did you lose a wager with him?"

He laughed. It sounded so gloriously merry she had to stop herself from laughing with him. "No," he said.

She frowned.

"Miss Faraday, I find you enchanting," he said. "Though I hope for more, much more in the future, I wish to take my second dance with you now, since that's all that is allowed to me. Please be at ease with me, unless you've taken me in dislike. I also wish to call upon your father, and ask to pay my addresses to you."

She gaped at him. His eyes were sparkling, dancing with dark light. But he didn't seem to be joking. She frowned again. "Pay your addresses to *me*? On such sudden acquaintance? But why?"

"You need ask?" he said. "After our dance?"

"The point is," she said, ignoring his questions, "the point is," she repeated, tearing her gaze from his, forcing her thoughts into line, "that I honestly don't know why you'd want to."

"Then let me show you," he said.

Eve paced her father's study. Then she stopped and wheeled around to confront her father. "He didn't say anything else?"

Her father ducked his head. "He asked permission to pay his addresses and I said yes," he reported again.

"And you didn't ask him why?" she asked, amazed.

He looked hunted. But that meant nothing. When it came to his children, Malcolm Faraday always looked as though he'd done the wrong thing, because he never was quite sure if he had.

He was a good man, but not a thoughtful one. He sat hunched in his chair: a tall, bland-looking, middle-aged man who seemed to have the weight of the world on his shoulders. He did, Eve supposed, with a wayward son and a clever daughter to raise by himself, all these years. A widower for decades, he'd never remarried, or professed any desire to do so. Her mother had been a forceful female, and one hard to replace.

Malcolm Faraday's primary love was fishing, and going round to the local inn to drink and brag about his catch and listen to his cronies do the same. But they were in Town now. So now his first love was his club, a glass of something bracing, a crackling fire in the hearth, and old friends to chat with. He didn't ask much from life, but his children always asked for things he didn't think he had: worldly wisdom and good advice.

"Why?" he answered finally. "Well, because you're a fine-looking girl, pretty as a picture and with a good head on your shoulders. And a nice body to hold it up," he added, his cheeks turning a bit pink.

"That's what he said?" she asked, relentlessly.

"Ah, no," he said miserably.

"He just asked for my hand?"

"And I said it was fine with me, if you suited," he said with more energy. "I added that you were a girl of firm convictions, and that I'd never force you to anything . . . even if I could," he added in a low murmur.

"You told him that last bit?" she asked.

"No," he admitted sadly. Then he perked up. "But why are you so angry, Evie? He's top of the trees. Talk of the Town. Even *I* heard of him. He's got looks, money, and brains. He's sophisticated, with the manners of an angel. Charming too. Even I think so, and I don't much notice charming gentlemen. Well, none of my friends are. And he isn't annoying, or foppish either. He's a man, with manners. So why are you carrying on when you should be dancing? Do you know something about him I don't? I won't have you marrying a cheat or a blackguard," he said with less conviction, because he realized he knew he had little to say about it if her mind were set.

"No," she said, plopping down into a chair facing him. "But can you think of any reason such a fellow would fall head over heels for *me*? And after just two dances? It doesn't make sense; at least, I can't make sense of it. Can you?"

"Easy. It's your sweetness and good temper that transfixed him," her brother, Sheridan, said as he strolled into the room. "Not hardly," he laughed. He sobered. "Lord! So you hooked Ashford? *The* Ashford? How did you do it?" He dropped into a chair, arranged his lanky form to his comfort, and looked at her with wonder. He was nineteen, bright, taller than his father, and no more studious; well enough looking, but no more spectacularly handsome than his sister was beautiful. And he was both as obnoxious and darling to her as the little boy she'd always loved, though his arrival had taken away their mother.

"I don't know about him being 'hooked,'" she said slowly, staring at him. "I asked why he was interested in me. He denied anyone but me influencing him. Did *you* have anything to do with this, Sherry?"

"Me?" he asked, astonished. "Why would an eagle look at a worm? I'm nowhere near his class. I'm a carefree lad and I know it, and I've just come down from University for the summer. I don't know anyone in London but my old mates. I couldn't influence a London rat, much less a fellow like Ashford. We don't go to the same places. Lud!

It's hard to believe we exist on the same planet. I doubt he knows of my existence."

"Well, I didn't think he knew of mine," she said seriously. "Yet he ups and as much as proposes after *one* dance, and then visits Papa to ask his consent after two? There's something shady about this, don't you agree, Sherry?"

"Yes," her brother said with heartbreaking honesty.

His father gave him a sharp look. Malcolm Faraday wasn't a strict man, but he'd never let one of his children hurt another.

"Not that you ain't pretty," her brother said quickly. "But what's pretty to a gent like that?"

Eve waved away her brother's comment. She knew him too well to think he was trying to hurt her feelings. He had, but even though it destroyed her hopeful fantasies, the statement at least cleared the last vestiges of doubt from her mind. There was no reason for the gentleman's sudden offer.

"You'll have to step out with him, old girl," Sheridan said merrily, "Find out what's to do. It's positively Gothic! Like one of those Minerva Press novels you used to read. What fun! Maybe our house has got a fabulous hidden treasure he found out about? Panels in the walls or secret parts of the basements, or something buried in the garden what? . . ." He stroked his beardless chin.

"Or it could be that you saw something you don't remember that could be bad for him if you did. I say, go with him, talk to him, but watch what you eat or drink in his presence. Keep company until you know what's up. But watch your back, my dear sister."

No, Eve thought sadly, *it's my heart I have to be careful of*, as she said, "Yes, I agree. And I'm going to find out, don't you worry."

Chapter 2

Eve was ready to see the man who had asked to court her. She thought she couldn't look better. Her green gown, sashed with rose and patterned with tiny yellow roses, was her best. A darling new bonnet covered her curly hair, and she held a green parasol, for support. Because although she was ready, it was the sort of readiness she might feel before jumping off a high wall. She thought she'd land right, but there was always the possibility she'd come to grief. She didn't want to break anything, particularly not her heart.

She had to see him. She *wanted* to see him. The whole thing disturbed her because the more she thought about it, the less sense it made. She feared it was a joke. She was afraid it wasn't. She stood by the front parlor window, a margin of the drape pulled back an inch so she could see the street, but no one in the street could see her. She waited, her expression already schooled to be polite and bland. She couldn't be more ready, or more terrified. She had to gather her courage and speak bluntly with him to find out why he was courting her.

Surely, they could speak more easily if she wasn't as surprised and overawed by him as she'd been last time. Definitely, she could talk more rationally if they weren't dancing. And certainly, he'd be less exotic by daylight.

He wasn't.

Her brother, who had walked soft-footed to stand behind her, whistled. Her shoulders jumped and she swung around, one hand on her rapidly beating heart. "Don't do that!" she whispered fiercely. "You frightened me half out of my wits! What are you whistling about anyway?" she asked crossly.

"You ask? Look at him," he said.

She did. Mr. Aubrey Ashford was something to see. He handed the reins for the two beautiful matched chestnuts that drew his high-perch phaeton to the boy who had jumped down from the back of it. Then he looked up at the house. He was immaculately dressed in a brown jacket, with dun breeches and shining boots, and a high beaver hat perched jauntily on his black hair. He carried a silver-headed walking stick. Never had a man looked less in need of one. He wasn't sportsman tan, or poetic pallid. Instead, he glowed. He paused. She could swear his gaze arrowed to where she was. A small smile quirked his shapely mouth, and he strode forward. She dropped the corner of the drapery and tried to catch her breath.

"Damnation!" she breathed. "He looks better in the light!"

Her brother frowned.

"Look at him," she said crossly. "Now why would *that* come courting me?"

"Maybe he has some disgusting habits?" Sheridan asked.

She gave him a withering look.

"Well, if he don't, then I agree," Sheridan said heartlessly. "It don't make sense. You have to find out. Maybe he did lose a bet."

She nodded, feeling better and worse at having her fears confirmed. She drew on her gloves. "You can bet I will," she said shakily.

"Mr. Aubrey Ashford," their butler said, coming into the front salon.

The man behind him walked into the room, smiled at Sheridan, looked searchingly at Eve, and then executed a graceful bow. "Good morning, Miss Faraday," he said in his melodious voice.

She stood still, barely managing to remember to nod a bow to him. Sheridan just stared at him.

"I am Ashford. You are . . . ?" he asked Sheridan, raising a thin black eyebrow.

"This is my brother, Sheridan," Eve said.

Sheridan bowed, while staring, like an automaton.

"Then do call me Aubrey. Pleased to make your acquaintance, Sheridan," Aubrey said.

That seemed to break the spell. "That's a bang-up rig you have there," Sheridan said eagerly. "Your team looks like prime goers too."

"Thank you," Aubrey said. "I'm pleased with them. And I thank you again because you give me an easy way to make my proposal."

Sister and brother went still again, eyes wide.

Aubrey smiled. "Since it was such a fine day, Miss Faraday, I thought we might go for a ride around the park."

"Oh," she said with relief. *That* kind of proposal. She thought about it. It was a way to get away from her brother's insatiable curiosity. He'd be sitting between them all morning if he could. But it was also unnerving to think of being alone with Ashford. Still, because of the things she had to say, she decided it was for the best. "Why, yes, so it is a lovely day," she said. "I'd be delighted. But will there be room for my maid?"

"If not," Sheridan put in hurriedly, "I can hang on to the back."

"But we'll be driving in an open phaeton," Aubrey said. "And so there's no need for a chaperone, Miss Faraday. Even the strictest arbiter of fashion can't think anything wrong in us tooling around London in an open carriage. We won't stop, I promise you, not even if my horse throws a shoe. And we'll have my tiger hanging on the back, Mr. Faraday. I'm afraid your additional weight would overbalance us. What if I take you out and let you try the reins another day?"

Sheridan looked like an excited puppy, Eve thought with disgust. If he had a tail it would be wagging.

"Yes, thanks!" Sheridan said. "And call me Sheridan, that is, Sherry. Everyone does."

"I will, and I'll be glad to let you run my team through its paces. That is," Aubrey added, with a glance from under his long dark lashes at Eve, "if your sister finds me fit company."

"That," Eve said crossly, forgetting her awe of the man, "is nothing more than blackmail, sir."

"Yes!" Aubrey laughed. "Exactly. Shall we go?"

They drove off into the heart of London.

"Yes, I agree," Aubrey said pleasantly after a while, as he steered his team around a corner. "London is enough to render anyone awestruck, not to mention dumbstruck."

Eve turned her head to look at him from under

the brim of her bonnet, and under her eyelashes, as though the sun was blinding her. She *was* blinded, in a way. She couldn't look at the way the sunlight teased dark moonbeams from his hair, showed the texture of his perfect skin, and mostly, showed the sparkle deep in his eyes.

"I'm not awestruck by the City," she said grudgingly. "Or dumbstruck. I'm accustomed to London. We always stay at our town house in Season. At least we have for the last several years. This isn't my first Season, you know."

"I do. More's the luck for me," he said fervently. "But you see, this is my first Season here in London in a long time. I've been living in Italy and touring the Continent whenever it's not at war with itself."

"Watch the road!" she said in alarm, as another coach came toward them from the other direction. She took a deep breath as he deftly moved their carriage to the side and looked at her, one brow lifted.

"I promise you I won't spill us into a ditch."

"It's not that," she said. "I'm quiet because I'm nervous. I'm thinking of how to say what I must say to you."

"Say away," he said. "I'm hard to offend."

"Well, I don't mean to offend you," she said in a rush, "but none of this makes any sense. You offered for my hand. After two dances."

"Yes. I'm a fellow who knows his mind," he said mildly, as he steered into the park.

"All very well for you," she said, staring at him directly. "But *me*? Please. Let us be realistic. I'm not vastly rich or titled. I'm certainly not a siren. I'm not spectacular in any fashion. I know my assets, and they are my mind. I mean, my brain. And at that, there are females who are smarter than I am as well. Mind, I'm not ugly. I do have my moments, and have had suitors, but why the most glittering fellow in the London social world should ask for my hand upon clapping eyes on me, I do not know. Nor does my father, or brother, and they really love me.

"Not glittering," she corrected herself. "That's tawdry. You're not that. You glow. You know it too. Now, please, before we go on with this farce: why me, why this?"

She sat back, feeling lighter, and light-headed too. He'd slowed the horses as they went down a single lane through the park, and was staring at her. And she was staring back, enchanted.

It was his eyes, she thought. They had deep hidden depths; more rich chocolate than mere brown, with starry lighter brown striations that ringed their centers.

"Because," he finally said, pulling up in the shade of an ancient tree. "Precisely because you are the only woman I know who would say such things about yourself."

"Piffle," she said, and wished she had the courage to say something stronger. "Hogwash," she added.

"Because though you underrate your looks, they give me great pleasure," he said, smiling. "Everything about you uplifts my spirits. Did you know your nose tilts up? Of course, I suppose you do. But did you know the bow of your lips tilts upward too? And your breasts, they also tilt provocatively . . ."

She gasped.

He fell still, but grinned.

She settled herself and gave him a gimlet-eyed stare. "Rot," she said. "There are dozens of females with tilted eyes and noses and whatnot. Try again. You know," she mused aloud, "the more you speak, the less enchanted I become."

"And because of that," he said.

She stared at him, crossing her arms over her chest. It was true. He no longer glowed. Not that he wasn't still wondrous to look at, but her anger was working like the wind blowing away the morning mists.

He cocked his head to the side. "You don't believe me?"

"Not by half. Look you, Mr. Ashford, you have

your pick of women here in London, and I suspect in Paris and Rome and, and—in Zululand too, for all I know. Mind you, I may not be a great beauty, but I'm content with what I am. Still, I know I'm not the kind of a female a man like you would single out in a crowd. Or even a small gathering. No sense beating around the bush. I won't be angry if you tell me the truth. Was it a wager? A test? Some kind of a jest? Whatever, tell me, and let's be done with it."

"You look wonderful when you growl," he said.

Her eyes narrowed. She wanted to throw her parasol at him, the pointed end first. He laughed and put up a hand in surrender. "All right," he said. "The truth is that I saw you, and you reminded me of someone I once knew."

"Oh," she said, growing quieter. "Someone you loved?"

"I was too young for that kind of love but, yes, I suppose, that's it too."

"Oh," she said again. "A relative of mine? I don't look much like my mother, as I recall. Or my father, for that matter. Maybe one of my cousins? I have distant cousins everywhere."

"Not your mother, not a cousin. The lady I recall is long gone. But I can't forget her. Do you mind?" he asked, watching her closely. "You look like the woman I was looking for. It's true that I don't know who you are. But tell me: how is a man to get to know a woman in your world if he doesn't keep company with her? If we talk too long at a party or any kind of social occasion, the gossips will have it that we're involved anyway. I can't dance more than two dances with you. The only way to get to know you is to become engaged to you."

She tilted her head to the side, again, considering this. She held up one finger. "But what if I didn't suit you, and I turned out to not be the kind of female you wanted?"

"Did you say yes to my offer?" he asked with amusement.

"No, I didn't say anything. That's why we're driving out today, to talk and to meet each other. And as to that, I certainly don't know if I will say yes," she said, sitting up straighter.

"And so I thought. And so where's the harm?" he asked, picking up the reins again.

"But what if I were the kind of woman who held you to your offer?" she insisted.

"I knew you weren't," he said.

"How?" she persisted.

"I have excellent judgment," he said, sounding a little bored.

His sounding displeased grated on her ears,

suddenly she wanted desperately to be in his good favor again. She mentally shook herself. It shouldn't matter that the fellow had a magnificent profile, a magnetic personality, and a melodious voice. But it did.

Still, who was he? What did he want? Should she believe his faradiddle about her resembling the woman he was seeking?

"Let me tell you a little about myself," he said.

And he did, as they drove round the park in the dappled sunlight. He told her about his estate in the countryside and made it sound beautiful and magical. He told her about his travels and made her laugh and sigh. He told her so much she had trouble taking it all in, and soon just sat, wide-eyed, charmed by his storytelling skill, lulled by his voice, pleased at the attention he was paying her, and slowly, but surely, wanting to move closer to him. She watched his wonderful face and found herself wanting to feel his breath in her ear, and feel the beating of his heart next to hers.

She knew what sexual attraction was, of course. She'd felt it for a stable boy when she was twelve, and a neighbor when she was thirteen, and Douglas McKenzie when she was sixteen. The stableboy had kissed her once, and that had been fine. Her neighbor had trapped her in the butler's pantry one night when she'd been visiting, and pressed an openmouthed kiss on her. She'd kicked him and stalked away, and that was fine too, because he'd been married. And Douglas had kissed her several times, and then rode off to war, and had never come back. He hadn't been killed, only married to a woman he'd met in Spain while recuperating from a war wound. It hadn't broken her heart. She hadn't been sure Douglas was good for much more than kissing. But she'd been very annoyed because he hadn't come back to her.

Eve had felt twinges of yearning since. But once she was of marriageable age, she'd controlled her desires. Now a stolen kiss could lead to marriage, and she wanted to be entirely sure of the man she finally wed. So she'd learned to suppress desire, and found that it wasn't that hard to do. Until now.

What could she make of Aubrey Ashford now? Except for the fact that so much as he lured her, she knew, deep down, that he was far too much for her, and she trusted nothing about him, from the top of his handsome head to his elegantly shod toes. Still, she couldn't help thinking about what his kiss would be like. He had such a beautiful mouth, such elegant manners, such a strong warm body. And surely, when he kissed, he'd close those knowing eyes, and she'd be more comfortable, not worrying about the notion that he was looking into her very soul.

The very idea of kissing him both thrilled and frightened her. He was not for her, though he insisted he was. Such a man could never be faithful, would never be constant. But he was such a man!

From time to time she shook herself free of her fascination and asked him questions. She hardly listened to his answers.

But as time went by she felt the need to be her own creature intruding on her pleasure in his company, and began to feel foolish and childish because of the way he so totally seduced her senses.

She shook her head to clear it. She felt like she was struggling out of a long, warm, pleasant dream. "Lord!" she said. "You can tell a story! So here I am, sitting mumchance, listening like a babe in its cot being lulled to sleep. No wonder you're so popular. I think you could have gone on the stage and made your fortune."

"But I already have one," he said mildly. "I told you about it, but you didn't seem interested."

She shrugged. "I'm happy for you that you're not in need, but not only is asking about funds vulgar, in truth, it didn't interest me. If we were going to be wed, I'd have to know. As for now, I don't. You know," she said, tipping her head to the side and considering him, "you've entertained me wonderfully well. But I can't say I know one more thing about you than I did before we set out on this drive."

"You are certainly not enchanted by me," he said ruefully.

But she did feel easier with him. "Well," she said, as a jest, "I do prefer blond gentlemen."

He looked surprised for the first time since she'd met him.

She smiled. "If *you* can actually ask for a stranger's hand in marriage because she reminds you of someone long gone and not find that odd, why should my preference in a fellow's coloring be considered trivial?"

"Right," he said with a crooked smile. "I'll have my hair dyed instantly. Gold or silver? Which do you prefer?"

She laughed. "Neither. You are who you are. As I am who I am. If we are to continue seeing each other . . . are we, by the way?"

"I hope so," he said.

"Then I'd like you to remember that I am myself, and not your lost lady."

He nodded. "I shall. Believe me, I shall. Now. Another tour of the park? I think we just have time to miss the rain I see approaching from the west."

"Yes," she said, sitting back, feeling very pleased with herself.

She asked a few more questions, he told her some more tales. Whenever she looked at his face and he turned his head to look at her, she had to glance away. Because the longer the time she passed with him, the more she wanted to be closer to him. As they rounded the last street to her house, she realized that she couldn't remember having a better time with a gentleman. She'd had a delightful morning with him. But she still didn't know him.

"I know," he said, as they drew up to the curb in front of her house. "I see it from your expression. Somehow, I've disappointed you."

"I still don't know you," she said with a slight frown.

He laughed. He stood, gave the reins to the boy who was his tiger, jumped down from his high perch, came around and held out his hand to Eve to help her down. "Good. Now you'll have to see me again. I may not know everything about you either, but I can easily see that curiosity is your besetting sin."

She stood, took his hand, and looked down at him. She paused. "You think curiosity is a sin?"

His face sobered. "I don't know what a sin is, exactly. I do know there are more than the seven deadly ones the priests go on about. But I'd wager my soul, if I have one, that curiosity isn't one of them."

She took his hand. "You don't know if you have a soul?"

"A figure of speech," he said, laughing. "Do I look like one of the undead? Or a devil?"

She stepped down and stood looking up at him, then said, "Undead? You must have been reading Monk Lewis or Mrs. Radcliffe's gothic novels. But no, never undead. A devil?" She cocked her head to the side. "Perhaps."

His smile was genuine. "Now *that*, my dear Eve, I can promise you I am not."

"And so you are . . .?"

"Your devoted servant," he said. His expression grew tender, and he took her hand in both of his. "Ah, Eve, what a courtship this will be. I'll have to beguile you a dozen different ways. Because I very much fear if you saw how ordinary my ambitions are, I'd bore you. I want to marry you. I'm convinced you're the woman for me.

"For some reason you don't trust me. I aim to change that. And if I have to do it by telling nothing but the truth, so I will. But you will allow me to embroider it a bit, won't you?"

She nodded, too busy thinking about how warm and strong his hands felt as he grasped hers to come up with a quick witty answer.

"You will see me again?" he asked.

"You know that," she said.

"But you won't say you'll marry me."

She drew herself up, and took her hands from his. "No. I don't know you," she said. "And I'm not a fool. Marriage is forever."

He hesitated, a faraway look in his eyes. "Nothing is forever. As close to forever is good enough for me." He straightened. "Tomorrow evening then? I've an invitation to a ball."

"I'm engaged for tomorrow night," she said with real regret.

"Then the night after? I've been invited everywhere. We can go to a musicale. Decent musicians will be there. After that? There's a ball in London every night this Season."

"You can't mean to see me every night?"

"I can," he said. "And do. How else are we to know each other?"

"I don't believe in rushing into anything," she said, drawing back.

"Reasonable," he said. "But how are you to get to know me? All right, if you have reservations, we can at least ride in the afternoons; and surely I can join you for tea, can I not?"

"Yes," she said meekly.

He took a small notebook from his pocket. "And so what about a ball too? Say, a week from next Saturday evening? It might be even more amusing. You'll have a week to get ready. You should know me even better by then. It's a costume ball. Will you come with me?"

"Yes," she said, bemused. "That does sound like fun. What will you dress as? Do you want me to match you?"

"Yes, I want you to match me," he said, looking into her eyes. "But however you dress will be right for me. Because you are."

She scowled. This was too much passion, too soon.

He nodded. "A misstep, yes. Too much, too soon. We'll speak more about it as time goes on. Until tomorrow night then."

He bowed, and left her at her door.

She looked after him as he strode back to his phaeton. She watched until he disappeared, still as wary as she was fascinated.

Chapter 3

She leaned forward in her chair, a smile on her lips; her eyelashes fluttering, though beneath them her eyes were fastened on his as she drank in his every word and watched his every expression as though experiencing a religious revelation. Eve wanted to shake her.

But Lucinda Thompson was her best friend in London. They'd met at a party and found something in common when they realized that Society had decided they'd both stayed a bit long on the shelf. Neither was as yet four and twenty, but young women in London Society had to be plucked fresh from the ranks of the eligible, or else people started whispering. Eve didn't care. Lucinda did.

And now, on her visit to Eve this morning, Lucinda had happened to meet Aubrey Ashford. She was entranced. She was fascinated. And she was obviously trying to snare his interest.

Eve found herself annoyed, amused, and yet strangely, a little frightened too. Because Aubrey had paid her friend strict attention since the moment he met her, and was obviously bent on amusing and enthralling her. Eve discovered she didn't like that. After all, the man was supposedly trying to win her hand. He didn't have to try to seduce her best friend too. And she didn't like the fact that she didn't like it. Why should she care? The man was stunning, his attention flattering, but she didn't really know him yet. The situation was getting more and more curious. He campaigned for her and then before he'd achieved his goal, set out to captivate her best friend? They hadn't stopped talking since they'd met. Eve sat and watched and racked her brain trying to figure out his game.

If it was a game. But what else could it be? Lucinda was not the sort of female to capture a man's interest. She was tall and thin, with a figure that was as straight as her lank brown hair. When she grew old, she might be considered "handsome." Now she was considered invisible, at least to suitors. Eve sometimes thought it was because Lucinda held herself too low, and practically fawned on any interested male, and usually frightened them away. If she were rich and a beauty it wouldn't matter. She had a tidy dowry, but nothing spectacular. She had no title, although she was related to many titled persons. But she was sweet and considerate. Still, how could a man know that on first meeting? Most didn't opt for two. Aubrey was acting as though he were ready to propose marriage to her too.

What was he thinking of? The mystery deepened, as did the spell he seemed to have cast over Lucinda. Although Lucinda acted like this whenever a single gentleman happened to speak with her, it didn't seem to repel Aubrey, as it did so many other gentlemen. He appeared to be hanging on her every word too.

Eve's own eyes widened. Was he an incorrigible flirt? Well, better she should know that now than later. That sort of a man was not one she wanted, however handsome and clever and charming he might be. She was very glad she'd found that out now, she thought with a sinking heart.

"But we are neglecting our hostess," Aubrey said, interrupting what he was saying to Lucinda.

"I didn't mean to," Lucinda said, startled. "It was only when I discovered who you were, and that you came from my part of the country, I couldn't help comparing impressions. Of course, I didn't know your grandfather, but I knew *of* him. Everyone in the district did. I can't wait to tell my mother that I met you. But I won't have to.

She's coming here to collect me this morning." She turned to look at Eve. "I honestly didn't mean to take over the conversation, Eve."

Aubrey rose. "You didn't. It was equally my fault; I found your recollections fascinating. But my rudeness is soon corrected. I've overstayed the allotted time for a morning caller. I look forward to my time as an evening caller. It's dinner for us tonight, Eve. And then the Swanson's for a musicale. Good day, Miss Lucinda. I hope to see you again. Good-bye, Eve, for now. I'll see you soon, but not soon enough to suit me."

He smiled, bowed, and left.

"Oh!" Lucinda breathed when he'd gone from the salon. She sat back and put a hand on her heart. "He *is* courting you. You lucky, lucky girl! There isn't a female at home who wouldn't envy you. The Ashfords are famous in our district. Such handsome men! Not that they ever stay around very long. They travel all the time. His grandfather charmed everyone, or so everyone remembers. They say his grandmother was a beauty, but when she began to ail they left the country to go to Italy for the climate. That's where your Aubrey's father was born. He came back to visit his estate once, but left soon again. I vow, I was only a child, but I never forgot the glimpses I got of him before he returned to Italy, which he considered his home.

I hear he married there. This Mr. Aubrey was his only child and now *he's* back. I vow your Aubrey is his father's spit and image."

"Not *my* Aubrey," Eve corrected her, sitting back, vastly relieved.

"Why not? He has everything. What fault do you find in him?"

"None," Eve said gloomily. "That's the problem. I've plenty of faults. Why should this magnificent, faultless person want to marry me at first sight?

"It's so romantic," Lucinda sighed. "Why not just accept it? I would, should such a person want to marry me, for whatever reason."

"He says I remind him of someone," Eve said. "A woman he obviously adored. But that's no basis for marriage either. I know you consider me mad, Lucy, but I want more from my husband. That's why I've waited this long. Marriage is forever. I don't want to make a misstep."

Eve sat up suddenly. "Tell me about his family. He's answered my questions about them, but not at length. All he says was that he was orphaned in Italy and came home to find his roots. I accepted that because, well, you know how it is when he's talking. He changed the subject and I never got back to it. I can now. Tell me all about them. Everything you know, or guess, or have heard."

"Didn't you hear when I was talking with him?" Lucinda asked.

Eve's cheeks grew pink. "I was distracted," she said. "Tell me now. And tell me all."

The dinner was delicious, the conversation witty, and Eve seldom stopped smiling. Aubrey was a wonderful host. The restaurant was elegant and in fashion. Sheridan was beyond thrilled to have been invited along. The newlywed young couple, friends of Aubrey's, were charming, when they stopped staring into each other's eyes and remembered where they were.

The musicale they went to next routed Sheridan after a half hour. He sat looking agonized, gazing around the room to see how he could make his getaway. Eve realized his plan even before he suddenly stood. He sat again when she tugged on his sleeve and whispered, reminding him that he'd agreed to be chaperone this evening. A maid wasn't enough for a well-bred young woman. She began to think that a cloister of nuns wouldn't be enough chaperonage for her when she was with Aubrey.

Sure enough, when they said good night to the young couple and returned to Eve's house, Sherry bowed, said his thanks, and dashed off to meet some friends at a nearby tavern. Eve allowed her yawning maid to go to bed. And all the while, Aubrey stood in the hallway with a slight smile.

"Thank you for a lovely evening," Eve finally said, looking up at him, suddenly aware that she ought not to have sent her maid to bed so soon.

"No, thank you," he said. "Ready to accept my proposal, Eve? Then you wouldn't have to look so stricken because we were left alone."

"You read my face, and not my mind," she countered, annoyed at how transparent she was to him.

"Did I?" he said in a soft voice, stepping closer to her. "I think not. Let us be done with the problem, Eve. Once we know, we'll know a lot more, and you'll either dismiss me . . . or not."

"Know what?" she said weakly as he bent to her, although of course, she knew. She closed her eyes, so as not to see his handsome face and be influenced by it or the tender look in his shockingly perceptive eyes. His lips were warm and soft on hers. Velvet and yet electrifying, she felt the tingle of first contact down to her toes. His mouth moved over hers, teasing, cajoling, gently urging her on. He was strong and yet under restraint. It reassured her. Soon, she felt entirely under his control and didn't resist, because to surrender brought her so much pleasure and it was so wonderful to be taken out of herself, to be able to stop thinking.

She stood on her toes to taste more, because he was so close and yet still too distant. Then he took her in his arms and deepened the kiss, and she opened her lips against his to seek more of the sweet dark taste of him. She'd never experienced such a kiss.

And yet, drowning in the bliss of it, she soon found herself wanting more. Her body itched and tingled and yearned. Even the stableboy had tried for more. Now, one kiss led to another, and yet another. But he didn't put his hands on her or over her, as she'd hoped he would. She crowded up to him; her thin gown allowing her to feel the heat of him. She knew he was not unmoved, but he made no further demands. Eve reached up and felt the clean thick silk of his hair under her hands, and sighed against his mouth.

Finally, her common sense started to over-whelm her senses. Why didn't he try to sweep her entirely away? Her breasts were peaked against his chest; her breathing was quickened, she was burning, and she clung to him. Couldn't he tell she wanted more? He who knew so much, how could he not know that? Impossible. He must be holding back. But why?

She moved back a step to look for an answer in his expression. But she wasn't as good at reading him as he was at knowing her thoughts. She saw his raised eyebrow, and could only guess that was laughter at the back of his eyes. It made her take a breath, step further from him, and raise her chin. "I amuse you?" she asked shakily.

"No," he said. "I'm only happy because I was right. Didn't you feel it? That knowledge that we're suited, mind and body?"

"I felt our mouths suited," she said crossly. "That's all."

He threw back his head and laughed heartily. "But, Eve, I didn't want to beguile your body unless I already had your mind, and I know I don't. Nor did I want to compromise you, and then have you saying you only married me because of that for the rest of our lives. The answer must come from here," he said, cupping her chin in one hand and raising her head, "and here," he added, touching a fingertip to her breast, right over her beating heart. "And so, your answer is . . . ?"

"I don't know," she said. "You stir my senses so much I find it hard to think. But then, when I do think, I have reservations. The same ones, and still with not enough explanation to ease my mind. Why me? Why so suddenly? I remind you of someone you loved? Surely that isn't enough, not for me, at least. Because I'm not her, and never will be, nor do I want to be loved for who I resemble."

"That spirit, that glow," he said, touching a lock of her hair. "That's the same. Little else is. And I do know you, Eve, apart from memories of yesterday. But if you want more time, I have all the time in the world to convince you. I only wish I didn't have to use it, waiting. I yearn for you, you know."

"I know," she said miserably. Because he'd finally said everything a suitor ought. Except he hadn't said he loved her, because it would be a lie. They both knew that. He wanted her, and that was very different. She knew that too, for herself.

"I'll wait then," he said. "Now then, my Miss Eve, you will see me tomorrow for tea?"

She nodded.

"And the next night, for the masquerade ball. Maybe you can learn more about me when I'm in disguise? You're so contrary, that may turn the trick. I can't wait to see what disguise you've chosen. Whatever it is, I'll wager I'll be your partner."

"At the ball, yes. But maybe not in our costumes. Unless you wish it?"

"Oh," he said, "I think you'll find we will match in everything."

"You have a spy in my house?" she asked in astonishment. "It can't be Sherry. I didn't tell him. But he has a way of talking the housemaids and the footmen around anything . . . he didn't!"

"He did not," Aubrey said. "I'm gambling on how well I know you."

"What's the wager to be?" she asked, hands on her hips. When they teased like this, she didn't mistrust him.

"Name it."

"So sure? This will be interesting. No material wager matters," she said airily. "I just look forward to victory."

"Then if material doesn't matter to you, a kiss will to me. That's the wager. If you win, you can come to me, anywhere, anytime, and kiss me. If I do, I get to kiss you, any time, anywhere. Agreed?"

"Yes," she said brightly. "There's no way I can lose if I win." She laughed. "And you won't win, we won't be a pair in our costumes. But I'll forgive you that."

He laughed, took her back into his arms, kissed her speechless, and left her looking after him. She watched him go out into the night, bemused as always at how much she could want a man, and how suspicious she could be of him at the same time.

She slowly went up the stairs to her bedchamber. She could have asked her brother or her maid to stay until Aubrey had left. But she'd wanted what she got, even though it turned out she didn't get half of it. He was still a mystery to her, but a more alluring one every moment.

Eve changed to her nightclothes, and then sat cross-legged on her bed and thought, her chin on her knees. She had a costume. She wouldn't use it now. He'd said he'd know. Which was ridiculous. He couldn't know. He didn't even know what costumer she'd gone to. Still . . .

She needed a new costume. A good one. This wasn't a public masquerade, where, Sherry told her, people dressed in unlikely costumes so no one would recognize them, so they could flirt and worse with their own maidservants and footmen or their best friends' husbands and wives. This was a top-notch affair, where people wanted to be seen in all their glory.

She had to think of how Aubrey would want to be seen, and then dress differently, so as to win her wager. Once again, she was aware of how little she knew him. One thing she did know, she thought as she scowled—she'd be *damned* if he actually came up with a matching costume to hers. He said he knew her. She doubted he really did. If he did, it would be unsettling. And if he didn't, she'd win. She loved winning.

That would show him she was her own person, not an echo from his past. She wasn't a copy of anyone. If he could accept that, she might even be able to accept him. That would be wonderful, because whether she knew him well or not, deep down she knew very well that she very much wanted to say yes to him.

A thought came to her and made her sit up straight. She shouldn't be thinking how *he'd* dress. She knew that. He'd said it. He'd be guessing her costume, and he'd match it. So she had to think and double think. First, she had to try to imagine what he'd thought she'd do, which was probably very likely what she'd like to do. Then, she'd have to do the opposite.

She'd been to masquerades before, but always wore one of her mother's antique gowns and a mask. She'd planned something different this time. With such a magnificent escort, she'd wanted to go to the ball a glorious sight, gowned in gold and silver and veils: a queen, a fairy princess. She'd decided to be an exotic Eastern princess, garbed in golden silk, and with satin silvery streamers capped by softly tinkling bells. She'd have a veil and a beautiful headdress. She'd tried on the costume. It had everything she wanted but the bells. Her only worry had been that she wasn't grand enough to carry off the disguise the way it should be shown. She'd tilted this way and that in the looking glass, cheered by her maid's exclamations. She herself had been blinded by the shimmer of the fabric. She'd convinced herself it would be glorious.

She sighed. If she did rig herself out like that, she now realized she'd look very much like other women she'd seen at masquerades, each trying to outshine the others. And if she dared dress like that, and Aubrey really could know what she most wanted to do, he'd dress like a prince, and they'd match.

Which was ridiculous. He couldn't know. Still . . .

So then, she thought, she should get a costume exactly unlike every other woman. A pirate, or a tavern wench, or some such, would be simple, and she'd seen those costumes too. But they'd been on women of lower repute, or scandalous females of the *ton*. That was out. She had her own pride to think about.

She could dress like a man: a pageboy, or a young fop of a fellow. But then she'd have to show her legs, and so she'd be like one of those wild, attention-seeking creatures. She didn't want to shame herself or look foolish. She wanted to look attractive, and yet not like anything Aubrey would imagine, however well he knew her.

Eve didn't get much sleep that night. But she wasn't tired in the morning. Instead, she leapt from her bed, and called her maid. She now knew what to do; she just had to find the materials to do it with.

"You look surprisingly handsome," Eve said, circling her brother.

"Dash it all, I *am* handsome," Sherry said.

"I never thought of you as a prince, though," his sister said.

He preened. And he had the clothes to do it. He was in scarlet and gold: a scarlet capelet, a gold tunic tied with a scarlet belt over black tights, with soft high boots, and a dashing sort of a slouched hat with a brave red plume sitting tilted back over his ear.

"A Renaissance Prince," she mused. "You know? It does suit you."

It did, making him look rakishly slim rather than awkward and lanky.

"I'm Robin Hood," he said proudly.

"That, you're not," she said. "The evil sheriff would have sent an arrow through you in a second if you'd gone romping through the forest in all that spangle."

He thought a moment, and then shrugged. "Dashed fellow at the costume shop said Robin Hood, but a Renaissance prince it is then. Now, let's get a look at you, whip off that hood and that cloak you've wrapped yourself in, and let me see."

"Not yet," she said, ducking her head. "I want it to be a surprise."

"Mr. Ashford," the butler announced.

She braced herself as Aubrey entered the salon where they were waiting. It didn't help.

She was stunned.

Had she thought he was magnificent before? It was not a patch on what he was now.

Aubrey was dressed as an Eastern prince. But out of some fantastical tale of derring-do. His costume was more magnificent than anything she'd seen in the costume shop. He wore gold and silver, and jewels at his wrists and on his hands, and they seemed to be the real thing. When he moved she heard the faint sound of the little bells that hung from the wide silver sash that went round his lean waist. He wore a white silken shirt, billowing at the sleeves, with a long, loose golden waistcoat over it. His silvery pantaloons were billowing too, and he wore golden slippers that tipped up at their toes. A silver turban with a startlingly bright green emerald at the center was wound around his head. What could be seen of his hair was dark gold. He looked like himself, but not at all the same. He didn't glitter; he gleamed. From behind his silver eye mask, his eyes glowed dark and mysteriously. His smile was pearlescent, he was wonderfully exotic, incredibly attractive, but more, Aubrey *was* a prince.

He smiled and bowed, to the sound of those far-away silver bells. Eve stared. Had she stayed with her first impulse and her deepest wish, she'd have been his match. This way, she'd won. It hardly seemed worth it now. It would have been wonderful to match him tonight. Still, she knew she never could, in any costume, and consoled herself with that.

"You look very grand, Sherry," he said, eyeing Sheridan's costume. And then those dark eyes flew to Eve. "And you in a cloak, Eve? Come, no pretending you've forgotten something so you can go flying up to your chamber to change. Let's see who you are to be tonight."

"You think I'm so craven?" she asked, and smiled. She threw back her hood, opened her cape, and let it drop to the floor.

Sheridan gasped.

Aubrey blinked. But then he threw back his head and laughed.

She wore a ragged old gown, torn in places, its hem all lengths, of a material that might have once been blue. The patches on it were several other shades. A long grubby apron was tied over it. Her feet were in scuffed torn slippers; her curly brown hair covered by a rag of a scarf. She bore smudges of ashes on her laughing face, and she held her ragged broom as proudly as any princess might hold a scepter.

"What the devil?" Sherry said, staring at her. "Your face is dirty!"

"I believe that's the point," Aubrey murmured looking at her appreciatively, for her wit. And, Eve thought, for more than that. Even though she was in rags, he gazed at her hungrily, as though she were dressed as a queen, or a siren.

She bowed to him. "Welcome, oh, dazzling Prince. I have won!"

He bowed to her. "I'm afraid you haven't."

Her eyes narrowed.

"You're clearly Ella of the Cinders. And I? Why, I'm your Prince Charming come to take you to the ball. Pay up."

She blinked, looking for a flaw in his reasoning. She hadn't thought of that. "But Ella didn't go to the ball in her rags," she said cagily. "She wasn't with the prince when she dressed like this."

"Yes, she was," he said, smiling. "The prince met her in her rags when he returned her shoe."

"He wasn't an Eastern prince," she persisted.

"Who says he wasn't?" he asked pleasantly.

She scowled as she thought, then lifted her head. "I see!" she declared. "But it's a cheat. Because a prince can match any female; he can match anyone in any costume."

"Yes," he said. "In almost every fairy story, in every folktale, there's a prince at the end who wins all. But there wasn't any penalty for cleverness, was there?"

"I wish there was," she said grudgingly.

"Don't sulk," he said seriously. "It was a good try. But I've been at this far longer than you. Even so, now you must pay up."

"Now?" she asked, glancing quickly at Sheridan.

"When I tell you. As for the immediate 'now,' shall we go? Or wait for your fairy godmother?"

"She obviously took the evening off," Eve said resentfully, tying on her mask. He held up her cloak for her to put on again, and even having lost the wager, she suddenly found her spirits soaring.

Chapter 4

It was a sparkling ball, masquerades always were no matter how inelegant the setting, or crude the guests. Masquerade parties were the current rage because everyone enjoyed them, and anyone could have fun at one. Even the popular public ones held at the opera, where dustmen in disguise could pay to dance with slumming duchesses, looked entrancing in the glow of gaslight. Stage light and gaslight made glass shine like diamonds, painted cheeks look milkmaid rosy, and dashing good looks seem real and possible on any man.

But tonight, at this London town house, the invitations were exclusive. The jewels the ladies wore *were* diamonds, emeralds, and rubies; the costumes were silk and satin and not tawdry substitutes, and when the ball ended, the sun would rise on splendor and not tatty stage effects.

There were harlequins and Cleopatras by the score. Bishops, nuns, and monks abounded. Venetian masks of the fantastical characters of *commedia dell'arte* were worn atop long black cloaks completely enshrouded identities. There were owl masks and peacock feathers, dancing girls and Elizabethan queens, devils and angels, courtiers from every year in English history, and even a few savages from the tropics and the New World thrown in for balance. The guests were wealthy, the guests were bored, and there was no expense they wouldn't go to in order to make the rest of their number gasp at midnight when they revealed their true identities. Except, of course, for those concealed so completely that they could leave before midnight and slink off into the night after their improprieties.

Not only could anyone look attractive, but anything could be done if one was in disguise. It was perhaps the prime reason why masquerades were so very popular.

Eve hardly saw the others at the ball. She couldn't take her eyes off her partner. He never left her side. This would have declared them engaged to be married at any other Society ball. Tonight, though, their masks allowed them to constantly dance together, stand together, and talk together without an eyebrow being raised.

Aubrey looked magnificent even in this crowd of splendidly dressed partygoers. He was thrilling to look at: a golden-haired magical prince, garbed in jewels so fine he might well have been a real sheik or an emir from a fairy story, visiting this mortal land for the night. Others noticed the magnificent figure he cut, and not a few wondered who the little ragged miss next to him was. Certainly not his wife. Such a man wouldn't partner a lady in life who made such mock of his splendor. Most people assumed she was titled, from their own set. Some thought it was a jest, she might actually be a light-skirt: a favored mistress come to the ball, only to disappear at midnight. After all, what female would poke fun at poverty if she weren't already rich?

Eve didn't notice. It didn't seem that Aubrey did either. They danced and looked into each other's eyes. Eve felt as though she was in his thrall, and tonight, in disguise, in this magical place she didn't mind.

"We dance well together," he finally said, in her ear, as they waltzed.

"That, we do," she said.

"We converse well together," he persisted.

"Yes, that too."

"But I'm afraid I can't judge more, at least not from just a few kisses."

Her head went up. "Then you'll stop asking me to marry you?"

He laughed. "No. I'll make more opportunities to kiss you."

The music stopped. They stood facing each other, both smiling: one widely, one less so.

A pirate stepped between them. He wore a white shirt with wide ballooning sleeves; a sash round his waist with a golden sword tucked into it, dark breeches and high, loosely fitted buccaneer boots. He wore an eye mask and a magnificent hat with a drooping feather. He swept off his fantastical hat and bowed from the waist as he looked at Eve. "The music's beginning again," he said. "May I have this dance, little Ella of the Cinders?"

She looked at Aubrey. Then she grinned. Dropping a housemaid's ducking curtsey, she placed her hand on the pirate's proffered arm, and with a backward look at Aubrey said pertly, in a countrified accent, "Aye, thankee, kind sir."

"So, Miss Sit-by-the-Cinders," the pirate said, as he led her into a country dance, "will you give me a hint?"

"A hint about what, sir?" she asked as the dance took them apart.

"Now, surely you know that the game is to give your partners a hint, and the one that guesses right gets a kiss at midnight?" he told her when the dance brought them together again.

"I didn't," she said. "But," she added, "I'm that glad to play the game. Because you'll never guess. Does it work the other way too?" she asked cheekily, as the music whirled her down the line away from him. She took the opportunity to steal a glance at Aubrey, at the side of the dance floor. He was watching and not smiling. She was.

When she returned to the pirate, he put one hand on his heart. "Aye, the game is the same for both of us. My hint then is that you'll never find me board a ship, but on shipboard I stay."

She laughed. "Very good! Then mine is that you've seen me before, but you've never seen me at all."

"How could I have been such a blind man?"

"But who would notice a kitchen maid, m'lor?"

"I should have," he said, taking her hand as they ducked their heads and stepped together through the end of the aisle the other dancers made, as each couple did in turn.

Eve was dizzy from the dancing, merry from the jest, and tickled that she'd possibly annoyed Aubrey. At least she'd showed him that he wasn't the first or last male in the world that wanted to dance with her, even in her rags. Which is why she didn't notice that after the pirate had whirled her down the line, he spun her away from the dance. They paused near an opened door, where a fresh night breeze tantalized them by cooling their faces.

"Come," the pirate said, tugging on her hand. "Let's go outdoors and breathe."

She wanted to, but giddy as she still was, Eve remembered this was a masked man who could be any man and it was decidedly not a good idea to go out into the dark with a strange man in London, or anywhere.

She forced a laugh and tried to pull back. "Thankee, sir, but no. I know me place. And that is in here, in plain sight, be it hot or not."

He tightened his grip on her hand and tugged harder, so hard that she was moved slightly off balance. "Come, lass," he said. "It's only a back garden. What can happen there?"

"Anything. Everything. Pray loose my lady, sir," Aubrey said, as he appeared in the opened doorway. He put one gloved and jeweled hand at his waist. "You carry a sword. I carry a scimitar. My weapon isn't too good for parry and thrust, but it can reap heads. So it might be awkward when I win, but I'm sure anyone would say it was a fair fight if we duel."

Aubrey's voice was soft but the pirate immediately dropped Eve's hand. He stepped back as though struck. "My mistake," he said, recovered enough to make a shaky bow. "I didn't know the maid was really spoken for. A thousand pardons. Good evening." He backed off, and away, and disappeared into the throng of partygoers.

Aubrey stood looking down at Eve. He held out a hand to her. "It *is* cooler out there," he said. "And you do know me. While it's true that anything can happen, nothing will unless you want it to. Will you come with me?"

She nodded, put her hand in his, and stepped out the door with him.

It wasn't dark, though the sky was. Dozens of flickering lanterns hung from the trees, more twinkled on the pathways that dwindled off into the distance: the night garden was like a starry sky. Eve stepped over the flagstones with Aubrey and watched a fantastical parade of costumed guests moving along the garden paths. Foxheaded men and glittering ladies, gentlemen with long furry tails and bird-headed women in ball gowns, clowns and ghosts and demons strolled in the garden under a bright half moon.

It was enchanting. But nothing fascinated Eve so much as her escort. His remarkable face glowed moonlight pure in the night shadows, and the eerie light made his hair shine white. The jewels on his turban and resplendent tunic smoldered with banked fires as they passed the lanterns and wandered under the moonlight. Eve again wished she hadn't been so humorous in her costume. She could have worn a golden wig too; she could have glowed as richly as he did. Because the longer they stayed in costume, the more they both adopted the mien of the people who might have worn the garb they had on. Aubrey looked more elegant and imperious by the moment, and she'd never felt so less than his equal, so much his to command.

He also looked utterly alien. She'd been drawn to his good looks, but now it was a shining stranger who paced at her side. He finally stopped beneath a towering tree. Stars and glowworms twinkled high above them between the tree's lacy leaves. And, for a miracle, there was no one else nearby.

"So," Aubrey said, looking down at her. "Again I ask. That's twice. I'll only ask thrice. Even Caesar was only offered the crown three times. It's a powerful number, three. Less, and I haven't really tried to win you. More, and I become a figure of ridicule. So, Eve, will you marry me?"

He held up a hand. "I know: you don't know me. How many years does it take for a woman to know a man? I've heard fifty isn't enough, I know one hundred isn't. Every marriage is a leap into the unknown, Eve. How well does anyone know anything? I know that we suit. I know I'm attracted to you. I know you're intelligent and well-spoken, good-natured and kind. You'd be a good mother and a good wife, simply because you're a good person."

He brushed his gloved hand lightly across her cheek and gazed into her eyes. "What can I tell you about myself that you don't know?" he mused. "I'm not cruel to animals. I try not to be unkind to people. I've never struck a mortal female. I won't cause you hurt, and I'd only ask that you never cause me any either. What else would you have of me?" He paused.

"Of course, if you aren't attracted to me," he added softly, "then we'll say no more. What would be the point? This wouldn't be an arranged marriage. Be sure, I want you body and mind."

"Where?" she found herself asking breathlessly.

He cocked his head to the side.

"I mean," she said, embarrassed at the spell his voice and words seemed to have cast on her. "Where would we live? If we did marry."

"Here, in London," he said. "But mostly at my estate to the west. It's beautiful there, so lovely all say it's magical. I know you will love it. Why did you ask? Where would you want to live?"

"I just wanted to know."

He nodded. "Now you do." He waited for her reply.

"Would you have a mistress?" she asked. "Many gentlemen of the *ton* do."

"No," he said. "That I promise. I would not. Nor would I want you to entertain any men in my absence. And certainly not in my presence," he added, with a curling smile.

"Don't humor me," she said seriously. "If you want my answer now, you have to answer questions that would normally come up slowly, over several conversations."

"Really?" he asked. "So far as I can see, and I have excellent vision, apart from those few gentlepersons who grew up together, most of them marry because of their family's plans. Or, if they're free to choose, they decide on their partner after a few dances and a drive or two round the park together. In fact, I think you already know me better than most women of the *ton* knew their spouses when they gave consent. But you need more than that, don't you? Quite right. That's only one of the reasons I want you, for your wisdom. Here then," he said, and took her in his arms.

She hesitated, her hands braced on his chest. "Have you loved before?"

He sighed. "I'll be honest. I've thought so. Who has not? But time, and meeting you, showed me my error. Don't make a face. I don't lie to you, it's true. There is no one to stop me from doing anything I wish now. And see? Here I am, yours to command. As to that, have you loved before, Eve?"

She shook her head in denial. He nodded as though he expected that, and smiled.

"You know. Am I so unpracticed then, that you knew it?" she asked.

He laughed. "Love isn't a matter of practice," he said, as he drew nearer. "It simply is. Let me show you."

His lips touched hers lightly. She was the one who sighed and stepped into his embrace. She was the one overwhelmed by the soft velvet of his lips, the warmth of his mouth, the thrilling sensations of his tongue touching hers. She was the one who burrowed closer to him, gripping his shoulders, rejoicing at the feeling of the lithe, strong frame pressed to her own. And when he lightly cupped her breast, she was the one who longed to drag off her ragged gown and press closer, skin to skin with him.

She realized what she was doing when she realized she wanted to do so much more than that. She stepped back. "Lord!" she marveled, touching her lips. "That's not fair."

"Why not?"

"Because I was trying to think," she complained.

He smiled. "Think then."

"You made it more difficult," she said slowly. "It's hard to recognize you. I kept thinking, who is this handsome fellow with such golden tresses?"

"You said you preferred blond men. But poor me. Dark as the inside of a cave. Do you want me to stay this way then? I can. All I need is some dye, and I can always be your fair gentleman. Or I can cast off the wig and be myself again. It's up to you. Or would you prefer that I nip off into the garden and reappear orange as a carrot, or red as a beet? Color is simple. Hearts and minds are not. What do you want, Eve?" he said more seriously. "I'll try to be that for you, but remember, I am myself, and I can't, I won't, change that. Not even for you."

"You don't ask me to change," she said. "Why should I ask you? I've grown used to you being dark-haired. And in truth, I've grown to love the look of you that way. That's not it." She hesitated, nibbled on her lower lip, and looked up at him.

"What is it about me—*me* in particular, that drew you to me? I must know, because that's the sticking point. I know myself. Please don't suppose I don't like myself, for I do, or that I underrate myself, for I don't. I'm actually pleased with who I am, but I know full well that I'm not that special and fantastic." She shrugged. "You are."

"I am? Thank you," he said, bowing.

"Oh, you know it," she said. "But I still don't know your motives in choosing me so quickly, and asking me to marry you."

The laughter faded from his voice. He took a deep breath. "Very well then. The truth. No lies. No protestations of eternal love. No more embraces, delicious as they are, to cloud the issue. Desire's a weed that flourishes in any garden, but love, I understand, has to grow in special soil. It has to be nurtured. I think I can do that; I think you can grow to love me. As for myself? I told you. I saw you and you reminded me of someone I'd been looking for a very long time. When I met you, I realized you were different, of course. All people are. I also realized that although you were very different from the woman I had sought, you suited me."

"And the other woman? The one I reminded you of?" Eve asked, trying not to sound disappointed. Because although she hadn't believed he'd been drawn to her immediately by some strange wonderful thing about herself that she hadn't known, she couldn't help feeling let down because she'd been right.

"That woman? She's gone," he said softly. "Oh, long gone. So don't think I deceive myself as to who you are. And I certainly don't want you for any reasons you might find in a Minerva Press romance. Don't start imagining discarded wives in my tower, or long-lost hidden treasures in your back garden that only I know about.

"I didn't choose you for revenge either, or to spite anyone, or to show anyone that I've gone on with my life. I know myself and my heart. I was drawn to you from the first because of a resemblance, that's true. But then discovered that I want you for yourself. For your company, and the comfort of being with you. And I know you are the one I want to bear my children."

"What if I can't?"

"You will," he said. "But why believe me? I'm not a physician. Say then that I vow any child you choose to call your own will also be mine. Now, will you be mine as well?"

She gazed up at him, so breathtakingly handsome, so clever and well spoken. It wasn't just the moonlight and the strange spell he seemed to cast over her. Moonlight, daylight, gaslight, or morning light, wherever she saw him, she liked the look of him. Dark-haired, light-haired, it made no matter. She loved the sound of his voice, his mouth tasted wonderful to her, he even smelled good to her.

So what if she didn't know him better? She was levelheaded, never one to leap into anything, no matter what the lure. And she knew there'd be time. Not only time in the years to come when they were wed, but time here, now, before the fact.

Because no one in the *ton* ever married in haste, unless there was a good reason, either parental objections that made them run for the border, or a child on the way, or an irate father that made them run to the altar. There'd be time enough during their engagement for her to find out more about him. And if, for any reason, and she prayed not, she discovered something bad, she could be free.

She wouldn't think about that. She couldn't, not here, not now, with his eyes looking into hers. One thing she knew above all. She dared not let him go. He said he'd only ask three times. She was afraid he might not ask again, or if he did, resent her for making him ask. And where on earth would she ever meet his like again?

"Come, Eve," he whispered. "Let go of harsh reality. Life's an adventure. Step into one, with me."

She stepped into his arms instead. "Yes," she said, letting all her pent breath out. "Yes, Aubrey. I will."

It was done. Aubrey rode home alone through the streets of London, smiling. He was relieved and exhilarated. He'd found her and courted her, and she'd said yes. He'd been sure she would, but still, people were difficult to predict, women twice as much so. He'd won her, and there'd been no coercion or magic about it. He hadn't had to delude her in any way. She wanted him. She was enough like him for him to know that. Her kiss good night had been filled with desire and impatience and eagerness to have him.

They'd have a good life together; he hadn't been lying about that. He hadn't lied about anything. He never did, or rather, he never wanted to. This time, he'd just not said those things she might have asked had she not been so taken with him, with romance, with her fate.

He was very pleased. Eve was charming. She wasn't as beautiful as some other females he'd known, but she'd appealed to his senses enormously, and for a wonder, she was also clever. That was a novelty and a joy. He knew he'd enjoy their time together. And, Aubrey vowed to the glowing moon above him, he would be as good to her as he'd told her he'd be. And he might, he thought, even come to love her. That was, to love her insofar as he was capable of it.

He rode home through the shadows, smiling.

Chapter 5

Eve shuddered. Aubrey's lips had left hers, his hands slowly drew away from her body, and now he sat back, only inches away from her. But he was far enough away to restore her to her senses. She took a deep shivering breath as he pulled up her sleeve and the neckline of her gown, and covered her.

"Why?" she asked, without looking at him. "Why did you stop? Did I do wrong?"

"No, too right. That's the point. You do too well. I stopped because we're not married. I can only go so far and no further."

She raised shaking hands to rearrange her hair. He'd run his hands through the tangle of it as he'd kissed her. It had felt as though each separate hair had a nerve of its own.

"We won't be wed for six months," she said. "So either we stop doing this entirely, or we do more. What's the difference? We'll be married soon enough." Before she could be startled by what had come from her own lips, he answered.

"Not soon enough," he said. "You want to walk down the aisle by yourself, not with our son in your arms, or at least, not with his imminent arrival visible."

"We don't have to go that far," she said.

"I do," he said.

"Why?"

"Because," he said patiently, "I don't like to feel like a boy stealing kisses in a darkened corner. And I have only so much control. I don't want to dishonor you; neither would you be comfortable with such a thing. But this kissing and nibbling, touching and withdrawing is not enough, Eve. There's satisfaction to be found that way, but it's furtive and unfulfilling. We can do much better, we're adults. Yet we aren't yet wed. And why is that?" he asked, as he reached out a slender hand and gently traced the outer whorls of her inner ear. "The settlements are made," he added softly. "Your father was too generous, by the way. Your brother likes me."

"You offered to teach him to drive your chestnuts," she said, trying not to shiver at his touch. "He'd have given you his soul for that."

"Indeed? I forgot to ask him for it. Well, let's see what else we've settled, besides any objections your family might have had. The guest list is complete. The banns have been posted, the church selected. We've been wined and dined and toasted to the sky by friends, family, and acquaintances."

"I haven't met your relatives," she said.

"Nor are you likely to. I told you," he said sadly. "There are few, and those are far between, or simply far away. There are no more impediments, Eve. Yet, now, because you want a spring wedding, we must wait longer, through autumn, winter, and then into spring. A season into another season, and then another." He said the last as though he were dropping the words slowly into her consciousness.

She quivered at his touch on her ear, and he took his hand away. She thought she saw a gleam of mockery in his eyes. She frowned. In that second's time, the gleam was gone, replaced with killing sympathy.

"But now," she said, "if we change the date, people will think the worst."

"And if we don't, the worst will be," he said. "If by that, you mean they'll think we've conceived a child. Because given time, it will become inevitable. The bond between us is that intense, the pull that strong. Do you doubt it?"

She said nothing.

He sat back and studied her expression. "So then, I think, my love, I really do believe that the best thing would be for me to leave you for a while. Just until time catches up with desire. As I said, I've hardly any family left, and those I do have are too feeble to travel far. I think I'd best go to see them, and then to see some more of the world. I could do that, carefully, I promise, because I don't want to be captured and made a prisoner of war. I can follow the sun and sail to the South Seas, or the Caribbean, or I could visit the new world, and yet still return in time for our scheduled wedding. Otherwise, I tell you, my Eve, with all my best intentions, and all my control and good will, I will not be able to keep my hands off you. My hands," he added, "my lips, and other more to the point attributes."

She drew herself up. "I am not a slave to my desires. I can resist your irresistible . . . attributes, you know."

"Can you?" he asked softly.

She looked down at her lap. She'd have sworn she could. But just before, in his arms, in his hands, drinking in his breath from his lips, feeling the warmth and power of the man, she'd been a heartbeat from giving him everything, with joy and delight. She couldn't deny it.

"And it will be a long, cold winter," he added. "I

hate the cold. I'll write, of course. I'll think of you. I'll travel abroad, wherever war is not. Then I'll return to you with the birds in the spring."

"No!" she said.

"No?" he asked quizzically.

He might travel into danger, Eve thought. The Continent was dangerous even with Napoleon pent on his stony island. There were pirates and storms on the seas, and unimaginable dangers even on the sunny shores of other lands. He might find risk to himself. He could discover trouble, or an old lover, or someone new, someone more to his taste, in his travels. She had the feeling that if he left he mightn't be back. She knew that if he didn't return she'd never wed because no one would ever suit her as he did, ever again. Worse, she thought he knew it.

"You're taunting me," she said.

One thin dark eyebrow rose. He looked at her with new respect. "So I am," he murmured.

"Worse," she said with more spirit, "you're threatening me."

He put his head to the side as a smile quirked his lips. "Excellent, Eve. I am."

"And you expect me to put up with it?" she asked, caught between anger and laughter.

"No," he said. "That's why I said it. But you know very well what I expect, Eve. Few other

women would. That's only one of the reasons I
want you so. And so . . . ?"

"You want me to tell you here and now that I'll
marry you immediately? This decision will be for
the rest of my life."

"So it is," he agreed.

"There are still so many things I don't know,"
she said anxiously.

He gazed at her curiously.

"Little things, but important ones. What do you
do?" she blurted. "Oh, I don't mean for a liveli-
hood. Gentlemen don't work, I know that. But how
do you pass the time? I know you don't frequent
London clubs, because you haven't been here that
long. We've never spoken of it. So, do you collect
butterflies? Collect horses, or great art, or dabble
in paints yourself? Are you political?"

"As to that last, not at all," he said. I've seen too
much of the damage done by both reformers and
those who don't want to change a hair on a wig
of the justices. Butterflies are better off in the sky
than pressed into a book, don't you think? I don't
collect creatures, but I like horses, dogs, cats, birds,
and fish. I don't have to own them to enjoy them.
I appreciate art too much to try to paint. But I do
read. I love music. I like to grow things. I ride and
swim, winter as well as summer. You don't have

to worry that I'll hang on your sleeve. I've many interests, but my foremost now is you."

He sighed. "Eve, do you really think time will make your decision easier? I don't think so. Not in our case. Either you know now, or you don't. I think time will not mend matters. It will only add frustration and distrust."

"Yours or mine?" she dared ask.

He shrugged. "And so?" he asked again.

"And so," she said, raising her chin. She thought another moment. "And so I think that an autumn wedding could be as lovely as a spring wedding. We can have autumn leaves instead of May flowers for my bouquet, and acorns and berries instead of peaches and cherries for dessert."

"And we can have joy in the winter instead of just longing," he said, as he drew her into his arms. "And maybe even a babe of our own by spring."

She drew away and gazed at him uneasily.

"What?" he asked to her unspoken question. "Where is the objection now? If we marry in September a June babe will be as safe from the gossips as you being a June bride would have been."

"It's not that. I just think that it's odd that you speak about a baby so much. Most men, I think, wouldn't be talking about babies instead of their honeymoon."

"I am not most men," he said, and kissed any other doubts, or thoughts, from her mind.

"But why such haste, child?" Eve's father asked her.

"He means," her brother said, from where he lounged by the window of his father's study, "is there need for haste? If there is, then Ashford's a fast worker, I must say. You've known him less than three months, and here you are engaged, bedded, and begging to be wedded."

"Sheridan!" her father said, shocked.

"Sherry," Eve said, clenching her fists and rounding on him, "you are going to die. But before you do, I'll have you know there's no need for haste." She colored, raised her chin and added, "Except perhaps, because I don't want him to get away and change his mind about me."

Sheridan looked genuinely shocked. "*You*, level-headed sister of mine? I'm the one who falls for crazes and has no sense at all. What has the man done to you?" he asked, so seriously that Eve believed him for once.

"He's made me love him," she said simply. "And I suppose, if love makes one crazed, so be it."

Sheridan's expression didn't clear. Neither did his father's.

"What could he have done to me?" she asked

impatiently. "No," she said quickly, "never mind that. He didn't do *that*. The point is that I didn't even imagine a man like him would ask me to dance with him, much less marry him. He's intelligent, kind, and witty; polite, well educated, and charming. And so handsome he makes people stare. Especially women. That's not his fault. He doesn't try to attract them. At least, I've never seen him do it. You approved his suit, Father, and now you look troubled to hear that we're marrying sooner than intended. I told you I'm not compromised in any way. So why are you upset? Do you know anything about him that I don't?"

"No," her father said slowly. "But I had thought to know all about him by now. I don't. I think that's what it is. He came to England not long before he met you. He's lived abroad for most of his life. So I thought time might provide any missing information. But now, this haste of yours, or his. I don't understand it. It isn't like you."

"What do you think could be discovered to his detriment?" she asked, her nostrils pinched. "He has a fortune, does he not?"

Her father nodded.

"His family is old and well thought of, is it not?"

Her father looked hunted.

"Then do you think he's some sort of Bluebeard, with headless wives littering a dungeon somewhere?"

Her father waved a hand at her nonsense. Her brother's eyes widened.

"He's eminently eligible," her father admitted. "But I'd thought you'd give yourself time to get to know him better."

"This isn't exactly a race to Gretna Green, Father," she said proudly. "We'll have known each other over three months by our wedding day. I know that isn't very long, but if you know your heart it is. I do, I'm no ingénue." She took a breath, controlled herself, and then asked seriously, "Father, am I that much of an antidote that this match is unbelievable to you? Never mind how I feel about him. Is it that odd that any woman would feel that way about Aubrey Ashford? Is it *that* strange that such a man would want me so much?"

She stopped because tears threatened. She wanted to know if there was a problem, and yet she didn't want to know.

Her father and brother eyed her. She wore a simple blue gown this morning; her curly hair was pulled back by a ribbon. Her eyes were shining, as they'd been since she'd met Aubrey Ashford. She sang as she walked about the house these days. She never had before. She looked younger and happier than they'd ever seen her too. In all, she was charming to look at, but even so, and though they loved her, they couldn't claim she looked spectacularly beautiful. Aubrey Ashford was incontestably spectacularly handsome.

"Well, I'd have thought he'd go for a dasher, Eve," Sherry said with truth, adding nervously, because of the looks he got from both his sister and his father, "Not that there's a thing wrong with you. Pretty as you can stare. But you're a pixie, and such a chap usually goes for the dashers, is all I'm saying."

"So why do you think he's asked me to marry him, and begged me to move up the wedding day?" she asked, one slipper tapping the floor in tune to her rising heartbeat.

"Maybe he doesn't like competition," Sherry said unwisely.

Eve's eyes narrowed.

"Because love ignores everything but the heart," her father said. "Hush, Sheridan. Your mother and I didn't always see eye to eye. Aye, she was a forceful woman, and I was content to let her rule our roost. But I loved her, even so. I never thought I'd come to love a managing female. Still, I did. I wish she were still here. She'd know what to say and do now."

He held up a hand. "But now there's only me,

and what can I say? No one's been able to explain love, though the greatest philosophers and poets have tried. So how can I? Ashford loves you, you love him, and there's an end to it. A happy end, I hope. I suppose," he said, looking at Eve, "I just didn't want to let you go so soon."

She was three and twenty, and he'd never paid much attention to her in her entire life, so Eve knew this was a lie. But she didn't care. If it was a lie, it was a kindly one, and she didn't want any more opposition. It woke too many doubts in her own mind. "Thank you," she said.

Sheridan levered his long frame from off from the wall where he'd propped his shoulders. "Father's right," he said simply as he stood up straight. "But remember, if there are any problems with him after the marriage, you can always come to me."

Eve gave him a misty smile. "Thank you," she told him. "The only problem will be that I'll miss you two so much."

"It's all for the best," Sheridan said, breaking the silence. "I'll get to know those chestnut prancers of his sooner too."

And then, relieved, they all laughed.

The groom, all said, was paler than the bride. He was as pallid and pained, as beautiful as one of the grave, stone saints that stood so patiently by the entrance to the tiny, ancient church. At least, so he was when he stood by the altar, side by side with his blushing new bride. This usually would have made the fashionable in the congregation whisper to each other, spreading rumor of a reluctant match, but the place was so hushed they were afraid their voices would carry too far. And for all his graces, Ashford was said to be an excellent swordsman, and a top-notch fellow with a pistol.

Still, in a few moments they reckoned it must have only been a usual case of nerves for the groom. Because once out into the bright autumn-light morning again, color came back to his face, and life into his eyes, which now sparkled in the sunlight.

"Welcome one and all," he said, as he stood on the front steps to the church and addressed his guests. "The weather's been kind, and with winter on its way, I thought we'd all enjoy an outdoor festival today."

Eve smiled. Her new husband's speech, she'd realized, fell into rhyming patterns from time to time. It was a thing that must have amused him. The guests loved it. Eve loved everything about him today. He was dressed in formal black and white, which made his hair shine blue black in the sun. He glowed; he gleamed and looked magnificent in the open air, which seemed to be his natural element. But so was candlelight and torchlight, she thought, and moonlight, especially.

She'd wanted to wear a green gown, because that was her favorite color. But there were too many jests to be made about "a green gown for a bride," since that was what a rustic lover was supposed to give his lady when he tumbled her in the grass. Anyway, superstitious people in the countryside considered green unlucky, since in legend it was the color of the mischievous, wicked elfin folk.

So the bride wore a rose-colored gown with long russet sleeves, and red roses twined in a crown on her curly hair. She looked delightful. But she didn't care how she looked. She had eyes only for her new husband.

"So come along, enjoy food and song," he went on, "the sun's shining and soft breezes play. Come join us on our happy day. This way," he said, pointing in the direction of Eve's father's estate.

The guests laughed, he bowed, and then, smiling, led his bride to his phaeton, bedecked with bright garlands of flowers and autumn berries; his horses crowned with asters woven into wreaths of golden leaves.

They drove off first, ducking their heads against the showers of petals, coins, and rice that the guests threw at them.

"That's done," Aubrey said, as they went down the winding country road to her father's estate.

"And done well," she agreed, untangling a wayward bramble from her hair. "But I worried there, for a moment."

He turned to look at her. "Why?"

"When we stood at the altar I looked at you. You were so pale and still. I thought you'd suddenly changed your mind."

"You could have cut off my head and I wouldn't have changed your mind," he said, laughing. "It's only that churches affect me oddly. They make me nervous. I think it's the enclosed space, the way sound and air is cut off by the thickness of the stones. It's hardly bearable for me. It's like a dungeon. The older the church is, the worse it seems. But I bore it bravely," he said, smiling at her, "and all for you."

"Well, we could hardly have wed in the churchyard," she said. "Don't worry, I'll go to church by myself of a Sunday, if you wish, although it will look strange."

"Not to the vicar at home," he said. "He knows my crotchets by now."

"Good," Eve said. She sounded nervous, no doubt realizing that after today her life would change in more than one way. She had a life partner now, a new name, a new home, and new people to become used to. "Anyway," she continued lightly, "you won't have to go back to church until our first child is baptized."

"True," he said, and thought, with a touch of sadness: *My first lie to you. Because no, never, Eve. That will not happen.*

But that was a long way off. Content at last, the aching pain in his bones finally gone, and the air clear again, Aubrey relaxed. He sang a sweet old country tune to make his bride smile as he turned to his team to drive them onward to their wedding breakfast.

Chapter 6

"**Y**ou're nervous," Aubrey told Eve as their carriage drove through the lingering twilight. This time, for their wedding trip, they sat in a well-padded barouche, a driver, a guard, and two outriders outside. "Don't be uneasy," he went on. "We'll travel slow and steady. We're going to stop at an inn when it gets dark, and stay the night before we move on. I've made arrangements. It's a decent place with passable food. And if you're worried about our wedding night, you needn't be. It's been a tiring day for you: a wedding and a reception to get through, and now this journey. So if you don't fall into my arms in a fit of passion the moment we're alone in a room together, I'll understand. We'll just go to sleep. But there's no 'just' about it. We're together at last."

"I'm not worried about our wedding night," Eve said. "Well, a little, because I don't want to disappoint you, and please," she added quickly, "don't say I won't, because that's just the sort of thing you'd say to be polite. But it's new to me and naturally, I feel a bit of trepidation."

"Naturally," he said, smiling. "So there's nothing to do but forget about it for now. Unless you want to start here and now?"

She looked at him in shock.

He laughed. "See? You forgot for a minute. Don't worry. We'll wait until comfort, desire, and privacy match, and you are absolutely willing—no, desperate, to begin. Don't make a face. So will I be by then. There's nothing wrong with that. You'll see," he said, drawing her closer to his side. "Now, what else are you worried about?"

She looked at her lap. "I'm anxious because I'm going to a whole new life. Oh, Sheridan promised he'd come visit us, and Father expects us to come visit him, and all my friends said they'd see me again. But Sherry forgets everything, and who knows when we can see my father again? And my friends have their own lives to get on with. I know no one but you where we're going, and nothing about your home. It feels like I'm stepping off the end of the earth. I wonder at my own bravery. Only I don't feel so brave just now."

"That's to be expected," he said. "There's nothing I can do about it but tell you again that I know you'll be happy at Far Isle. Come, move closer, lean against me. Maybe that will help you feel brave again, seeing that you're not alone."

She moved to his side.

"Eve," he said, putting an arm around her, "I tell you there's nothing to fear. You're a lucky lady. You'll have no mother- or father-in-law to trouble you. Those few relatives I have are distant. We have no ghosts or specters rattling around. No near neighbors either. You'll be queen of our manor, with no one to impress but me. And you've already done that. Don't worry about being lonely. We'll travel to London whenever you wish. But in truth, I tell you I can't like being gone from the Hall for too long."

"Then how did you manage all those years before you came back to England?" she asked curiously.

He was still a moment. "I meant," he said, "since I've come back, no place on earth pleases me so much. You'll think so too. It seems the grass is greener there, I swear it even looks like the sun even shines more brightly. The dew sparkles, even the rain seems like silver drifting over the land. The gardens are beautiful and the forest, deep and cool. It's the way England itself looked long, long ago. Or so I think it must have been. You'll see for yourself. But not today, it's north and west, on the border between England and Wales, so we'll stop to play at being tourists before we get there."

She yawned. "Excuse me," she said quickly.

He laughed. "Excuse me for nattering on. It's been a long day. Here, rest against me." He moved her closer. "Close your eyes. I'll wake you when we stop at the inn. There's a good dinner and a soft bed awaiting us there. Now sleep."

"I couldn't possibly sleep now, here, on my wedding day," she protested. "I can never sleep in moving carriages anyway. I feel if I close my eyes I'll lose control and something will happen. It's as if I keep the coach on the straight path if I'm awake, by the sheer force of my will. And if I sleep, how will I know if the coach goes into a ditch?"

"I'll tell you," he promised. "Now try."

She rested her head on his shoulder.

"No wonder you can't sleep in a carriage," he said with a smile in his voice. "Shoulders are to cry on, not to rest on. They have too many angles. Here, put your head on my chest. It's not softer, but there's more room. You can put your hand on my heart and rest your head on that.

"Now relax and close your eyes. I'll take the reins by thinking as hard as you ever could, and I'll make sure the coach doesn't go into a ditch. If it does, I'll wake you, I promise.

She gave a sleepy chuckle and burrowed into

the comforting solid warmth of him. He began to hum that old country song, and she smiled to herself, pleased he was serenading her. It was like a lullaby. She felt the vibrations thrumming through his chest. She slowly began to close her eyes. In fact, she found it harder and harder to keep them open. When he fell still, she heard his strong slow heartbeat against her ear, the rise and fall of his chest, and snuggled up closer. Then, breathing in the clean fresh scent of him, of deep forests and fresh meadows, she sighed, and slept.

"Wake up," he whispered in her ear, after what seemed like minutes later. But when Eve's eyes fluttered open, she saw it was entirely black outside the coach windows.

She sat up quickly. "It's night? We've stopped. Is everything all right?"

"We're here," he said. "We've stopped at the inn."

"Already?" She stretched and yawned. "I haven't slept so well in days! In truth, now I can tell you, I was thinking so much about our wedding, how it would go and such, that I stayed up nights worrying."

"I wondered if it would go on at all," he said. "You were so hesitant to say yes that I sometimes imagined I'd find myself standing up at the altar, alone."

She stared up at the face so softly lit by the glow of the carriage lamp by the window. As if any female would ever disappoint him. But she was glad he'd said it. "This is all a great adventure for me," she said seriously. "Forgive me if I sometimes seem ill at ease, but remember that I haven't been many places or done much."

"You are as you are and how I found you is how I love you."

She tilted her head to the side. "You almost speak in poetry sometimes, did you know that? Do you write any?"

"No!" he said, throwing up his hands. "I leave that to Mr. Byron and his friends. It's just a tic, a habit of mine. You don't mind?"

"Mind? I love it."

"Good, now come, let's get out," he said, rising to stand half crouched over her because of the lack of height in the carriage. He offered her his hand. "We'll rest here for the night, and we'll be able to reach the Hall by nightfall. Is that all right with you, or would you rather go slower, and in shorter stages?"

"I can't wait to see it," she said.

"Good," he said. "Neither can I."

It was a comfortable old inn; the floors and ceilings tilted by the weight of centuries, the rooms small, but clean. The air smelled of woodsmoke and good things cooking.

"You wash, change, whatever you want," Aubrey said. "You won't have to share. There's a room down at the end of the hall with a wooden tub, for me. Or do you want me to assist you? Your personal maid didn't want to leave London. We'll find you a new one when we get to my home. Since the servant's carriage stopped a while back on the road anyway, there's no one to lend you a hand, but me. Do you need any help now?"

"Help?" she asked, puzzled.

"Assistance. Getting off your gown, undoing the catches and hooks, and the rest."

She laughed. "I'm not helpless. And there aren't any hooks, stays, or cinchers these days, or at least I don't use them."

He paused, and then grinned. "What was I thinking of? I suppose you can imagine. Don't look so stricken! I'm joking. Now, do what you will, but please don't take forever. I'm hungry."

She went into the bedchamber and bit her lip. He hadn't seemed to be joking. He'd seemed surprised, and only then amused, as though he'd just made a recover. She hoped she hadn't displeased him.

It didn't seem so.

He was charming at the dinner table, and made her laugh and drink, and toasted their marriage until she was dizzy with merriment and wine.

The only thing that bothered her was how the serving girl was eyeing him, simpering, casting him glances beneath her eyelashes. The landlord's wife and little daughter had ogled him too. So had the few old women in the common room they'd passed. She didn't blame them. He was something to see. Tonight he was dressed in autumnal colors, the gold of his waistcoat and the brown of his jacket complimenting the deep color of his eyes. They all must be wondering how a simple curly-headed young woman had snared such a magnificent male, even for a night. Eve knew many of her own friends wondered about that. She couldn't blame them. But somehow she *had* snared him and rejoiced in it.

She sat back and waited for dessert. Lud! She thought, looking at him but he was a magnificent looking male. Would she ever get used to it? It was odd that sometimes she didn't notice and other times she couldn't take her eyes from him. She hoped that as she grew accustomed, she'd be less stricken by his masculine beauty. And she hoped that would never happen.

He leaned forward. "You look wonderfully well tonight," he said.

She was just merry enough to answer him with a peal of unrestrained laughter. "Just the right thing to say to a bride," she said when she'd done, and he sat watching her, puzzled. "You're either so in love that you can't see straight, which I don't see. Or you're foxed. Or you're trying to make me feel better about how our serving girl is mooning over you. Because I think that any minute she'll serve herself up on a plate with your pudding." She giggled, picturing it.

"I look neat, tidy," she went on. "But not much more, I seldom do. I'm wearing a russet frock, and it's true that it's very nice. I brushed my hair and it curled right up again. Still, in no way do I look *wonderful*."

"To me," he said simply, "you do. So. You think I ought to order up cakes instead of pudding, for fear of getting a lass in my dessert?"

They laughed. By the time they'd finished, it was quiet in the old inn, the serving girl had finally, with many a backward look, left them. Only the sound of the crackling hearth fire competed with their murmurous talk. Eve had one more glass of port.

"If you were trying to make me addled," she said with a lopsided grin, "you've succeeded."

"Come," he said, rising "I wasn't trying. And it's definitely time for you to sleep."

This time he escorted her up the stairs and into the bedchamber. Then he bowed and said, "I'll be back soon. Go to bed, Eve."

When the door closed behind him, she looked around, made sure the shutters were closed, and quickly drew her gown over her head. She hurried to her trunk. She tossed open the lid and found the finely embroidered gown she'd gotten from a friend for her wedding night. She flung it on, and shivering, jumped into the bed. One lamp was lit. She wondered if she should lie down or sit up, waiting for him. He'd said they wouldn't make love tonight. But they were going to sleep together. Who knew what would happen? She could hope, or worry. She did both.

The room grew chill, so she lay down and pulled the coverlets up.

She was drowsing, between sleep and ragged bits of dreams, when she felt the high feather tick tilt down on one side. She sat up, surprised, blinking, trying to rub the sleep from her eyes. Aubrey sat in the bed beside her. He wore a white nightshirt.

"Sleep," he said, gently turning her, guiding her down to the feather tick with him. "We'll both sleep, together, as though we've done it all our lives." His voice became soft and dreamy as he drew her down into his embrace. He lay behind her, an arm tucked over her waist, his lips to her ear. "Sleep now," he purred, "sleep as though we were two birds in a nest, two fawns in the heather, two sheep in a clover-filled meadow, sleep, and dream of morning. Sleep, Eve. Sleep."

When she finally lay breathing slow and steady, he laid his own head on the pillow behind hers.

Her hair smelled clean and lightly perfumed. He felt the stirrings of desire as she sighed in her sleep and drew up her knees so she could curl up closer, pressing her rounded bottom until it fit tightly and so sweetly into the curve of his body. He suppressed the urge to wake her with kisses and caresses. He'd waited too long and worked too hard for such simple surcease. Desire was nothing to him. What he wanted was everything. All had to go right. However much he wanted her, he would not conceive his first child here. They had to go home.

He lay awake, eyes open, planning. He didn't sleep for a long time. But he was not unhappy.

"It's nothing like I thought it would be," Eve blurted.

"Disappointed?" Aubrey asked, as he lay back so she could see it better.

"No, fascinated," she said, bending to look out the window on his side. She turned her head and gazed out the other window as the coach turned in the drive. His estate was nothing like any other stately home she'd ever seen. The front of grand estates she'd seen were bare of trees and their drives were barren twists of roadway made of shells or sand.

Aubrey's home was huge, surrounded by ancient trees, and the road to it was more like a drive through a meadow. The house itself was made of grey stone, and huge. But it didn't tower over the scene. In fact, it seemed longer than high; shaped vaguely like an inverted U, with the sides going off behind the front. It glittered, but only because of the last of the sunlight echoing off all the windows. She could see a huge glass dome in the center of the house. Behind and to the sides were trees, a wood full of them. A soft mist had begun floating up from the forest in the last light, making the scene look magical.

The carriage drove to the front of the house, and stopped. An assemblage of servants stood waiting there. Aubrey smiled, and sat up.

"Welcome, my lady," he said, "to our home."

Before she could answer, he bent, scooped her up in his arms, and carried her out of the carriage. He waited a moment with her held high in his arms, looking at the assembly in front of the house. "My bride," he announced with pride. "Your lady."

Eve was charmed. The estate looked to be as unique, beautiful, and different as was her new husband. "I'll take you on a brief tour," he said after he'd introduced her to his servants. "We have things here that were accumulated over the centuries. It will take almost that for you to see it all, but there are some things I thought you'd like to see now."

She thought that some of his servants might also have been relics collected by his ancestors, and smiled to herself. But they all seemed happy to see her, and as polite as she could wish. So she took his arm, and followed him through the house.

What first struck her eye was the huge dome over the entry she'd set foot into. It covered the high ceiling the way murals and frescoes did in other great houses. But instead of painted clouds, or lofty pagan gods or dancing cherubs, she saw the sky itself. She saw the darker clouds of the coming night high above her, a slice of a new moon, and the first far off glints of early stars pecking holes in the purpling sky.

"In the daytime, it's even more impressive," Aubrey said, watching her face as she looked upward. "You'd think it would get hot under the dome during the summer. It might in any other clime. But this is England, and so that's rare. It wouldn't matter if it blazed. My people love the light of sun or moon."

"It is magnificent," she said. "I seldom see sky so clearly even when I'm out of doors. Is it the height, or the curve of the glass? It must be terrifying in a storm."

"Terrifying? Maybe, at first. Later, you'll find that lightning decorates the hall for us. You'll become used to it. Now let's go on, there's too much to see in an hour, or a day. But I want to show you some of your home before you grow too weary."

The downstairs rooms connected each to each and led in a path through the house. Aubrey took Eve through rooms where Elizabethan chests stood next to twelfth -century ones, where ancient hand-hewn high-back chairs surrounded intricately carved inlaid wooden tables. There were spindly Chinese consoles of modern design, and massive wooden chairs that looked as though they'd be perfect in a hall of ancient kings. The walls held pennants from bygone wars and murals of modern design, all that lacked was martial body armor. Yet somehow, some way, it all fit together. It was a history of England, all ajumble, and all equally prized.

She gaped. "Your ancestors were like magpies," she finally breathed. "But magpies with good taste."

He bowed. "Thank you."

"Where are the family portraits?" she asked, suddenly realizing that though she'd seen landscapes and portraits of flowers, horses, and haystacks, she hadn't seen what most great houses held: a corridor of ancestors.

"We weren't vain," he said briefly. "Look at the shadows! It's time for dinner. I'll show you upstairs to your chamber, and then we'll dine."

"My chamber?" she asked, stopping in her tracks. "You'll live elsewhere?"

He looked down at her. "I have my bedchamber, of course," he said.

"I wish you didn't," she blurted. "That is, I ought to have mentioned it before. I didn't expect . . . I don't want to be alone."

He stared at her, consideringly. His lips quirked. "You're saying you wouldn't have married me if you'd known we'd have separate bedchambers? Most of the *ton* does, you know. People in highest Society always have, for ages. When this place was built—and that was so long ago no one quite remembers when the first stone was laid down—there were the master's quarters, and his wife's, just as the ancient kings and queens had it. But don't worry. We'll share part of the night, of course," he added, smiling.

She looked down as her heart sank. The house

was huge, and he'd be far from her through all their nights. The size of the place wasn't really the point. When he was beside her, she questioned nothing. Long nights apart would surely feed her doubts about this hasty union. She couldn't tell him that, it would be insulting. Besides, she wanted to be near him day and night. Especially night.

"You want to change that tradition?" he asked softly.

"I didn't know about that tradition."

He looked bemused, then shrugged. "You're very different from any female I've known. Or any that has ever lived here, in fact. But that's why I chose you for my bride. Very well. Off with the old. It's time for something new. I'll have your night things moved into my chamber, or mine into yours. There's a connecting door, it won't be that much work or take that much time. Just decide where we'll sleep and there we will always sleep together. Come, I'll show you both rooms, and you decide."

He offered her his arm.

She took it, and stepped more confidently into her new life with him. She'd won a small point. It boded well.

He led her to the stair, and looked down at her, smiling slightly. She'd managed to surprise him. She was changing things here, things that no woman had ever thought of doing. That boded very well for him; it lifted his spirits, and made him hope, once again, that this time, he'd made the right choice.

Chapter 7

She woke to a kiss, a light warm velvety touch on her lips. Her eyelashes fluttered open. She saw a pair of soft brown eyes smiling into hers, and she felt like a girl in a fairy story.

Then Eve realized who she was, where she was, and who he was, and she flung her arms around his neck. "Good morning," she said with joy.

Aubrey smiled, but backed away.

She dropped her arms, her eyes widening. She put a hand in front of her mouth, remembering she hadn't yet rinsed her mouth or brushed her teeth.

He laughed. "No, your breath is as sweet as the morning breezes, but this morning we have things to do. We have the night to come for loving," he said in a gentler voice, "and all the nights to come, after that. But *this* morning," he said, as he straightened to stand beside the bed, "you have to see more, learn more about this hall and the lands around it. I don't want you wandering out and getting lost a foot from home. Tonight," he added, touching her nose with one finger, "is also the night of a full moon. Very propitious. Now, breakfast with me?"

She realized he was fully dressed, and very fine looking even in casual garb. He wore a blue jacket, a light gold waistcoat, white linen with a carelessly tied neckcloth that looked so well it might become the latest fashion. As he walked to the door, she saw he also wore brown breeches and high brown boots.

"I'll get up and dressed in a moment," she cried, flinging back the bedcovers.

"Don't rush, I'll wait for you. I'm sending a maid in to help you. If you like her, she's yours."

She laughed. "I hope you don't really mean that. I don't want a slave, but a good maid would be just the thing."

"She says she's never been a lady's maid before," he said. "I think she was a dairy maid before. But she's certainly anxious to please."

So she was. Betty was plump and strong, wore her hair skinned back into a crown of braids, and looked like she was well used to working with cattle. But she was so eager to please that Eve was charmed. Betty didn't know that silence was a hallmark of her new trade either, and so Eve learned a lot about her new home while getting dressed. Betty babbled incessantly as she helped Eve pick out a gown to wear, and helped to do her hair. Eve didn't have the heart to silence her. She stopped listening after a while. But then something caught her attention.

". . . And a tight crew they are here, ma'am," Betty was saying as she brushed Eve's hair. "Right friendly, but thick as thieves 'cause they been together for ages. Didn't have no one to use as a lady's maid, though, and no one else young enough to help you, so here I am. I hope I please you. Some girls didn't want to work here. I s'pect it's because there ain't many young people about. But I already have a fellow in mind, and I need a dowry. Now, the master's mother was a real lady, and she had a real lady's maid, but they both went abroad and never came back. Since there wasn't no need for another lady's maid before you came, they put word out into the village, and down through the crofts, and here I be. Don't that look fine, though? You're so lucky to have such curly hair, ma'am, it's a treat."

"Mr. Ashford's mother was a real lady?" Eve asked curiously.

"Oh, to her fingertips, or so they say. You are too, 'course, ma'am, but there's ladies and ladies, y'know. She acted just like one. I never saw her 'cause I weren't born yet. She was high in the in-step; she didn't have a kind word for no one, and kept to herself. She was stately, she was, beautiful as she could stare, so say all. It were a great pity, all said, that she couldn't have a babe. But when she got older, Mr. Ashford's father, he took her to Italy, or somewheres abroad for her health. And lo and behold, but she has a baby after all, and after all that time. 'Course it wrecked her health, and she never come back. Mr. Ashford's father, he took it that hard, he never returned neither.

"But here's our new master and if he ain't the spit and image of his father—'cept'n one was fair as an angel and the other's dark as a handsome devil, pardon me saying so—I ain't standing here, and so says all. And what a sight he is, if you don't mind me saying, ma'am. Anything else you want me to do?" she asked, as she put down the hair-brush.

"I think the housekeeper must tell you the rest. I have to go meet my husband now," Eve said. "Thank you, that will be all for now." She took one last look at herself in the glass. She wasn't a stately beauty, but he knew that. And she looked about as good as she could in her newest green gown. She hurried down the stairs to meet her husband.

Betty was right; he was a sight to see.

But Eve just went to him and kissed him good

morning, as though she'd been greeting monstrously handsome gentlemen every morning of her life.

After they breakfasted, they walked down winding green paths beneath ancient trees. They strolled beside babbling streams that made bright music to compete with the birdsongs above them, and walked through sunny meadows busy with butterflies and bees. There was a pond filled with lilies and carp, and a lake in the distance. Aubrey's estate was beautiful, but in time an enchanted Eve noticed that though it was undeniably magnificent, it had no formal gardens, no rose arbors, no iron gates, mazes, classic statues, Roman fountains, or any of the other usual accouterments to a great house. She asked Aubrey about it.

"You think we should have some?" he asked in return.

"I don't think they fit here," she said. Then she held out her arms for balance as she stepped behind him, toe to heel, across a fallen log that bridged a sparkling stream. "There," she said, when they reached the other side. "That was fun. I haven't done that for years. What would you have done if I'd fallen in?"

"Considering that it's only about four inches deep here, I think I'd have laughed," he said, sitting down on the grassy bank.

She laughed, and sat beside him. "This place *is* magical," she said, looking up at the lacy canopy of willows above her. "Untouched. I only asked because most English aristocrats start with houses that are like yours, I suppose. Or else they're Elizabethan, medieval, or actual castles or such. Then they make their houses Roman or Grecian or into the latest fad. Speaking of that, lately they fill their grounds with artificial nature, to try to look as yours do now."

"Ours," he corrected her.

"Ours then. But did you know the lengths they go to? Some even have man-made hermit's grottoes. I actually saw one once. All fitted out with a cave. And a specially hired hermit, all beard and bushy eyebrows. When guests were led by on a tour, he'd poke his nose out and scowl at them." She grinned. "Actually, the poor fellow was always sneaking down to the local pub when he thought no one would notice."

"Disappointed because I haven't a hermit, much less a grotto?"

She cocked her head to the side. "No, not at all. But surprised? Yes. It's rare to find such a beautiful place, untouched. Or seemingly so."

He looked into the far distance. She watched as the dappled sunlight played with his hair, making it gleam like moonbeams were in it. "We never added anything to disturb the place. As I said, I think this was how England looked long, long ago."

"Have you any Druid grottos then?" she asked whimsically.

His expression grew cold. "No. And they wouldn't be satisfied with a grotto, they wanted everything. They weren't a pleasant people. They crushed all who opposed them, even as the Romans crushed them."

She stared at him. "Are there any more of them around?"

He turned his head to her. "No, they're long gone. Why do you ask? Are you worried?"

"I worried at the look on your face. Why do you hate them so?"

He laughed, and stood up, offering her his hand. "I heard about them from my father, who heard from his father and so on. It's an old story in my family."

"Tell me about your family," she said as she rose.

"I have. I did. There isn't much more to tell. We're not prolific. One or two children at most a generation for generations now. So it's up to us to change things."

"Shall we have a hundred or two hundred babies then?" she asked as she fell into step beside him.

"And that," he said, stopping to kiss her, "is

why I love you so. Not just for this, but for the laughter. I need that."

Dinner was magnificent. Aubrey said so, and complimented his cook. Eve thought so too, but then, she would have found any food taken in his presence to be delicious. She was, she realized, falling more in love with her new husband by the minute. She wondered if this was true of all new brides. She doubted it. Aubrey was the most handsome, intelligent, and kind groom any female could want. And he knew so much. Had she known a particle of that before, she'd have married him even sooner.

As they'd walked and talked, she realized that he knew the names of every plant, from the merest mosses to the tallest trees. He knew the birds, the animals whose tracks they saw, and having seen so much of the world, he knew which ones were to be found only in England. And which could be only found on his grounds at Far Isle.

He knew great literature and the men and women who had written it, so well it was as though he'd actually known those authors from so long ago. And best of all, he knew about her: her moods, her fears, her joys. When he looked at her she could feel it to her marrow.

By the time the sun had set, and she'd played the pianoforte in his music room, Aubrey accompanying her in his low, strong tenor, she was so in love and in lust that she shocked herself.

She sat back as the song ended, and felt a soft kiss on her ear. She turned her head, and he sat beside her on the piano bench. He slid a hand around her waist and pulled her close, and kissed her properly, and then, she thought with pleasure, very improperly too.

He ran his lips alongside her neck, and she shivered.

"It's early, but I think it might be time for bed," he said quietly.

"Oh, yes," she said.

He rose, lifting her in his arms. She squeaked with surprise.

"Think I'll drop you?" he asked.

"Well, I think it's possible," she said.

"Then hold on tight," he said, and walked out of the salon to the long stair, and from there, down the hallway to their room. She clung to him, and reveled in how light she felt in his arms, how right she felt in his embrace.

"I dismissed your maid hours ago," he said, as he entered their room and kicked the door shut behind them. "Do you mind?"

"Mind?" she managed to say as they sank to the bed together. "Mind what?"

He laughed. But there was no gloating his tone,

and nothing but love in his eyes. The fashion was for light gowns, and no stays or corsets. He had her gown off in moments, with her help. He sat, for a moment, looking at her naked form. She wished, in that moment, that she had something more to show him. And without knowing she did so, she raised her hand to cover her breasts. He took her hand down and held it gently in his own and looked at her.

"Perfect," he said.

"Well, smallish," she said in a low voice.

"Perfect," he said again, cupping one in his hand. "Tilted and firm, and lovely. You are so lovely," he said, lowering his mouth to her breast.

She shivered, and opened her eyes. "Thank you. And you are so . . . dressed," she said with a touch of uneasiness.

He laughed, and sat back. "True. You wish it to be otherwise?"

"Well, of course," she said. And then she blinked. "Shouldn't I?"

"Some women do not— Forgive me, I shouldn't mention any other women now."

"Well, if I'd done this before, I'd certainly be comparing, in my mind, of course," she added fastidiously.

He shook his head as he began to remove his jacket. "My level-headed Eve. You astonish me."

"A great many?" she asked in a smaller voice, as he shucked off his waistcoat to follow his jacket.

"A great many what?" he asked as his head emerged from his shirt.

She was so busy looking at his chest she almost couldn't answer. His body was contoured like that of the statues of ancient Greek gods that she'd seen in the new museum in London. "A great many lovers," she murmured absently, watching as he removed his boots, and then stood to remove his breeches.

His hands halted on the buttons on the fall of his breeches. "Would it matter?"

"I'd like to know. But if it isn't done, never mind," she said, suddenly horribly embarrassed by her lack of knowledge of what to expect, as well as what was wrong or right to ask him.

"Anything we do is done," he said. "Yes. A great many. But I have no diseases, if that's worrying you."

She raised a hand to brush his words away. "No. I know you too well to expect that. You're too honorable to surprise me with that."

He looked, in that instant, pained.

"I shouldn't be talking about this at all, I know, I know," she said in an agony of discomfit, scooping the coverlet up to cover her, and lowering her head to her bent knees.

There was silence and then she felt the mattress tick move as he sat on the bed beside her. "You may ask me anything," he said, his hand brushing back her curls from her forehead. "I can only tell you the truth."

"Then, I know I asked once before, I must know, did you . . . ever love anyone like this before?" she asked in a rush.

"Love anyone like this before? No," he said, against her ear. "To my sorrow and to my woe, no. And in all truth this is so. I vow it."

She raised her heated face, and she was beaming. "What a fool I am," she said, and came into his arms.

"Never," he said, as he gently lay her down against a pillow. "Never," he said as he joined her there.

He kissed her softly, at first, and then, because he felt her body straining to get closer to his, he deepened his kisses, and felt the warmth of her mouth against his. He touched her tongue with his own, and found her arching toward him, offering much more than her mouth. Her nipples were hard and crested against his chest; her hips arched into him, she laid one hand on his back, holding him closer to herself, the other at the nape of his neck. And all the while she murmured his name into his ear. When he felt his sex rising and straining toward her, he kept it trapped between them so he wouldn't end this luxurious searching too soon. She was wonderfully responsive to him, but then, he'd known it could be no other way with her. He hadn't guessed the absolute sweetness of her complete surrender to him, though, and he was charmed.

He was patient with her, Eve knew it. But she was ecstatically impatient with him. She knew the plain fact of what was to come, she was no fool. But she hadn't known how she'd react to it. She feared the pain she'd heard about. That had been before she knew the bliss. Now she did, and was eager to get on with it. He made her feel that ever more so. His lips on the peaks of her breasts, first one, then the other, was thrilling; his touch was so exquisite it set her aching, but with a sweet pain she loved. There was no holding back, none of the shyness she'd feared, nothing but such complete willingness that it even shocked her.

And then, too short a time, and far too long a time for her, she felt him raise himself, part her, touch her and set her trembling with weakness because of the strength of her desire. At last he brought himself to her, and she felt a slight pang, the first reminder that she'd never done this before. It brought her back to herself, she withdrew from him, if only in her mind, and her body began to tense for the first time, not with expectation of ecstasy, but fear of it.

He murmured something. She hardly heard it. He passed his hand over her hair, her face, as he kissed her, and then murmured more. Love words, she thought dazedly, they comforted her even as they aroused her. There was then no pain, no discomfort, only Aubrey filling her until they were as one.

Her body, relaxed, then tensed and shuddered. As he began to move, she moved with him until she felt herself gathering toward some incredible storm. Then at last, she felt the long slow shudders of a pulsing release. She uttered a short cry against his shoulder, and clung to him as waves of pleasure washed over her, and brought her, at last, to herself again.

Only then did he move more quickly, rocking into her, until he too shivered and groaned, and finally arching his back, released.

They both sank to the softness of the bed, and lay entangled, too overcome to speak, too much in pleasure to move from each other.

"Oh my," she finally said.

She heard his laughter, silent and deep in his chest.

"That was wonderful," she said.

"Yes," he said.

She bit her lip. "But there was no pain. Only joy. And a person who hasn't done it isn't supposed to feel such pleasure. That's supposed to come in time. But Aubrey, I swear to you that I've never done this before."

"I know," he said. "And pleasure comes when it will."

She disengaged from him slowly, and looked down at herself. "Oh!" she gasped, turning this way and that. "There's blood," she whispered, "but it didn't hurt. I vow it isn't my time of the month, I never knew a man before you."

"Hush," he said, taking her in his arms. "I know. And it doesn't have to hurt. I would never let myself hurt you."

She sank to her elbows above him. "I'm surely the luckiest female in all England," she whispered, gazing down at him.

"So I hope you will be," he said, but there was a trace of sorrow in his voice that made her frown. "Who can tell the future?" he asked briskly, sitting up and laying her down again. "I'll get some water, we'll clean up, and then you can dream in my arms. What you heard was partly right, tomorrow will be even better for you."

"How could it be?" she said.

He laughed. Then he rose and stepped from the bed. "We shall see. You haven't felt all we can do together. There's more, much more."

Her grin was touched with a little nervousness. "Can I bear it?"

"Oh, yes," he said. "You were made for me."

The night was at its height. Aubrey lay in bed with his bride asleep in his arms. The moonlight kept him wakeful until she'd fallen asleep. But she'd had question after question for him, as honest and eager as a child to know how she'd done, what did he think, was she what he'd wanted? The slice of moonlight that came through the window lit his smile. She was exactly what he wanted.

He rose from the bed in one smooth move. He kissed his sleeping bride lightly and whispered one word—"sleep"—to her.

Then he threw on a night robe, left the room and the house, and walked out into the broad moonlight at the back of his house. He stood basking in its cold glow. It was high midnight. The moon shone whole and full, white, and clear, and for those with eyes that could see there was sufficient light for living and dying. There were no sounds but those of the breeze-fluttering leaves in the trees in the forest; an occasional chirrup of late crickets, and the shivering sounds of those things that moved almost soundlessly on wing or feet through the night to devour them.

Aubrey put his face up to the moon and let his night robe fall from his shoulders to puddle at his feet. In that moment he looked like any of the glorious statues Eve had seen in cold marble in the museum. But he was cool living flesh. He closed his eyes, and sought answers.

She wasn't with child yet. He'd never really thought she could be, even she, not this soon.

But soon, he wordlessly promised to the moon.

He'd waited for her for so long. He still couldn't believe his good fortune in finding her. He'd pored through books, and tested memories, his own and others, and at last he'd found her. She would conceive his long-awaited son, if not at first, then at last. And at last, he'd be content. He hoped she would be too. He could assure it. Though in some small way, he regretted it. That surprised him; he never had regretted anything he'd done before.

But that was why he'd sought her out, and why he so prized her. Because she was like him as no other mortal woman had ever been. He treasured her and would continue to, for so long a time as they would have together. And, he thought, with sad surprise, maybe for long after too.

Then, refreshed and reborn in the cool quiet night, he caught up his robe, donned it again, and went back into his house.

He stepped softly into the bedchamber, and paused by her side. The moonlight lit her face where she lay dreaming on her pillow. He looked at her with tenderness. Those tousled curls framing her face were silvered by the night. Charming, she was, he thought, innocent and wise, honest to a fault, and utterly giving.

He was sorry for many things, but even so, for all he pitied her, he couldn't be sorry for having her. They would together change the world. His world. He'd make sure she'd find peace and happiness in her own as well. He bent to kiss her. Her eyes fluttered open and looked at him with a steady gaze. He was surprised.

"Where were you?" she asked, touching his dew dampened hair.

"I went out into the moonlight, to think," he said truthfully. "I didn't want to wake you by stirring too much in our bed," he added, lying.

"Why couldn't you sleep?" she asked.

"Because I couldn't be sure of dreaming of

you," he said, knowing it was the perfect thing to say.

And it was. They lay down together, and he took her back into his arms. She shivered at the chill of his body, but her own warmth soon warmed him. She slept again. He closed his eyes and gave thanks, again.

Chapter 8

The night was almost done, and gray shadows in the sky showed the coming dawn. Eve woke and stretched and yawned. She felt Aubrey stirring beside her, so she rose on one elbow to peer over his shoulder and look down into his face. He turned his head.

"Is it wrong to love what we do as much as I do?" she asked worriedly, glad of the dim light that hid her blushes.

"It's the rightest thing in the world," he said.

She sighed. "But I shock myself. I used to be such a proper young woman."

"Loving lovemaking with your husband is perfectly proper," he said. He sighed too now, growing weary, wondering how often he'd said that before, other places, other times

"Is it wrong to do the things we do *when* we make love?" she asked seriously.

"We do the things that please us. We were told to worship each other with our bodies and our hearts, weren't we?"

"But some things . . ." she said doubtfully.

He studied her carefully. "Have I ever made you do anything that frightened or disgusted you? Have I ever asked you to do anything against your will?"

"You've only ever pleased me and showed me how to please you, which pleased me more," she said.

"So why are you so sad? Do you feel guilty? Misused?"

"No. Just surprised at myself. You know, I think I have it. You," she finally said, "have ensorcelled me."

He'd been smiling but now his eyes widened and his breathing stilled.

"Yes," she said, planting a light kiss on the tip of his nose. She put an arm on his other side, framing him, and raised herself until she lay half atop his hard body. She looked down into his face. "Bespelled me, you have. Cast a web of sensual pleasure upon me so that I forget time and place. But I've fought free of it. It's been exactly three weeks since we married, and already I can see more clearly. The truth of it is that you could have saved all your black magic. I just love making love with you." She flopped over on her back again, and laughed.

He turned to her, and pulled her back into his arms. "Are you sure it isn't magic?" he asked, his lips on her neck.

She shivered. "Yes. But if love is magic, then it is. But the problem now is . . ." she paused and buried her head in his chest, "I don't know how to tell you this, or if I should . . . but we can't do more now, I don't think. The thing is that I woke an hour ago and discovered that I've got my courses," she said in a rush. "And so I don't know if we can now, can we? Well, but even if we could, my stomach aches. Now, if you've any magic left over, please use it now, will you?"

He laid her back on her pillow and kissed her lips. "You should tell me, and you have told me, and the only magic I know for that is willow bark tea, and warm compresses. Later, when the pain is eased, I'll show you I can please you anyhow."

"I believe you can," she said in a small voice. "But it makes me sad. And not just because of the discomfort. Do you think this means I'll have difficulty conceiving our baby?"

He laughed softly. "Eve, my love, we haven't been married yet a month. If babies came so easily, there wouldn't be room to put a foot down there'd be so many people on earth."

"But my friend Chloe conceived the day she was wed," she said nervously.

"Probably a few weeks before," he said. "It can happen the first time, but usually it takes much longer. Don't fret. We have a whole life ahead of us."

She knew he was right, but she was melancholy anyway. It was odd because she'd never felt particularly maternal before, beyond getting along with certain children. Now she discovered herself yearning for a child. Not just any child: a boy that looked like Aubrey, with inky black hair that fell into his big brown eyes. She had brown curls and eyes, but she'd never found it attractive. She still didn't want a copy of herself. She wanted his image in her son or daughter as she had seldom wanted anything before.

He put one large warm hand on her abdomen. "Now, go back to sleep. So we won't greet the dawn in our usual fashion. What of it? We have years full of mornings to come. Sleep. The sun isn't full up yet. Sleep."

She sighed, and snuggled close to him, fitting her bottom into his lap, holding his hand on her stomach. Soon he could feel her even breathing as she slept again. Only then did he relax.

* * *

"So there," Aubrey said later that morning as they walked down the lane by the great meadow. "Now I think you've seen all of it. What do you think? Do you still want me to put up statues and gazebos, fountains and succession houses?"

She stopped. "I never said that!" she declared, her hands on her hips. "I always said this place is enchanting as it is, and so it is. It's natural and beautiful, and magnificent in its way. I don't want anything more. But . . ." she hesitated.

"But?"

"But it would be nice to meet more neighbors," she blurted. "And see more people too. Not that I'm lonely. Please don't think that for a minute. How could anyone be lonely with you around? We read, we talk, we walk; I've never been so happy. All that is positively true. But I want to show off. I want to show *us* off," she added, truthfully.

"Wouldn't it be nice to have a party?" she asked him. "Not that I'm a social butterfly. I'm actually more a bee, because I like to do things, not flit from party to party. Still if we have a party, we can invite some of my old friends, and my brother too. I don't know if my father would stir to come so far, but I do know Sherry would jump at a chance to see where I live. He's written me, hinting about it. And I want to share my joy. If we did have a party

I could get to meet some of your friends too. Our honeymoon will last forever, I hope. But we've passed the first moon of it, haven't we? So it isn't really a honeymoon anymore. Though it feels like one," she added quickly.

"So it does and so we have," he said.

He smiled at her. She was still adorable to him, and that was so unusual, so charming, and so pleasant that he himself had forgotten how much time had passed. She was a delight. Saucy and pretty, and best of all, she never bored him; she made the world seem new again. Her manners were impeccable, her conversation was amusing, her intelligence keen, her constantly busy mind kept him on his toes. She was all fire in his bed, and all warmth in her heart. Nothing embarrassed her if he asked it of her, but then he never asked anything of her he wouldn't do himself. Nothing displeased her if it pleased him, and everything she did pleased him.

And yet, they could and did argue. They disagreed about politics and literature almost as often as they agreed, and it was a treat for them both. Because they never got really angry at each other. She'd come to him without fear or artifice, and was honest with him and with herself. He regretted he couldn't say the same for himself. But they were happy as it was. He'd known so many females, but no one exactly like her. She gave love even as she took it. Unlike the beauties and the titled females in his past, and some he had lived with far longer, Eve had already found a niche in his heart he hadn't known was there. He reasoned it was because of how alike they were, more than he'd ever believed possible. His heart was high, now he believed all things were possible, even his life's dream of content.

Today she wore a russet gown, the color of the turning leaves. With the breeze in her curls, and her light step as they walked, she reminded him of some wild creature that had just stepped out of the wood. It made him feel even more comfortable.

"And it's a beautiful autumn," she persisted. "There's been little rain and I think the good weather will hold at least until winter. When winter comes, everyone in London goes to his or her own homes for Christmas, or they go off to huge Christmas parties at country estates. I don't think I want to go to all that trouble, what with guests staying over for twelve nights, and Yule logs, and caroling. And gathering the holly and the ivy to decorate the place, giving gifts to everyone, feasting every night, and arranging carriages to take the guests to and from church. Just listing the things to do exhausts me. Do you want to go to such lengths?"

"No, not at all."

"Are you cold?" she asked, cocking her head to the side.

"Why should you say that?"

"I just saw you shiver," she said.

He smiled, she watched his every move. It was flattering, and dangerous. Perhaps she did need diversion. "I think a party held on All Hallows Eve would be pleasant," he mused. "That's coming up soon. We could decorate the Hall and feast and have games, and yet keep our London guests happy for only three or four days, not twelve nights. It isn't customary to stay so long for that kind of party anyway. Nor would anyone want to go to anything but a churchyard, and if they did, there'd be no carriages to arrange because they could walk to that. The guests I'd invite live closer by too, so they wouldn't stay overnight in any event. Would you like that?"

"Yes!" she said excitedly. "What a good idea. We could have our guests bring costumes, like the night when we agreed to marry," she said, as he'd hoped she would.

"And will you come as a ragged kitchen maid this time?"

"No," she said seriously. "I'd like to come as your queen."

He repressed a shiver. She was at times so close

to the truth without knowing it that he wondered if she really knew more than he thought.

"So you shall be my queen," he said. "Now, I think you were right. It's early autumn, and I never get sick. But the chill of the day does seem to be getting to me. I must be coming down with something. Or it's just that you and your insatiable demands have worn me out," he said, just to see her blush. "Shall we go in and have some tea, sit by the fire and warm up while we plan our gala?"

She grinned up at him. "I wish I could warm you completely, no matter the consequences. But soon, in a few days, I can."

He took her hand in his. "Just seeing you happy warms me, Eve."

"Does it? Then you'll never be cold again," she said.

He wished that were true, but was too wise to say anything, and far too wise to believe it.

"Aubrey," Eve said. "There's a door we can't open."

He looked up from the papers he was studying.

She was standing in the doorway to his study, her hair hidden under a kerchief, an apron tied around her waist. She looked like the ragged Ella of the Cinders she had played those months ago. Mrs. Hood, his housekeeper, stood by her side.

"I see. And you want to open it to find my beheaded wives?" he asked.

"No. I wouldn't think you'd be so sloppy," she said impatiently. "I want to open it because we're clearing house for guests."

"Where is the door?" he asked, laying down his pen,

"In the back of the house, near the kitchens. If it opened, I think it would be a room that exited to the kitchen gardens. But I can't be sure. There's no window on the outside there. We shoved and pried, and Mrs. Hood went through all her keys, but the door won't open."

He stretched. "I'll come along and see, but it's probably just another one of the rooms that my ancestors bricked over." He laughed. "Your eyes will fall out if they open any wider. I'm sorry to disappoint you, Eve, my love, but there's no pirate treasure or skeletons behind those doors. They were either priest's holes that were closed after the burning of priests stopped being such a sport, or simply rooms my ancestors no longer had any use for. When there's a house this big, it's easier to close a room than to tear down part of the house to be rid of it. Some of my forebears were as miserly as some were reckless spenders.

And it's more amusing to add new spaces than to recover lost ones. We've doors to nowhere all over the place. But let's go see this one. It may be just a stuck doorjamb."

He nodded to his aged housekeeper, and followed her and Eve to the back of the long house. They stopped in a corridor in front of a dark wooden door that fit seamlessly into the wall. Only a latch on its side showed that it had ever been a door.

He nodded. "As I thought. It goes nowhere, and never opens. The others in the house are mostly unnoticeable because they don't have latches. They've been painted or papered over. But not here, and that was odd. I used to dream about what might be behind this one when I was a boy. It enlivened my life quite a bit."

"I thought you grew up in Italy," Eve said, her forehead wrinkling.

The hallway was suddenly silent. Mrs. Hood stared at the floor.

"So I did," Aubrey said easily. "My father told me about this door, because he'd tried to open it when he was a boy. I dreamed about it so much that I swore the first thing I'd do when I came here would be to hack down that door. But I only found others like it. And then I found you, and the thought went out of my mind. Do you want me to

call in workmen now so we can have a peek? I
suspect all we'll find is a brick wall behind it, and
when we knock those down, we'll only have an
empty room."

"Lord, no!" Eve said. "I don't want to start any
new work now. I just want to get rooms cleared
for our guests. Oh, this will be such fun!"

"So it will," he promised. "I was just writing
out my invitations. Mrs. Hood, Far Isle will have
more guests than it's had in many a year. You'll
need more help than we have. Ask at the stables,
and ask the cook, and then get some of the villagers to come work here for a few weeks."

Mrs. Hood lowered her gaze.

"I understand, of course," he went on in a
smoother voice, "it's a busy time of year for them,
getting the slaughter done, killing the cattle and
hogs that wouldn't get through the winter, bring-
ing in the last of the crops and so on. So I will, of
course, pay very well. I'll pay everyone double for
their trouble."

The housekeeper looked up. "Aye," she said.
"For that, they'll do it."

"I thought so," he said. "That will include you
and the staff, of course. Guests are more trouble
than you bargained for. Now, Eve. Have you finished your guest list? How many may we expect?"

"I don't know how many to expect, because you

never know who's coming. I know Sherry will come, but my father won't. He's not much of a one for traveling, and less of a fellow for parties. He's very happy to be home in the countryside again at his own manor, and I don't think anything would budge him—except for Christmas, and then only because he could stay for a fortnight. But everyone else is curious, both relatives and friends. You were a sensation in London, Aubrey. Still, we'll be competing with parties in London at that time of year. So, I'd think about two dozen."

"I'll only have a handful of guests, if that. My Italian family and my friends from abroad probably won't come. But I still have a few here in England."

"They haven't been here in many a year, sir," Mrs. Hood said repressively. "Not a guest, nor family nor friend, not since I come here," she added. "If you'll pardon my saying so."

"Oh, some will come, if only in disguise," he said. "They're shy, but as curious as anyone. More so, perhaps."

She blanched. "I've got to see to dinner, ma'am," she said to Eve. She ducked a curtsy, and hurriedly left them.

"That's peculiar," Eve said, looking after her. "She looks worried. Is she afraid of your friends or anyone in your family?"

"Well, you may as well know now, as later," he said on a resigned sigh. "The local folk are superstitious. Far Isle was built on what was thought to be a fairy mound, eons ago. At any rate, for years it was thought to be a place for the gatherings of the elder folk of all kinds. The stuff legends are made of. The hill probably started out as an ancient burial barrow, or such. Then myths were laid over it. At any rate, it was considered a place of primeval magic. Often such places were made into holy sites, like martyr's holy wells, churchyards and such, in order to subdue pagan practices of worship. But the church never claimed this place. It may be why my ancestors never changed the nature of it either.

"And since it's been unoccupied for so long a stretch of time, since I was born," he said, "I suspect the locals have some fantastic tales brewing again about Far Isle and its master. What else is there to do here in the countryside but gossip? If there's no gossip, then they make some up. Disregard it."

"I thought fairies were good luck," Eve said. "When I was a little girl I was told that when the lawns showed a circle of mushrooms, that meant fairies danced there in the night."

He shook his head. "Little pretty people floating about with wands and gossamer wings? No, in the old days, fairies were thought to be human size and cold-hearted, and they were much feared. It was said they could be cruel. Remember *A Midsummer Night's Dream*? Everyone tried to clear out of the forest by nightfall. Shakespeare and his audience thought the fairy folk were powerful creatures with great magic, but no charity, and no concern for anyone but themselves. Don't worry. We'll fill this place with human laughter, that's enough to chase all evil spirits away."

"I thought that lured them," Eve said.

"Ah, now I've frightened you. Want to go to London instead?"

"Never," she said. "This is my house now. I won't let fairies or brownies or goblins or ghosts chase me away."

"Hush," he said, laughing. "Don't tempt fate."

"You're just saying that so I stay close to you in the night."

"You need fear in order to do that? Where have I failed you?"

She came into his arms, and kissed him. "You?" she said when she could speak again. "Nowhere. Never."

"Stay close to me, Eve," he said, holding her tight, his voice suddenly dark and serious. "Always, at all times, here, and there or anywhere. I will never let anything harm you."

"Nor will I let anything harm you," she said.

He laughed. "My brave Eve. Thank you. I know. That just exactly why I married you."

And each having spoken the truth, they laughed, and walked away together, discussing the guests, and menus, and the coming house party.

Chapter 9

Sheridan, for once, was speechless. He looked up and down and through the rooms as he paced through Far Isle with Eve, and said nothing.

"Well?" she finally said, stopping in a side parlor to look up at him.

"Well, you've landed on your feet," he said.

"What a vulgar expression," she said, wrinkling her nose.

"Didn't used to think so before you got so grand," he commented. "But lord! My brother-in-law has got everything: looks, funds, and a family estate to beat all—and you," he added sheepishly. "Missed you, Evie, I did, really."

They hugged briefly, and then grinned at each other. Eve always wondered how her parents had produced two children so unalike. Sherry was handsome in coltish fashion; tall and lanky. Gray-eyed and with an aquiline nose, he had his sister's curls, ruthlessly cut short. But otherwise, it would

be difficult to tell they were siblings. Sheridan
was also happy-go-lucky, although he had a kind
heart, he never took anything too much to heart.
But then, Eve thought, he was still young. As tall
as he'd grown, Eve never thought of him as anything but her baby brother.

"This place is in the back of nowhere," he commented now, "but it's a gem. Don't you get lonely,
though?"

"Well, I didn't," she said honestly. "I was on my
honeymoon most of this time, you know."

He flushed.

"And so I haven't had time to meet the local ladies yet," she went on, to spare his blushes. "Nor
have I yearned to, to tell the truth. Aubrey takes
up my time, and very nicely, thank you. But now
that everyone's coming to our party, I guess I do
feel as though I'd forgotten what the rest of the
world was like. I'm so glad you came, Sherry."

"Wouldn't have missed it." His brow furrowed.
"You're not trying to get me leg shackled, are you?
You haven't got some female ready to pounce on
me, do you?"

"Sherry," she said impatiently. "You're only
nineteen. Far too young for marriage."

"Well, that's a relief," he said. "But sometimes
newlyweds can't rest until they get the rest of the
world in the same state."

"Not me," she said. "Anyway, I haven't yet met the woman I think deserves you."

He laughed. "Good old Evie. I can take that two ways, can't I?"

She grinned.

"Sheridan," Aubrey said as he came into the salon. "Greetings and welcome. I wondered where you were?"

"Lud!" Sherry said, taking his proffered hand and eyeing him. "Marriage suits you, Aubrey. You're handsomer than ever."

"More handsome," Eve corrected him.

"Thank you both," Aubrey said, bowing.

Eve made a face at him.

"Say, any chance we can go riding?" he asked Aubrey. "I saw your stables. Looks like you've got some real beauties there."

"I do, and we will, if you like," Aubrey said. "You didn't have to pour a bucket of butter over me, I'd have asked you if you hadn't asked me."

"Me? Flattering just so I could get a ride?" Sherrie asked. "Ha. As if flattery would move you. Bet you've heard every compliment in the book. But I'd like a go to shake off the dust of that coach ride here."

"Good. Do you want to join us?" Aubrey asked Eve.

"I do but I can't. My old friend Lucinda and

her sister are due here soon, and I want to spend some time with them. Oh, Aubrey, this was such a good idea! We'll have such a wonderful time. I can't wait for the actual masquerade, but I also want lots of time before it so I can talk to my old friends again, and even pass an hour or two with this scapegrace here."

"There's time for everything," Aubrey said. "And if he wishes, this scapegrace here can stay on after the ball for as long as he likes."

"Well, I don't know," Sherry said. "Haven't seen what your cook can do yet."

"Oh, wonderful!" Eve said, ignoring his jest. "But now, I have to be sure Lucinda's bedchamber is ready for her. See you both later. Have fun." She stood on her toes and kissed Aubrey's cheek. Then she dashed away down the hall.

"She is something, isn't she?" Sherry said, watching her leave. "Not in the common way or the usual style, but something wonderful, even so. I'm glad you saw that, Aubrey. I'm glad she's so happy. She means a lot to me."

"Anyone can see that," Aubrey said. "Never worry about her, I'll always be sure she's content. Now, shall we ride before any more guests get here and ruin our fun?"

* * *

"I thought you said you weren't laying traps for me with your friends," Sherry told Eve later that night.

"Mmm?" Eve said. They were slowly pacing along the paths in the back garden, after dinner. It was late. The other guests who had arrived were variously preparing for bed, still gossiping in the salon, or playing billiards with their host. Eve's duties were done and she was sharing some time with her brother. The night was so dark, the stars so far, and the moon such a sliver that it was hard for her to even see her brother at her side. Her own gown looked like a pink aura floating around her. Sherry, in customary black evening dress, was a shadow by her side.

"Your friend Lucinda's sister fluttered her eyelashes so much at me during dinner that I thought she might actually leave the table, rise up, and fly," Sherry said.

"I had to have her here, Sherry. There must be even numbers at the table, and you're a bachelor. And Grace is lovely.

"Never said no," he protested. "She's a pretty little thing, and a charmer too. But I don't want to marry yet. And she's the kind you have to marry. And that Turner woman! Has she run through all the married males in London by now, that she even considers me? As if I would! I don't mind being considered a rake, in fact, might do me a world of good, come to think of it. But an adulterer? I think not. At least," he said conscientiously, "not for the likes of her."

"I didn't notice."

"You don't notice anyone but your Aubrey."

She turned to look at him. "You think I'm neglecting you?"

"No, you're true blue, Evie. You *are* happy here, with him, and all?" he asked.

"Yes, and yes, here and with him, and all."

"You'd tell me if you weren't?"

"First thing," she promised. "Why? Is there anything you find amiss?"

He patted her hand where it lay on his arm. "With Aubrey? Nothing. Except he's so damned good-looking makes a fellow feel like a goblin next to him. But I have to say he don't seem to notice, though he must. He's a prime one, and no mistake."

They walked on in silence. They'd already discussed their father's state of health, and the latest London gossip, all of which was, they agreed, much the same as it had been when Eve had left. Now they walked in a comfortable silence. Until Sherry shivered.

"Lord!" he suddenly said, "But it's night out here."

Eve gave him a quizzical smile. "It *is* night. What did you have to drink this evening?"

"That's not what I mean," he said, raising his shoulders as though to deflect a blow. "It's darker than most nights. The stars are always closer in the countryside, but here, everything is. I don't know. It's hard to say. Your new home is a smashing place, everyone's all envy. But it's mysterious. It's almost as if you turn a corner, you can get lost forever, inside or out. Especially outside. Or something like that. Ah, I'm no good at words. Don't you feel it?"

"You think we're *haunted?*" she asked, laughing.

"No. I've been to haunted houses, castles and such. Good fun. Ghosts don't bother you much. They just go sailing around, rattling things, wanting to be noticed. Here, it's like someone's watching you all the time. Let's go back."

"You?" She stopped and stared at him. "My baby brother is still afraid of the dark?"

"Not afraid, Evie. Just that the back of my neck prickles. Not a good sign. How many times have you been out here by yourself in the night?"

"Never," she said. "I'm always with Aubrey."

"Well, see?" he asked.

"No," she said. "But we'll go back right now. I want you comfortable. What are you going to wear to the costume party on All Hallow's Eve?" she asked, to change the subject.

"Don't know yet. There are a few days to go, right? I brought some things along, but they don't seem to suit. Aubrey said there are heaps of old clothes and costumes in the attics here. I'll look them over. I fancy togging myself out and looking, well, splendid."

"Good," she said, linking arms with him. "So do I."

She parted with him in the hall, looked in on the last lingering guests, gave them a good night, and went up to her bedchamber. She'd sent her maid to bed hours before; the girl was overworked with all the company. Even though they'd gotten extra help from the village, few village maidens could play ladies' maid to Eve's guests. And even those guests that had brought their own maids with them always wanted more personal service.

Some lamps in the bedchamber had been left lit, lending a rosy glow to the darkness. Eve took off her gown and shift, and then stood staring into the looking glass.

She studied herself dispassionately. Nice breasts, she thought, but small. Firm, though, and they titled upward. She put a hand on the curve that defined her trim waist. Not much use for that, these days, she thought sadly, what with fashion's decreeing gowns that tied under the breasts. She could have a waist round as a carriage wheel and no one would know. Her stomach was flat . . . well, slightly rounded, only that. Her hips were in proportion to her breasts. Nicely defined, but nothing extraordinary, in her opinion. She sighed.

Aubrey entered the room and came toward her at once, smiling. She didn't shrink or try to cover her nakedness. He'd taught her not to be ashamed. Anyway, he did it for her; he stood behind her and put his hands over her breasts, cupping them. She shivered. His moved his hands to her shoulders, and frowned.

"You're tense. You look troubled. Why?" he asked, watching her reflection in the mirror.

She saw him in the glass in front of her, where he stood behind her, glowing like a candle in the dim room. Again she wondered at his masculine beauty. Somehow, seeing his reflection made him seem even less real, even more perfect, even slightly dreamlike. And yet she knew how very much flesh and blood he was. He was her husband, she knew him well, and still again, found herself wishing she knew him better, wondering if two people ever could be as close as one except in the act of love.

He gently kneaded her shoulders. "What is it, Eve?" he asked when she didn't answer at once.

She shook herself from her reverie. "I don't know," she said, with a shrug.

"Something anyone said? Tell me who. I'll turf them out this minute."

"Don't you dare. Actually, I suppose it was Sherry, and he didn't mean anything by it. We were walking outside and talking just now, but he was so uneasy we had to come in. He said that though the house was wonderful, he couldn't like the night here. He said he felt as though he was being watched."

Aubrey's hands stopped for a moment. Then he went on gently kneading her shoulders. "Did he, though?" he said. "Curious. I think he had either too much wine at dinner, or too many longing glances from Miss Morris, Miss Pennick, and probably Lady Turner too. Poor fellow must be feeling hunted, if not haunted. I'll go riding with him tomorrow and find out what's troubling him. It's likely that he saw something he didn't like by day and didn't consciously take note of it, and it came back to bother him in the night. But by then he didn't know what it was."

She tilted her head back. "You have an answer for everything."

He bent and kissed her shoulder, lightly. "Except one thing."

She tilted an eyebrow.

"Will you make love to me now?"

"You knew the answer to that too," she said, turning to put her arms around him and kiss him fully.

"Tonight," he said, as he picked her up in his arms, "let's try to make you forget tonight."

She laughed into the hollow of his neck as he carried her to their bed.

Within minutes she had forgotten the night, and the day, and herself. All she could feel was exquisite pleasure and infinite joy she always found in her husband's embrace. She could see his splendor even with her eyes closed, but she seldom closed them, because she wanted to look at him forever, or at least, until rapture at last gave way to sleep.

Eve yawned, stretched, put out a hand, and found her husband gone. She opened her eyes to find the sun well up. So he was with his guests, riding or showing them the grounds. She'd slept late, but didn't worry. Her female guests were from London, they'd sleep longer. She rose and went to the window. Another glorious day, as though autumn itself was in league with her and her plans.

Betty helped her select a pretty blue gown sprigged with green, and Eve went down the stairs.

Eve heard strange female voices and cocked her head. The men were either out riding or still sleeping. No one was stirring except for all the hired help, who were busily preparing the great house for another day. But these women spoke in rough accents. She realized they were the workers hired from the village, and they were chattering as they did their chores in the dining parlor. She paused to listen to them.

"Well, I says it's a good way to earn the extra coin," an unfamiliar voice was saying. "Imagine getting money just for polishing up bits of old silver."

"It's better than slopping a hog, I'd say," another agreed. "And a rare old chance to see the place. I heared of it since I was born, but never seen the like, inside. A room for everything, just like my Gran said."

"Good way to see some real ladies too," another said excitedly.

"Best way to see the master," the second female said, giggling. "Ain't he something for sore eyes? I seen him from afar, but up close? Lord!"

"My Gran says he's the spit of his Da, and his Da were the spit of his, and he, of his, so far back as anyone can remember. They're like as peas, except for their hair, her Gran told her, she says," another put in. "The old folks say there be some-thing weird about 'em, that's the truth."

"Weird about being so wicked handsome? Lord, I could wish all the men hereabouts were weird then!"

"And the ladies of the manor, they was all grand ladies of wealth and title, so I heard. This new little one be nothing like that."

"Yeah, but the others they was all sickly, wasn't they? Not one child never born in this place, 'cause the ladies had to go abroad to have them. And then, they never returned."

"How's that? You've rats in your noggin. Why, there's the master of the house, I seen him just this morning."

"Clunch! I meant the ladies of the house never return."

"Good thing then, I say, that this one is not so grand."

"I beg your pardon!" said an annoyed voice that Eve recognized. It was one of the servant girls who had come with her from London.

"Didn't mean nothing by it," the first speaker said. "She's a lovely bride, all like her right well. It's just that Gran said . . ." Eve had to move closer to hear the low whisper, ". . . that Far Isle itself were weird. In the olden times, I means. What with the Old Folk of the forest and such living here since forever."

"And such?" asked the maid from London. "What 'and such' do you mean?"

"Fairies and the like."

"What?" The London maid laughed. "Little folk dancing on pansy petals, you mean, and you're afraid? Get away with you."

"It's more serious, it's pure evil, and they ain't little at all. And although I don't like to be the one to tell you," the other woman said in tones that clearly gave the lie to what she said, "but you being from Lunnon and all, you likely don't know. My Gran says that there was all sort of mischief and wickedness done in this place and on this here very spot afore the house was ever built. Strange magic," she said with evident pleasure, "wickedness in the night, and all."

"Ha!" said the London maid. "Pull the other one. There ain't nothing worse than what's on the streets of London by night. It would turn your hair white if you seen what we have out in the night in the streets of London Town!"

This caused much laughter.

"Done with your chores, are you?" the housekeeper's voice said clearly and coldly. The room fell still as she went on. "I see. The epergne polished enough to see your face in? The forks and knives clear as crystal? All the candlesticks free of wax and gleaming? Why no, that isn't so. You'd best get on with it instead of having a party, because no matter how lenient the master and the mistress of this house, I do not pay for services not rendered."

They got back to work, silently, as Eve ducked back up to the stair. She took the last step down slowly, looking thoughtful as she did.

"Now what can the matter be?" Aubrey asked her as she entered the breakfast parlor and he rose to greet her.

"Ah, she's always a bear in the morning," Sherry said. "Give you good morning, Eve. I see the country life has you rising before noon."

She made a face at him. "I never did like to sleep that late, and you know it. Good morning all. Today, I have to be sure everyone we wanted to have come here is here. So if you have anyone you want to our Halloween Ball it's now or never. Let me know, please."

"I sent my invitations," Aubrey said. "They'll be here soon enough. Pitiful few there are too. I hope your list is longer."

She beamed at him. "We have twelve guests here now, and there's room for many more, so I'll invite them. It's not too late. The only problem was thinking of whom not to ask. I want everyone here, so that they can envy me."

"Then I have to put a sprig of ash over the door," Aubrey said. "To ward off jealousy and evil intentions."

"You don't believe in superstition, do you?" she asked.

"No," he laughed. "Knock on wood."

At luncheon, the company was told about more guests arriving. They were delighted, especially since they'd be at the house when the others arrived, and so would socially score one over the rest of the party. They passed the day riding, playing cards, and walking. In the evening they danced, and sang. At last, the company got to bed, and in some cases, into each other's beds. Even though the guests were known for living London hours, the outdoor life they'd led made them all seek their beds, or someone else's, much earlier than was their habit in Town. All seemed quiet and content in the Hall when the old case clock in the green salon chimed the eleventh hour.

Eve stirred in Aubrey's arms.

"When?" she asked sleepily, tracing the curve of his naked back with one finger, "Whenever shall I get used to this ecstasy?"

"Never," he said, burying his face in her neck.

She chuckled. Then she spoke again. "Aubrey?" she asked lightly, so lightly that he listened closer. "I heard . . . well, I overheard some gossip. Is it true that your mother was a great lady, and very beautiful?"

"It is," he said.

"And your grandmother too? And her mother as well?"

He propped himself up on one elbow. "Just who were you overhearing?"

"Never mind," she said. "Is that true?"

"It is. Or so I hear. Why do you ask?"

"And that they all grew sickly, and so had to go abroad to have their babies? And," she added in a rush, "that none survived to come back to England?

He was still. He lay back on his pillow. "True," he finally said. "Are you afraid you'll get sick if you stay with me, and conceive a babe with me?"

"No," she said. "Well, maybe not. I don't know."

"No," he said, turning, and holding her close. "I promise you, no. You'll stay well, and if you wish we'll stay here until you're very old. Or, if you want, I can take you to see the Continent too. We don't have to repeat history. We won't. And you're nothing like the others."

"So I heard," she said sadly. "They were all grand titled ladies."

"You are my lady," he said. "You and I were meant for each other. I know it. I feel it in my heart. Don't you?"

"I do," she said, as she had when they'd wed.

He kissed her to reassure her, and then he kissed her because she clung to him, and then he kissed her because he was impelled to. They made love slowly, quietly, as they were each trying to convince the other of their honesty and desire.

When she arched and cried her completion, he allowed himself to join her, and they clung even closer until their throbbing bodies calmed.

In moments, she was asleep in his arms.

He was falling asleep when his eyes suddenly opened wide, and he shivered. He looked at her to be sure she was sleeping. He passed a hand over her closed eyes to ensure it, and then rose from bed. He pulled on a dressing gown, and left the room.

Aubrey quickly made his way downstairs and paced through the darkened Hall until he came to a back door. He went out and walked through a copse of trees that flanked the great house, until he came to a clearing. Then he shrugged out of his dressing gown and stood alone under the moon, and raised his arms, until he looked like a pale luminous pillar reaching to the sky. He stood, waiting.

He threw back his head, filled with exultation. He'd known it! He'd felt it. It was true, at long last. He'd conceived a child! A son.

He whispered a silent incantation of thanks, and opened his eyes. They gleamed silvery as the sickle moon above him. It was done. Soon, he could live his own life again, free of the compulsion that had carried him this far. There was no one he could share this with, and the furious joy he felt was almost too big to contain. There had never been anyone to share with. He'd never cared before. Now he did. But that was likely because there soon would be someone.

He picked up his dressing gown, put it on, and hurried back to his bedchamber.

Eve was still sleeping soundly, of course. He curled up in the bed behind her, his hand on the gently rounded abdomen that contained such riches. His own heart was still beating wildly. A sudden realization sliced through his jubilation. He pressed his lips to her hair. In that moment, he loved her as never before. And the best part, and the worst part, was that he realized he'd come to really care for her.

Chapter 10

The night of the ball finally came, and when it did, when Eve first saw her husband in his costume, in their bedchamber, he took her breath away again. Would she never get used to it? She lived with the man, she slept with him, saw him morning and night, and still she experienced this feeling of utter wonder when she beheld him. But tonight, he was something to behold.

Aubrey was dressed as king of Far Isle Hall. His costume subtly referenced the mystical history of the place. His costume might have been out of the Renaissance, but it was too ethereal even for that colorful time. He looked entirely royal, impossibly handsome, and magnificently unearthly.

He wore a closely fitted long silver tunic over green tights. The tunic showed the breadth of his shoulders, and the tights, his strong legs. A silvery cape was flung carelessly over one shoulder, and he wore green slippers. A silver crown sat atop his black hair. That was all, and that was almost too much. Although his costume was outrageously foppish, even for the Renaissance period, he was entirely masculine, and beautiful, of course.

He made Eve feel lust, and pride, and excitement, all as usual, she thought with the usual astonishment she felt when she really looked at him. But tonight, in fantasy, he had become what she always saw him as in her imagination: too exotic, too splendid, too wondrous to be true.

Then she looked down at herself. She wore a diaphanous green gown, and silver slippers. A silver crown and small white flowers had been woven into her curls. Simplicity suited her. She might not compare to Aubrey, but she felt she didn't shame him. She glowed too, and the simple elegant clothing showed off her lithe form and graceful step as nothing she'd ever worn before.

Aubrey had selected their costumes, and she pleased him, so she held her head high.

"The king and queen of Far Isle Hall," Aubrey said with satisfaction, as they stood and gazed into the glass in their bedchamber. He offered her his arm. "Shall we go and await our guests, my queen?"

She nodded, took his arm, and feeling oddly light, and strangely reassured, she followed him down the stairs into the main hall.

To make the fantasy of All Hallow's night complete, the hall was hung with rowan, willow, and wildflowers picked from nearby meadows. Late roses and asters, plumy weeds and scented herbs, gourds and red haws, nuts and blackberries were strewn, artfully but seemingly artlessly, on tabletops and mantelpieces. Ropes of leaves were strung through the stair rails, and overhead hung gilded apples and silvered pears. Everywhere too, there were vases of silver overflowing with trailing vines and wildflowers.

The punch bowls were filled with blood red wine and hot crabapples steaming and hissing. Fires were lit in every hearth, strewn with herbs and boughs of fresh fir to make the house redolent, the scent wild and refreshing. Lamps and candles were lit and strategically placed, so it was not too bright, but all could be seen. Here and there a long window was left ajar so that the draperies and candle flames stirred with the breezes, as though spiritual guests were streaming in.

Eve looked around as she descended the stairs, as amazed as she was delighted with her first real duty as hostess. The last conceit they'd thought of was to make the houseguests leave the house through the back door and come in again through the main door, so that they'd appear like visions let in from the magical night. And a spectacular night they had for it too: cool and clear, the sky hung with stars and a bone white moon.

Sherry was the only guest who awaited them in the hall, because he was the only family member there. Eve covered her mouth with her hand when she saw him.

Aubrey took a reeling step back, as though he'd been dealt a mortal blow, and hung there, looking astonished and theatrically pale, one hand against his heart. His shock was so convincing that for an instant Eve couldn't tell if he were genuinely ill or just pretending. She only relaxed when she saw him stand up straight again.

Sheridan bowed. With difficulty. He creaked, because he was dressed in a suit of armor. "I thought this would be great fun," Sherry said, somewhat hollowly.

"It's a good way to stay away from Lucinda's sister," Eve said, also with difficulty, because she was trying not to howl with laughter.

"Yes," Aubrey said, still pale and coming no closer to Sheridan. "All that iron does make it impossible to cuddle. But it is a wonderful way to stay away from all other females too. Where did you find that . . . machine you're wearing? Not in the attics here, certainly."

A groan came from the helmet of the suit. "No. I rented it from a shop in London. It seemed like a good idea at the time. You don't have to pretend to be so horrified, Aubrey. I hate it too. Can you wait until I get upstairs and change before you let the guests in? I want to be on the reception line with you, meeting everyone firsthand and all."

"You've met most of the guests staying here, or know them from London," his sister said. "But we do have some guests coming from the village too."

"Do we?" Aubrey asked.

"Of course," Eve said smugly. "I got the names from Mrs. Hood. We've the vicar coming, Squire Thompson and his family, Mrs. Culpepper and her three daughters, and some others. All the girls are charming and lovely, by the way, Sherry, or so Mrs. Hood says. Their families have been here for years. I've asked other local gentry I can't remember right now. It would be rude not to have them, Aubrey, don't you think?"

"I think it was rude for them not to ask us to their homes first," Aubrey said. "But I know little about modern manners. I suppose it's time I got to know."

"Please wait for me," Sherry pleaded. "I have a Robin Hood sort of get-up in my room too. My valet suggested it if I grew weary of this . . . walking mausoleum. Gads! How did they fight in these things?"

"Carefully," Aubrey said. He waved a hand and drew further back from Sheridan, as though he smelled like a tin of old fish. "Go. We'll wait. Hurry, if you can."

The suit of armor clanked stiffly to the stair. Sheridan's valet was already standing there, waiting to help his master decant himself.

Eve giggled. "You didn't have to act *so* appalled, Aubrey, although it was funny. He couldn't stand it himself."

Aubrey smiled, wanly. "I was just trying to save his life."

She looked at him oddly.

"He would have suffocated in there," Aubrey said. "Or starved."

Sheridan rushed downstairs a few moments later, resplendent in scarlet and green, a Robin Hood from the jaunty feather atop his cocked slouchy hat to the tips of his pointed shoes. He took his place next to his sister and her husband. The ballroom stood ready; the musicians hired for the evening sat behind bowers of ferns and flowers and tuned their instruments.

It was a cool night, not a cold one, but the guests could be heard complaining about the chill as they lined up outside, at the front door.

"They only walked from the back of the house," Eve said.

"They're hothouse flowers," Aubrey said. He signaled to the two footmen by the front door. "Allow our guests entry," he said, and stood waiting.

They rushed in like autumn leaves blown by a gale, a colorful crowd of Halloween party-goers, eager to greet their host, ogle his new bride, marvel again at the wonders of Far Isle Hall, and show off their costumes. They were such a colorful collection that it took Eve a few minutes to sort them out in her mind, much less recognize them. Unlike the masquerades she'd been to in London, this crowd of guests seemed to stay with a certain rustic theme. There were fewer diamonds and jewels and more feathers and fur to be seen this night. It seemed that the history of the place had influenced some of them too.

There were milkmaids and goose girls, serving wenches and princesses, all of whom wore costumes that showed tantalizing glimpses of ankles and more than glimpses of bosoms. Gentlemen dressed as princes, looking to waken sleeping princesses or ready to discover princesses in disguise as goose girls, were there in plenty. Sherry wasn't the only Robin Hood, by far. He and his merry men were well represented this night. There were many portly elder gentlemen dressed as good Friar Tuck, and not a few rakish middle-aged fellows preening and leering as they played at being the wicked Sheriff of Nottingham. Patient wives favored medieval costumes to match the merry band.

More basic folklore was given a bow as well, to judge from the many Morris Men and Druidical get-ups. Some guests wore amusing owl or hawk heads. Some wore fox heads and tails, others wore hound's heads and tails, and when they spied each other they pretended to chase each other into the ballroom.

As a final bow to the spirit of the night, the butler announced them as what they were dressed as tonight, rather than their true names, which led to more merriment. There was laughter and barking, baying and giggling as the crowd went one by one to meet their hosts and ogle the Hall.

"Now this," Sherry said with enthusiasm as the last guests were introduced, "is going to be some party!"

And so it was, or at least the best one Eve had ever attended.

"I'm not used to being the center of attention," she confided to Aubrey at one point. "If this was an ordinary ball, I don't think I could stand all the scrutiny. But everyone is so keen on staring at each other to see who's wearing what, that I don't feel uncomfortable at all."

"You don't see how many are admiring you because you don't expect to," Aubrey said.

She shook her head. She wasn't an ingénue or a fool. She knew to the last decimal how many balls she'd attended before she'd met him. She'd been popular, in a quiet sort of way. She was well liked, but she'd never been a sensation. He was the one who had made her fashionable. She'd never forget the night they'd met. He'd stunned her by his presence. Now she realized that the fact that he'd singled her out had not only stunned her, but the fashionable world even more.

Now, as host and hostess, they began the ball by dancing a waltz together.

"This is a grand success, isn't it?" she whispered to Aubrey.

"Grand," he said, smiling.

"The food at dinner should be good, the ballroom isn't too warm, the guests are enjoying themselves," she said. "And just look at Sherry, will you? He did the right thing and is dancing with Grace. Good for him."

"I imagine he knows there are a bevy of other young girls waiting to be singled out by him next," Aubrey commented with a chuckle.

"Oh, good!" she said again, and danced, and laughed, and thought there was no woman in all England luckier than she. She had a loving husband, who just happened to be the most handsome man in the world. She had a beautiful home, and her dreams of a blissful future were becoming daily more than just dreams now. They danced, he held her tenderly, and gave her up with a comical show of resentment when she had to go to new partners in the country dances. She couldn't be happier.

As host and hostess, they danced with their guests too, and it was with relief that she came into Aubrey's arms again for another waltz just before dinner.

"Isn't this wonderful?" she asked him again.

He smiled down at her, all his pleasure in his eyes, along with all sorts of promises of future pleasure.

And despite all her experience, she blushed. "Look at Sherry," she said, to change the mood, because it would be hours before she could be in his arms in their bed together tonight. "He's the belle of the ball. He's danced with every wallflower, every unknown, and every diamond too. He's behaving just as he ought. And now look at him. *Oh my!*"

She stared at her brother as he waltzed by with a beauty in his arms. The woman was so exquisite that Eve almost lost her step in the dance. She didn't have to worry. She kept to the right steps.

Aubrey was the one who didn't. He stopped and stared.

Eve saw her husband's dark eyes grow darker with rage. His fair complexion grew white. He dropped his hands from her and knotted his fists at his side. "How *dare* she?" he whispered fiercely, but it seemed to Eve that he spoke to himself.

"Who? What is it?" she asked, confused.

He didn't answer her. He took her back, and continued dancing, but though she was in his arms, he might have been miles away. He didn't stop looking at the exquisite woman Sheridan danced with.

Sherry stared at his partner, also transfixed, but he was obviously rapturous. And with cause, Eve thought. The woman wore a green gown with a gauzy silver overskirt that floated as she danced. She had long flowing golden hair tied up with flowers and then left to cascade to her creamy shoulders. Her eyebrows were thin dark gold arcs over her small black eye mask, her nose small and straight. Her lips, red as autumn leaves, showed off the perfection of a camellia-petal complexion. She was all grace, and her curved yet slender figure was all that was alluring. And when she laughed, which she did often, it sounded like lovely bells chiming in the wind. In fact, Eve thought in alarm, the woman looked like Aubrey's perfect consort:

dark and light, grace matched with grace, and beauty triumphant. They had the same instant appeal. It was as though she should be the mistress of the Hall.

"Who is she?" Eve asked, watching her.

Aubrey said nothing; he only kept staring, now expressionless, at the woman in Sherry's arms.

Eve grew cold. Could this beautiful creature be an old love of his? Or was she someone he still wished were his lover? Had he lost her, or was he finding her tonight? Eve couldn't wait for the music to stop so she could know. And yet she never wanted the music to stop, because she suddenly didn't want to know the truth. Her dream had been too delicious, she had celebrated it too much; this was, she thought, the end of vanity, and such impossible rosy dreams as she'd been having.

The music finally ceased and the musicians rested. Servants rolled the doors to the dining salon open. Long tables covered with steaming dishes filled with savory treats could be seen. A buffet dinner was being served.

The guests poured into the dining salon, some removing their masks so they could eat, and some keeping them on, obviously able to dine through them, or wanting to keep their appearances secret until midnight in traditional fashion. Aubrey and Eve waited at the doors to the salon, watching their guests enter. Aubrey maintained a statue-like stance until Sherry and his lovely partner approached.

Then, at last, Aubrey moved, and spoke. He laid a hand on the woman's arm. "I did not expect to see you," he told her icily.

She stopped, looked up at him and laughed. "Why not?"

"I don't recall your being invited," he said harshly.

Eve and Sherry looked at each other. This didn't sound like the Aubrey they knew.

"What?" the woman laughed. "But of course I was invited." Her tilted eyes slewed toward Eve. "I *had* to meet your bride. So sorry I couldn't come to the wedding. But she is a darling!" Beneath the mask beautiful eyes narrowed a fraction. Eve felt cold as the woman studied her.

Then the woman smiled. "Of course, I see now. It makes perfect sense. I hope she's as good for you as she seems to be. Oh! Where are my manners?" she cried in a bright voice. "My dear child. I am your sister-in-law, Aubrey's sister, Arianna. I live afar, but nothing could keep me from returning home for this occasion. Welcome to the family, Eve. Have you met any of Aubrey's other relatives?"

"Why, no," Eve managed to say, looking up at Aubrey.

His face was tight, his eyes cold. He never stopped staring at his sister.

"Well, you may meet some, or many, tonight," Arianna said, laughing. "Or none at all. They do dearly love a disguise, and who can say if they'll reveal themselves tonight? Now, I am famished. Sherry, my sweet, wilt thou take me in to eat?" She laughed again.

Sherry bobbed his head, transfixed by her. "Of course," he said.

"I'll see you later, my dear little sister," Arianna told Eve. She looked down meaningfully at her arm. "So overcome with emotion, Aubrey, that you forget your manners? You hold me back? How comes this? Or do you not want me to dine at your table?"

Aubrey looked down at the hand he still had on his sister's arm as though he had forgotten it. He drew his hand back. He bowed. "I will certainly see you later," he said coldly.

Arianna and Sherry went into the salon.

Eve stood frozen. "Why didn't you tell me you had a sister? Why wasn't she at the wedding? Where does she live?"

Aubrey let out a breath. "There's much to tell. Too much for here and now. Later, please." And he led her into the dining salon.

Eve ate without tasting and listened to her

guests without hearing them. She watched Sherry and Aubrey's sister. Sherry was fascinated. Aubrey saw the direction of Eve's gaze.

"That would not be a good match," he said, as though he saw Eve again for the first time. "Don't worry. I'll make sure it comes to nothing."

"Why wouldn't it be a good match?" Eve asked.

"First of all she is . . . she is much too old for him," he said, and smiled, but there was no humor in it. He saw Eve's expression of confusion and doubt. "My sister and I don't get along. We don't see each other for years on end," he went on in that curiously humorous, humorless voice. "She travels widely, changing her name with her lovers. Now it amuses her to be 'Arianna.' I've known her by other names. She travels the worlds for amusement, and to make mischief."

"The world," Eve corrected him.

"Ah, yes, the world," he said. "Now she's here, and obviously amused to play at being a concerned sister. She is not. She will not be." He turned and looked at her keenly. "One thing I must ask you to vow to me, and now, Eve. I may have been wrong not to mention her. My only excuse is that the mere mention of her brings me pain. Forgive me. But do not meet with her alone, or when I am not there. Ever. Can you swear to this, for me?"

Eve nodded. "Yes, I'll try, but why?"

"Because she's treacherous. Because she means you no good. Because," he said, with effort, as he watched Eve's face, "the plain truth is she wants to be mistress of this Hall, and that she can never be. Not while I live."

"Or I do," Eve said suddenly, her eyes widening.

"Precisely," he said. He shook his head. "Just look at you. And listen to me! I've ruined the party for you. Don't let that happen. This is all merely family matters, my love. Disregard it all, except for your promise to me. Let's continue to be merry, be a good host and hostess, and let the rest of the world spin on as it may. I'll protect you; I'll keep you safe from spite or ambition. Believe me."

She did. "But what other relatives did she mean?" Eve persisted. "Do you have other relatives here? Do you get on with none of them?

"I get on with many of them," he said. "I have seen none at all tonight. My sister likes to be mysterious. She loves to lie. And now," he said, "let us forget her. And then when the dancing begins again, I have to find all the Ellas sitting by the cinders, and dance with them, and pretend they're all you I'm dancing with at the masquerade where we met."

"But what am I to do?" she asked. "In order for

me to recapture the moment, I have to dance with the most handsome man in the room, and that was, and is, you."

"So then," he said reasonably, "when the music starts again, dance with me."

"But we're host and hostess, we do have duties and we have danced."

"And will again, and again. Come, see," he said, taking her hand and rising. The strains of a waltz began as the musicians began to play. "Recapture some magic with me."

They rose and returned to the dance. Eve forgot the guests, his sister, and her cares as she moved with him and smiled up into his eyes. She was startled and a little lost when the music finally stopped. She stood next to him, swaying, loathe to leave his hands.

"What shall I do now?" she whispered hoarsely.

"I know what I should like you to do," he said in her ear. "But you're right. Duty calls. Go dance with your brother. Tell him my sister has fleas. Tell him worse and better, as you please. Now, we'll go to amuse ourselves, and make this night memorable for more than meetings ill met."

"And your sister?"

"And I'll speak to her too."

"Is she staying the night?" Eve asked, suddenly

remembering her duties as hostess. "I can have another bedchamber made up for her."

"No, and never," Aubrey said. "Neither she nor I want that."

"But where will she stay? Whatever she is, we can't turn her out on the road in the night."

"She has her friends, everywhere," Aubrey said. "Never worry about her."

"Shall I worry about you?" she asked seriously.

He smiled, and touched her cheek. "Never," he said.

But she did.

Chapter 11

If Far Isle were in London, the ball would have gone on long after the midnight unmasking, and then the guests would have dragged their weary bodies home at dawn. But it was the countryside, where the local lights blew out their bed lamps long before midnight most nights. Many of the local worthies were yawning as they left the Hall soon after the unmasking. Even the London guests, their day having been filled with riding, walking, or traveling to the Hall, retired to bed before their usual times. The ballroom was deserted by an hour into the new day. No one in the house was abroad by the second hour except, of course, for servants cleaning and clearing.

Fewer guests had been there for the unmasking than at the start of the ball, but that happened in London too. Many an uninvited clever lad or lass had sneaked into a fine affair, in both senses of the word, by attending and then leaving a masquerade before their trickery was discovered. But this time, at midnight, there seemed to be fewer guests than before, an exodus even more marked than at the most crowded London masquerades. Likely, Eve thought, some villagers had managed to get in to rub shoulders with the exotic class that was usually ordering them about.

It didn't bother Eve. She had better things to worry about than some uninvited guests at her table. She was more fully involved with a new problem. Where was Aubrey? She'd left him only for a few moments to ready herself for bed. She'd gone to the convenience. Trust Aubrey to have indoor plumbing here in the countryside! She'd washed and put on a night rail in her dressing room, dismissed her maid, and come back into their bedchamber again—to find he wasn't there. His valet, in his dressing room, had no idea of where his master was either. Eve pretended she remembered, laughed and left, to save face. Now she paced, and worried, and wondered. She had so much to talk to him about.

How could Aubrey have neglected to tell her about his sister? She obviously didn't live that far away if she'd come to the ball. But why hadn't she been at the wedding? And she was so magnificently beautiful, and yet she didn't look at all like her brother. They were dark and light, night and day.

All her insecurity returned as Eve paced. The nasty little worm of a thought that the woman mightn't be his sister at all ate through all Eve's rational reasonings. Now that promise he'd extracted from her: to never speak to the woman alone, seemed unjust and perhaps sly. How had Arianna heard about the ball if she lived far away? Had Aubrey told her?

Now too all her fears and doubts returned in full force. How had she captured a lover like Aubrey, much less a husband like him: the most beautiful and the brightest man she'd ever known? And she, a simple shadow of a woman, at least, compared to him. Eve remembered his lovemaking and shivered, recalled his words of love and sighed, and saw his face when he'd seen the woman he'd called "sister," and found tears gathering. She wiped her eyes, angry with herself, not with him, never with him. She loved him, but began to think she'd been a deluded, lovesick fool. But why had he deluded her?

Even more important, here and now, it was two hours into the new day, and where was Aubrey? More important still: where was the woman who'd claimed she was his sister? She'd promised to see them again soon, thanked them for their hospitality and, with some of her still-masked friends, had left the Hall before midnight with a secretive smile on her lovely face. As he'd gone to his bed-chamber, a starry-eyed Sherry had told Eve that they'd both see Arianna soon again. That was too soon and too late for Eve. She had to know what happened now, or she'd never sleep easy again. And where could Aubrey be?

Rather than to keep wondering, Eve decided to find out. She threw on a robe, a soft gray one, the color of cobwebs. Then she went silently out of the bedchamber, light-footed, glad for once that she was a mere slip of a brown-haired, brown-eyed girl; easy to ignore, able to melt into the background whenever she chose. She'd discovered long ago that her unspectacular looks made it easy for her to be unnoticed. That was only one of the reasons why Aubrey's unexpected attentions had shocked her. Like a beggar who turned a limp into his fortune, she'd sometimes used her unremark-able appearance for her own purposes. When she wanted to, she could move like a shadow, and hide herself even in the light. She seldom did, ex-cept when she and Sherry were young, in order to give him the occasional sisterly fright of his life by leaping out of closets or doorways at him.

Now she floated down the stair, and drifted through the hall, toward the voices she heard.

There were servants in the ballroom, quietly gossiping as they cleaned. There were servants in the kitchens and the salons too. Though the great hall seemed to sleep, servants ran everywhere, like busy mice, cleaning, clearing, squeaking softly to each other, hurrying so that they too could go to sleep soon.

Tempting as it was to listen to the gossip, most of it scurrilous, Eve ignored them. She had to find the master of the hall. She wound through the rooms, invisible to anyone not expecting to see her, searching for her husband, hoping not to find him if he was with the beautiful woman claiming to be his sister, but expecting to, even so.

She heard voices, and one was the one she'd been searching for. Narrowing her eyes, she went straight toward them like a hound on an invisible trail, moving past furniture and obstacles as though they weren't there. That was Aubrey's rich tenor. She'd know it in a raging storm; she would hear it above a cannon's roar, she'd know it as she heard it in her happiest dreams, as she heard it in her ear when they made love and she was in ecstasy. The dulcet, laughing, bell-like tones that accompanied it were Arianna's.

Eve never questioned her ability to find them. It was as though she were born to the task. She went to the back door, the one by the kitchens that led to the gardens. She eased it open, and heard them clear. Worse, she opened her eyes and could see them clearly, standing there together in the moonlight like a pair of characters in a play near the footlights on a darkened stage. Arianna's gauzy gown blew in the slight breeze, Aubrey, as ever, shone even in the faint starlight.

Eve stood, one with the concealing shadows, and listened. She felt guilty, but she was, after all, keeping her promise to Aubrey. She wasn't going to meet with his sister, alone. She wasn't meeting with her. She was eavesdropping on her and Aubrey's conversation. She'd been brought up to believe such a thing was wrong. It wasn't. If it concerned Aubrey, then she knew it was right.

"And so why didn't you attend the wedding?" Aubrey was saying.

"I wasn't invited." Arianna laughed.

"That never stopped you before," he said. "Or tonight."

"I didn't know who or what she was," Arianna said lightly. "Then I began to hear things about her, even where I abide. She's not in your usual style. First of all, she's very clever. And too, they said she wasn't a noble, stately, proven beauty of the first water. And so she isn't that either. How odd, for you. Not that she's unattractive. Quite the opposite. She's fey, in a strange way. But not beautiful at all, not exotic, surely never the sort to make a man pant with lust, especially not the sort to appeal to you. And for a wife! I confess myself fascinated.

"But she has something," Arianna mused. "I don't know what it is. I intend to find out. You're particular, Aubrey. I can't see any particular reason you should have chosen her this time. But I'll discover it in time. Unless, of course, you make matters easier for yourself and tell me now."

She impudently put her face up to Aubrey's and laughed at his expression. Yet he was, so far as Eve could see, expressionless.

"I married her because I needed her," was all he said.

"Ever more fascinating. Why didn't you bring her to see me?"

"It's not yet time. That will be a very, very long time from now," he said curtly.

"Before you go abroad with her? Ah, I see from your face that's exactly what you intend, again. You changed the style, but not the content."

"How could I?"

Eve frowned. She hadn't any idea of what they were talking about and didn't have the time to think about it. They'd lowered their voices and she had to strain to listen.

"And, of course," Arianna said, "you've forbidden her to talk to me. Why? What difference if she knows now or later? Or is that something you refuse to change too?"

"Again," Aubrey said wearily, "you ask what you know. I can't and you know it."

"So," she said thoughtfully. "This one is special because she's so unlike every other one. So," she repeated with real humor in her voice, "I expect her brother is special too. He'd have to be."

Aubrey stood up straighter. "I have no idea," he said. "I do know that you are to leave him alone."

Arianna cocked her head to the side. Her laughter filled the night with bright music. "Ah, brother," she said. "What's sauce for the gander is not sauce for the goose? I hardly think so."

Eve caught her breath and then stifled a sigh of relief. They were brother and sister. Whatever other strange thing there was about this meeting, that, at least, was balm to her soul.

"Leave Sheridan alone," Aubrey said in a deadly cold voice.

"I may, I may not," Arianna said lightly. "You can't forbid me what you feast on. And he so wants me. But let's not quarrel. How long has it been since we've met, by day or night?"

"Not," Aubrey said, "long enough."

She laughed again. "Time to remedy that, certainly. Your wife will wonder at the estrangement.

The other women never would have, they had little curiosity and never strayed from their proper places. This one, I think, will. Have a care, brother. If you take up with a clever creature you have to face new problems. That's why I never do. That's why I like her brother. He's charming, and not stupid either. He's just too young and fired with lusts to use his brain. But who needs it? Not I, certainly. Ah. I see I've vexed you. Then I will leave you. It's not seemly for us to quarrel. 'Till next time then, brother. Adieu."

She backed away, and faded into the darkness.

Aubrey stood there, looking after her, obviously deep in thought.

Eve, deep in the shadows, knew she had to leave too. She backed up and drifted slowly away, not making a sound. She stole back into the house. She fairly flew up the stair to her bedchamber. She closed the door quietly behind her, took off her robe with shaking fingers, and sat on the bed. Then, shivering, she realized her feet were damp with dew. She caught up her robe and used it to dry them before she slipped into bed. She huddled under the covers, shaking with more than the chill of the night.

He'd kept things from her. Important things she couldn't understand, but she knew they were things she must know. Should she pretend to be sleeping when he returned? Could she face him knowing she'd spied on him? And worse, knowing that he'd spoken of things he'd never told her.

No, she thought, she wouldn't pretend to be asleep. Because maybe he would tell her now, tonight. She couldn't wait until morning to talk to him, in any event. So she lay awake, waiting for him to come back to their bed, for him to come back to her and tell her what he surely should have, long before.

But at the last minute, she lacked courage. She watched him through her half-closed eyelashes as he came into the room and took off his robe. She tried not to sigh, as she always did at the sight of his naked body. She lay still, waiting for him to slip into bed beside her.

He surprised her by gathering her into his arms. His hands were as cool as the night outside; his hair was damp with dew, he smelled of ferns and forest, but his breath was warm and sweet on her face as he whispered to her.

"Wake up, Eve. Ah, I knew it," he said, a smile in his voice as her eyelashes fluttered open. "I knew you couldn't get to sleep until you knew where I was. No need to pretend otherwise. I'm flattered. Thank you. But I only went for a walk in the cool of the night. I bade good night to my sister too," he added.

He ran a hand lightly over her body, and each place he stroked peaked and prickled at his touch.

"Parties and balls call for me to be on my highest form," he said. "It's a strain to smile when I don't feel like it. And a host must smile and smile. My head ached too. The musicians were fine, and deserved their fee. But the guests were louder. So I needed time to cool down and collect myself. Getting some exercise always does that for me. I was hoping," he breathed into her ear, as his lips touched her earlobe to set her shivering, "that you could help me further."

"Why didn't you ever tell me about your sister?" she blurted, amazed that her body could be so willing when her mind was so distressed. He hadn't lied to her, exactly. But he hadn't told her about his meeting with his sister. And because she'd been a secret onlooker, neither could Eve tell him that she'd been there. She could tell him, she supposed, and maybe should. But suddenly it seemed a bad idea, precisely because he kept it secret.

"Because she's someone I like to forget," he said, interrupting every other word with a breathy kiss on each new place he touched.

"Why?" she persisted, her senses warring with her logical mind.

"All right," he said, sighing. He drew away from her.

She wanted to pull him back, but pulled herself together instead, and waited for his explanation.

"My sister is a troublemaker," he said. "She has been since birth. She's vain and callous, self-serving and clever. And she loves no one, no one, but herself. She can do people injuries and think nothing of it, because she lacks a heart. Or so I've always thought. And yet, she must have some family feeling, because as you saw, she manages to keep finding out news about me. Don't let her disturb you, Eve. I'd give my life for you, if I could, and willingly. I'll never let her hurt you."

And now, because of the earnestness in his voice, and because in her love-starved state Eve couldn't think clearly, she dragged him back into her arms. "You're cold," she said, burying her nose in his neck and breathing in the scent of him.

"So warm me," he whispered, and lifted her so he could kiss her.

She responded to him as always, with her whole heart. But tonight, there was something more, be-cause even in the haze of physical joy he gave her, and even though she loved him utterly, she knew, in some deep place in her heart, that she still didn't know everything about him; that he should

tell her more. But she also knew she couldn't bear
him not touching her.

"This time," he said, as she kindled in his arms,
"we'll try letting you set our pace. Here," he said,
lifting her higher, and placing her on top of him.
"Do you know what to do? Do you feel where I
am?"

"How can I not?" she gasped.

"Oh, Eve," he said on a strained chuckle. "Here,
this is how you do it. Ah, yes, right there. Now
sink down. Can you, do you wish to?"

She shivered and laughed, and shuddering
with newfound sensation, leaned down her head,
until her nose touched his. "I can, I do, I will, is
there no end to the joys of this?"

"No," he said, and raised her in his hands only
so he could lower her again, until she did it for
him, and they forgot the night and the secrets of
the night between them, in their pleasure.

"More," she said later, when their bodies were
at last relaxed, and they still lay entwined.

"What have I created?" he laughed. "A de-
generate monster that wants nothing but my
body? Wonderful," he said, stretching his long
body against hers, so she could tell he was again
aroused.

"No," she said. "Or maybe, yes. But that's not

what I mean. I need to know more about your family. How can it be that you know everything about me, even those things I didn't know? Like my appetite for you? And yet I know so little about you?"

"Ah," he said. "What would you know?"

"Everything you haven't told me."

He ran his lips down to her left breast, and placed his mouth on the puckered flesh he'd created.

"And you can make love to me ten times more tonight," she said breathlessly, "and in fact, I wish you would. But at the end of it, I still will want to know."

He stilled, and then slowly disentangled himself from her. He propped himself on one elbow and looked down into her face. "Most women would sleep now. The rest might forget the question in their weariness. Or else, they'd discover they wanted more pleasure, and then they'd sleep. But not you. You're like a little terrier or hedgehog. You're tenacious."

She sat up. "And comparing me to a dog or a hedgehog, complimentary as you might think it, will not make me forget either. Neither will speaking about your past lovers, though that's rude, but tantalizing, and something I'd usually want to know more about too. Why are you so loathe to tell me about your family?"

"I married you because of that damnable streak of level-headedness," he said, smiling. "I'll have to tell you then."

He lay back, his hands behind his head.

She almost lost her train of thought at the sight of his bared body on the sheets. He was muscled and firm, all in proportion, and beautiful to see. She clenched her hands at her sides, and willed herself to lie down beside him and not on him once again.

He chuckled; as though he knew one more ploy to distract her had failed. "I apologize for speaking of other females," he said, seriously enough. "It was beyond rude. It was boorish, given our world and your sensibilities. Though some women do enjoy hearing about . . . I'll stop right there. I'm only trying to make you laugh. You look so serious I have to keep myself from kissing you into giggles. Don't get angry. I spoke out of turn, and I'm sorry for it. Not one word about my former lovers shall you hear from me.

"What to tell you then, about my family that you don't already know? I know my sister was a surprise, and I apologize for that too. My family is a small one, though I've many cousins. We are not a prolific troop, to our sorrow. In fact, it's only my sister and myself on earth now. She has had a husband, and then lovers, but no children. And as you should know, I have none either. I haven't been a holy monk. But *that* I would have told you."

"I'm older than you, you know that too. I was brought up in another land, far away from here. I've traveled widely since. And so my life has taken many twists and turns. But now, and this I vow, I've found you, and I'll never be untrue. For so long as you live I am yours, with all I have to give."

"And your family?" she persisted, knowing he was serious, because of the odd poetry that he had spoken, always spoke when he was so sincere.

"What else would you know of it? My sister is of my blood, and in no part of my heart. And you are in my heart, and every other part. And that's all," he said. "Now, speaking of those other parts . . ."

He rose to sit in one swift smooth motion. "Would you like to make sweet, slow love to me? There's so much more I can show you."

She laughed. He hadn't told her much. But she didn't know what else to ask. "Yes," she said as she went into the promised sweet oblivion of his embrace. "Yes, Aubrey, please."

But joyous as it was, and so much as she was eased, when she finally closed her eyes, to sleep at last, she couldn't forget what she didn't know enough to ask.

And neither could he.

Chapter 12

Aubrey was gone when Eve awoke in the morning. He had duties now that he was living at the Hall again. He had tenants to discuss rents with, servants to speak to, whether there were guests at his home or not. So he left a sweet, silly note for Eve on her dresser table, all in rhyme, about how he'd see her at dinnertime. She was delighted. A decision had come to her. It was there, whole and reasonable, when she opened her eyes to the sunlight, the way all her best decisions always appeared.

She had to get up immediately, dress well, order a light curricle, and hunt up Sherry. He'd probably be in the morning parlor having his breakfast. He'd go with her, if only so he could drive the curricle, and he'd lend her courage and countenance. She'd make sure all her remaining guests were happy and well occupied, and then she was going to steal off to the village with Sherry to meet everyone she could and learn by artfully posed questions all she could about the history of the Ashfords of Far Isle Hall. She knew a great deal now. But she had a nagging feeling there was more she must know.

The breakfast parlor had a few gentlemen guests already there when she arrived. They were either sportsmen, up early so they could ride or explore, or simply gentlemen who were eating early so as to be ready to leave for their own homes. They rose when they saw her. She gave them a good morning and signaled for them to sit again.

"But wasn't she beautiful?" Sherry was asking as she sank to her chair.

A hearty gentleman, a local squire, his fork laden with beefsteak, paused it on the way to his mouth. "Thank the lord you're here, Mrs. Ashford. Your brother will have someone new to sing her praises to. This fellow has been prosing on so much about your husband's sister that our heads are aching. We were about to order up roasted onions to put on our ears to soothe them."

"But you ought to have said something!" Sherry exclaimed, his cheeks turning ruddy.

"Didn't give us a chance," another gentleman said. "Don't worry about it, lad. All of us have suffered calf love one time or another."

"It's not that," Sherry said. "I'm sure it's more profound."

"As were we all," the gentleman sighed, as all the others laughed.

"I tell you what, Sherry," Eve said, seeing a perfect opening. "I need an escort this morning. I've an errand to the village."

"But then when shall we make our farewells, and give you our thanks for such a delightful stay?" one of the men asked.

"I hope this evening, at dinner!" she said, as a good hostess ought. "But should cruel fortune part us before then, we'll be back by afternoon. That is, if my wretched brother helps me, as I asked."

The gentlemen smiled at her. Ashford had his pick of all the beauties in London and had chosen her. Their wives might wonder why, but to a man they thought they knew. Mrs. Ashford was charming, and she made a fellow feel right at home, and when you really looked at her, as one whispered to another, she wasn't bad on the eyes at all.

Eve stopped listening to Sherry's praise of Arianna after a while. She had learned one thing: to add a note of caution or warning was futile. The first time she did, he turned to look at her as though she'd run mad.

"What?" Sherry had asked, eyes wide.

"Watch the road!" she cried, "You'll have us in a ditch."

"You think I'm clunch enough to force the issue of seeing her again?" he said, ignoring her warning. "She's miles above me, Evie. Miles. I don't deserve to touch the hem of her gown. That she danced with me at all is a wonder. I'm not rich or madly attractive, and I know that I'm too young for her, thank you very much. Mind, that doesn't mean she's too old for me." He turned attention to his team again and murmured, "It's just that I know a woman of such beauty, poise, and experience would be mad to think seriously about a fellow like me. But a man can dream, can't he?"

All Eve could do was nod and mumble agreement. And then listen to him continue to carol about the wonders of her husband's sister as they drove to the village together.

She had to broach the topic of their visit to the village to him before they got there. And so when he fell into a somber reflective mood, and stopped talking for one minute, she did.

"Actually, Sherry, I have an ulterior purpose in going to the village this morning. I don't know many people here, and I ought to, I really ought. The Ashfords have lived here forever and . . . well, the long and short of it is that I want to know more about them. Now, seeing as I'm mistress of the Hall, I can hardly go in and ask anyone directly, can I? It would make them nervous. So I was hoping that you could go to the tavern, have ale with the regulars, and just mention the subject of the Ashfords. You can find out more about your Arianna too that way, you know. And I can go to the dressmaker's or the market and do the same. Unobtrusively, mind. As though the subject of gossip never entered our minds."

She looked at him. His mouth was actually open. But not as wide as his eyes.

"What!" he thundered. "You want me to spy? And on whom, I wonder? Not on your Aubrey, I'm sure. Why don't you come right out with it, Eve? It's all so you can spy on his sister. Well, I won't. How could you ask me?"

She straightened her shoulders. "I want us to find out about both of them. Understand, Sherry, I never knew Aubrey had a sister until last night. It made me realize that though I love him dearly, there's too much I don't know. He's not a Bluebeard or a liar. But I just have this *feeling* that there's something too painful for him to tell me. And it's not spying. It's . . ." she paused. "It's research. Now, are you with me, or not? Never fear, whatever I discover I will tell my husband."

They argued about it all the way into the village.

Then Sherry heaved a sigh. "All right. I've only the one sister and so does he . . . I think. And I'd certainly be mad at you if you hadn't told him about me. But just today, just this once, and never again."

"I love you, brother," Eve said sincerely as they rode down the main street of the little village.

Sheridan sauntered to the tavern. He'd be sure to get an audience. The rig he drove was spanking new and fashionable. Eve didn't doubt he'd caught every man's eye as he'd tooled it toward the center of the little town. And she'd remembered who had known the most gossip near her father's country manor, and so she went to the vicar's neat white house near the ancient village church first.

If the vicar had a wife, she'd know everything. Even if she didn't, and even if the vicar himself was closemouthed as a clam, that was where the truth about the Ashford family was recorded. They were the grandest family in the district, and so there she might find the most myths and rumors about them.

She was in luck, though she wouldn't think so later. The vicar was in, and alone except for his housekeeper. He was very old, and trembly, and terribly lonely, and eager to talk to the new mistress of the Hall.

"I'm so sorry you couldn't come to our party," Eve said when his housekeeper had shown her in.

"Thank you for the invitation. Too kind," he said, "And thank you for coming to see me so soon. But I'm not invalided, only a trifle old for such festivities. Do come in and take some tea with me."

After she'd been seated in his study with a cup of tea and some little cakes and biscuits on a plate between them, he settled in his chair and looked at her.

He was a thin little fellow with spectacles and not very much white hair atop his head. He looked dignified and wise. He wasn't. Or maybe he had been, but loneliness and increasing age had eroded his discretion. Eve sat still and listened as he happily told her everything he knew about her husband's family, or had ever heard conjectured about them.

"The family has been here forever." He chuckled. "Well, almost. There were Ashfords here when the Romans came. Why, I do believe they were here even before that, when Far Isle was just a mound." He gave a dry cough of a laugh, dipped a biscuit into his tea, popped it into his mouth, and went on. "They always had funds too. Now, here's a strange thing: they never contributed to the church. That may be because they were never a devout family. The truth is, they've always ignored us. We could have had a cathedral here, but we have the same small church we had in the eleventh century. A little treasure, one guidebook has it. Built when the Normans came, and untouched since. But still . . .

"At any rate," he went on, "the Ashfords were said to have been a much larger family in the distant past. They were always said to be beautiful people, and charming, when they wished to be. They were known for their revels and their love of company, but only company that they chose. Many wild stories were told about them then, as you may imagine."

He licked a crumb from his quivering lip, shook his head, and smiled at some memory before he continued. "As time went on, there were fewer of them, and those that were there settled down. Far Isle grew larger, but quieter, and more remote. They never had much to do with us. They still don't. Which is why, my dear Mrs. Ashford, I am so delighted with your visit here today."

"Thank you," she said calmly. "So I take it you didn't know my husband's family? His father and mother, or his sister?"

"Oh, no," he said. "I knew his father, and your husband is the image of him, as was his grandfather. They must have been strong men to pass on such perfect resemblances! Except for the hair, of course. Odd, that. And his mother looked nothing like him. She was not terribly friendly, but then, she was a lady born, and we were sorry to see her leave the country nevertheless, and sorrier when she never came back. She was quite old, however, to have had a babe at all. As was your husband's grandmother. I do hope you have many children, my dear, and early, to change the family history."

"And my husband's sister, Arianna?" Eve asked through tight lips. The more he spoke, the more she disliked the vicar, and the more she disliked herself for having come to him. But she was driven now. She had to know more.

"His sister? *Arianna?*" the vicar said, his head to the side. "But I never heard of her. I always thought Mr. Ashford was an only child."

There was a silence in the room, broken only by the ticking of an old clock on the mantel.

"Ah, but she was likely born abroad too," the vicar said. "That must be what it is. You must have her come here, or your husband, if he wishes, to enter her name in the church record. I should like to see a true Ashford again. They were such handsome men: almost too perfect to look upon. Their wives were beauties too, but not in the same fashion. They were more substantial, so to speak, by which I mean not perfect at all, but perfect for their times. Their style of beauty changed. The men of the family never did. And the ladies were, well, toplofty, that's a fact. Whereas the gentlemen were known for their agreeableness and charm.

"It is a great pity when the masters of the Hall so disregard the people of their village," the old man mused. "It leads to talk. The things that were said! That are still said! That the Ashfords were allied with demons and enchantments, black masses and strange cults, or so it was whispered in days gone by.

"And because the family never came to church, even more dreadful things were said. The beauty of the Ashford men smote the women and inflamed our men. Local girls were forbidden to go there, even to work, and the men still don't like to labor there. But I understand the wages paid to workers for your masquerade were enormous, and these are modern times, after all."

Eve sat still, trying to make sense of what the old man was saying or trying to tell her. She didn't care for any of it. The wrongness of seeking gossip about her Aubrey suddenly came to her, and she was ashamed of herself for listening to this foolish old man.

"Thank you," she said, rising from her chair. "But I've overstayed my visit. My brother must be seething, waiting for me. Thank you for your hospitality, but I must go."

He stood at once. He seemed to realize he'd said too much. "Jealousy," he suddenly said. "That explains much of it, if not all. The Ashfords always had such unearthly beauty and so much money, and the village girls were easily seduced by both, and the men forever envious. I'm sure of it. Forgive me any nonsense I said that might have alarmed you, my dear Mrs. Ashford. And pray, don't disturb yourself of Mr. Ashford about it." He wrung his hands together, looking at her fearfully.

She said she would not, and left him, unsure of whether he had asked for forgiveness out of a long forgotten sense of duty or out of newfound terror.

Sheridan looked upset when she came hurrying back to where he stood pacing by the curricle.

"Nothing," he said when she came up to him. "They never heard of her. Imagine that! The locals never heard a word about Arianna. Now, I like Ashford, but that is beyond anything. He didn't invite her to your masquerade, and I thought hard of him for that. But now it turns out that's nothing new. Why did he keep her from Far Isle all these years?"

"Get in," she said through tightened lips. "Drive. We'll talk on the way back."

They argued all the way back.

"I don't care if she was born abroad," he kept saying. "She's here now. Why does he keep her a secret?"

"Maybe she wants to be one," Eve said. "Why don't you ask her?"

His anger disappeared. Now he looked sad. "How can I? I doubt I'll ever see her again. So you have to find out, Eve. You're the only one that can. Or has he enchanted you, the way they all said he can do?"

She glared at him. "I like the clunch you are when you're hopelessly in love, Sherry. Not the idiot you are when you're thwarted."

It felt very good to both of them as they began to call each other names, as they had when they were children. And they did as they rode all the way back to the Hall.

A surprise awaited them there, in the drive in front of the Hall. No guests were seen, but a new one had arrived again.

"Sherry, my dear boy!" Arianna trilled as she neared the curricle.

Sherry almost fell off his high perch in his haste to get down.

"I've returned, but alas! The party is breaking up. Thank heavens you're still here," she said to them both, but smiling at him.

She was as beautiful in sunlight as she was in moonlight, Eve thought. Her eyes were blue as a summer sky, her golden hair glowed radiantly where the light touched it, and her skin could be seen to be perfect, unblemished, and smooth. Her lips were true red, her gold gown was sashed with green and showed a perfect lithe figure: she was, in a word, magnificent.

"Oh, and how good to see you again, little sister," Arianna told Eve. "It struck me as dreadful of me to come to your ball and then leave so promptly and ungraciously. I came back today to tell you that, and beg your forgiveness. And when Aubrey returns from wherever he is, I'll be gone. I think he won't mind. He's obviously eager to continue his honeymoon. As though I would dream of interfering! I only returned to get to know you a bit better before I left again. And," she added, "to ask you to come to visit with me one day soon."

"You live nearby?" Sherry asked eagerly.

"Not far," she said. "But secluded. I like my privacy. I love this part of the land. I won't live with my brother because I like my independence too. But I have a charming home of my own."

"Miss Arianna," Sherry blurted. "Why didn't he—I mean Aubrey—tell us about you? Even my sister, his wife, didn't know. And just now, in the village, it seemed no one had ever heard of you."

"Sherry!" Eve said angrily. "This isn't our business. It's a family matter."

"But we are family now." Arianna laughed. "Don't blame Aubrey. He was away from home so long he must have forgotten me. I'm only joking. I'm sure he would have remembered to tell you, in time. But I love this place and would never go so far away as he has done." She stopped talking, and then looked full at Eve.

Eve fidgeted under Arianna's suddenly rapt gaze. Those blue eyes seemed to look straight through to the heart of her.

"Ah," Arianna said, as though stricken. Her eyes grew wide. Then so did her smile. "I see. I mean to say, I see why my brother forgot me. Who wouldn't when he had such a lovely bride? The lamplight doesn't do you justice, Eve. You are a woman made for sunlight. Come," she said, taking Eve's arm. "Walk with me in the gardens, please, dear sister. I can't stay long, and I would know more about you and have you know more of me."

Eve had promised Aubrey she wouldn't meet with his sister alone. But Aubrey had told her Arianna had lived far away, and Arianna had just denied it. It would be craven, not to say downright childish, to walk away now, especially with Sherry looking on. And she hadn't promised Aubrey, exactly, Eve remembered. She'd said she'd try. She had. But she couldn't be so rude without better reason.

Sherry stood irresolute as they began walking across the drive to the side of the house.

Arianna looked back over her shoulder. She laughed. "Dear Sherry. Will you wait for me? I'd like to have a private word with you too."

"I will, I shall, I mean, I will be here, right here, waiting," Sherry called after them.

"My brother," Eve said, "is smitten with you." She felt awkward, walking with linked arms with anyone but Aubrey, but she continued on down the path with her sister-in-law. Arianna, she noted, smelled of jasmine, night flowers, and spice. It was a refreshing perfume, but nothing like her brother's intoxicating scent.

"It was very wicked of Aubrey not to tell you about me, but very, *very* wicked of him not to tell me about you," Arianna said. "I forgive him, of course. His head must have been so completely filled with thoughts of you that all else was lost. But I mean to come to know you better, Eve. Is it just you and your brother? Or do you have other sisters and brothers?"

"It's just Sherry and myself," Eve said. "Have *you* any other siblings that Aubrey neglected to tell me about?"

Arianna looked surprised, and then she

laughed. "Well done, turnabout is fair play. No, it's just my brother and myself. But we have a great many cousins, and so I hope you will see them when you come to visit with me. Tell me, is your mother still with us? Your father?"

"My father," Eve said. "Our mother died after Sheridan was born."

"And you are a Faraday, your father's name. What was your mama's maiden name? Forgive me," she added quickly. "One of my hobbies is genealogy."

"There's nothing to forgive. My mother's family name was Tragacanth."

"From Wales, or near to?" Arianna asked.

"Why, yes. The family had its roots there. And her mother's name was Peagle. I much prefer Ashford," Eve said with a laugh.

"Interesting, indeed," Arianna said. She looked up suddenly, as though hearing something, though Eve heard nothing but the usual midday sounds of birds, late crickets, and rustling leaves

"Oh, this is dreadful. We must go back," Arianna said. "I see from the sun that the day is more advanced than I realized. I wish you'd been home earlier, so we could have had a longer visit, but at least I had this time with you. I invite you to visit with me, Eve. Oh, you must come! With Aubrey, of course, if he wishes. But he never comes to visit me, so it may have to be just you and Sherry. I have such an interesting home, I'm sure you'll enjoy yourself mightily. The beds are soft; I have a garden that blooms all year; my friends and cousins are delightful company. We have such delicious parties. No! Don't say a word yet. I won't hear no. I'll send word to you to ask again.

"I must hurry now," she said, as they neared the drive again. "My carriage is waiting on the other side of the stables. Tell Sherry I'll see him again, and invite him personally as well. Take care, dear little sister, be sure to give Aubrey my love, and come, do come, to visit with me soon." She rushed away, to the stables, and was soon gone from sight.

Eve turned, and walked to the drive. She saw Sherry and Aubrey waiting there. She braced herself and hurried to them. She wouldn't lie. "Arianna's just left," she said breathlessly. "You can still catch her if you hurry," she told Aubrey. "Not you, Sherry. She said she'd see you again soon. She'll be inviting us to her house, she said."

Aubrey didn't move. He stood tall and still. "I won't catch her, nor do I wish to," he said. "What else did she say to you?"

"She just wanted to be acquainted," Eve said. "She asked about my family, my mother's maiden name, the sorts of things that people interested in genealogy often ask. But I don't think she was being high in the instep or snobbish at all. Just curious."

"And you told her," he said.

"Of course."

He hesitated. "My sister," he finally said, "is not quite normal, Eve."

"I beg your pardon!" Sherry said icily. "I saw nothing amiss with her, and it does you no credit, Aubrey, to speak against her."

Eve was shocked at how adult Sheridan suddenly sounded.

Aubrey put his hand to his forehead. "True, Sherry. Calm yourself. I only meant that it's hard to explain. She has fancies and superstitions, and peculiarities. She would drive you mad with them. I don't want . . . That is to say, I'd suggest you never meet with her alone again."

"I shall meet with whom I choose," Sherry said, and strode away in the direction of the stables.

"He won't find her," Aubrey said.

Eve shook her head. She looked up into the beautiful stern visage of her husband. "It won't do, Aubrey," she said. "Not at all. I tried to avoid her, I could not. It was a poor promise to try to extract from me. And as I recall I didn't take any vows about it either."

"I know," Aubrey said, with a slight bow of his head. "I stand corrected."

"Thank you," she said. "Especially since she says she lives so near. There are things you haven't told me, things I ought to know. If you don't tell me now, I'll find them by chance or accident. So I ask you to honor me with truth. I will have no such secrets between us." Her expression was grave, her voice deliberate. "Give me truth, Aubrey, for the sake of our marriage. I won't be kept in the dark anymore."

"I'd rather not," he said.

She blinked.

He scowled. "Are you sure? Sometimes ignorance is bliss," he said.

"Ignorance may be bliss, but lies are hellish."

"I'm not lying."

"You're not telling me everything," she said.

"True. And so then if you insist, I will. I meant to, in time. I imagine that the time is now. I hadn't expected it. But you, my Eve, are cleverer than most, and harder to fob off with excuses than any. So, later, I will. For now, we have guests to see off, and your brother to pour ice water on. And then I vow, I'll tell you what you want to know. Whether you believe me or not."

Chapter 13

He came to her in the night, to their bed, when the house was still and all their guests were gone away or gone to sleep.

Eve was waiting. When Aubrey put his lips to hers, she turned her head. He stopped and drew away.

"No," Eve said. "When you kiss me, I want to make love, and when we do, I forget everything. Then I'd sleep, and it will be yet another day when I don't know what I should. Just talk to me, please. Please tell me truths. About you and your sister, and the rumors that fly about the Hall. And then, if you please, make love to me."

"Will you want to then?" he asked slowly.

She sat up. "Will I?"

He stood and paced the bedchamber. "There are some things I haven't told you," he said. "Some, because I didn't think they'd matter. Some, because I wanted to wait until you know me better.

Some, because I didn't think you'd believe me. But ask me now, and I will tell you."

He sat on the edge of their bed, and waited.

"All right," she said, slowly nodding. "First. Why didn't you tell me about Arianna? And why doesn't the village know about her? Even the vicar doesn't. So, is she your legitimate sister? And why is she a secret?"

"I didn't tell you about her because I doubted you'd ever meet her. She's a moody creature, and only makes friends where she feels she can make some good for herself from it. She surprised me as well.

"The village and the vicar—my, you've been busy," he added with laughter in his voice. "Yes, they've never met her either. She was born in another country, and likes it so much there that she seldom comes here and when she does, she seldom stays long enough to know anyone here. She's my sister, and if by legitimate you mean, is she my sister from both my parents? Then, yes. She is. And she's secret only because she chooses to stay that way, and so I honestly forgot about her. And I thankfully forgot her spite and malice as well. Maybe I wanted to forget. But there it is, and that is it. Any other questions?"

"Why don't you want me or Sherry to see her, or go for a visit to her home?"

"As I said, she's vicious and petty. I'd rather you didn't deal with her alone. One day, I'll take you, if you wish, and Sherry too, if he's still infatuated by then. We'll visit with her. That is, if she still wants us to. She forgets her fancies as soon as she forms them. But that's the only way I'd feel you and Sherry were safe from her machinations."

"What of these rumors about your family?"

He had stood, preparing for bed, and now paused, his hands on the sash to his night robe. "Which rumors?"

"The villagers. . . . Well, I hear they say . . ." she paused, trying to think how to say what she'd heard.

"Ah," he said. "Let me see, which distressed you the most? The black masses held here at the Hall? The pagan magic worked, and the enchantments chanted? The dissolute parties at midnight? The sounds of music and dancing when decent working folk are sleeping? Or was it the maidens stolen away and the handsome youths disappearing after a dance with someone at a party here? Or is there something new I haven't heard?"

She hung her head.

He discarded his robe, and came to sit beside her. He put a hand under her chin, and looked at her directly, the glitter in his eyes dancing with the flickering lamplight. "That's why I, and my kind, seldom stay here, or at least, for long. We're distrusted and reviled. I suppose it's because my ancestors were rich beyond most kings, and a merry, feckless clannish troop. They were arrogant too, as well as heedless and selfish.

"Still," he said, "what village maiden would want to return to her humble home after she'd made love to a gifted lover with money and charm and music in his voice? Why wouldn't a handsome local young farmer or farrier's son with little future want to run away with a beautiful, exotic and erotic woman of means who wanted him? Yes, it happened. And often as not the young folk never returned, or if they did, they were older and wiser, and bitter about what had happened to them."

She looked up. She'd never heard that.

"What had happened was usually only that they were discarded when they grew boring," he explained. "I never said my folk were constant or kind. They were, in fact, like many other rich and careless lovers. So the villagers still don't trust us. How can I blame them? When such things happened we were whispered about and lied about, and feared. Not unnaturally, we don't trust them either."

This sounded true to Eve. But still, even with

his hand and his eyes upon her, she wasn't satisfied. There were things he wasn't saying. She knew it, but how she knew she didn't know. A thought came to her from nowhere. "The vicar said all the women your ancestors married were noble beauties. Why didn't you marry one? No," she said quickly. "No more flattery, because I don't believe in it. Why didn't you choose a wife as your father and grandfather did? Someone fabulously beautiful and titled?"

"I found you," he said so simply and honestly, that in spite of herself, she believed him.

"You never loved before?" she asked, because this she couldn't believe.

He hesitated.

"Ah," she said. "So tell me, as you promised you would. Why didn't you marry her?"

He lowered his head. "I vowed the truth, and truth you shall have. I've been married before. Before I returned, before I met you. She died long ago, on our travels."

"Oh!" she exclaimed, as though all the air had been punched out of her chest.

"Eve," he said, looking at her again. "I was younger. I was looking for different things in a woman. But now? What I felt for any women before I met you is nothing to what I feel for you."

There was music in his voice, as well as an under-current of sorrow. He was pleading with her to understand. "I found you," he said. "And you are all I ever wanted, whether I knew it or not."

"Why?" she cried, because there was still that small stubborn part of her logical mind that refuted what he said. While all the time, she yearned to believe him. "Why me? I am inconsiderable."

He smiled. "There's a lie! I've told you nothing but truth but you're not being as honest with me. Oh, my dear little liar, you *are* considerable, and deep down, you know it."

"But I'm not titled, neither am I a great beauty."

"And note that you said 'great,'" he said, laughing. "Because you know you're not without charms, and you didn't mention your wisdom and your good sense. You're without vanity, but not without pride. And not without a title: it is 'beloved wife.' You can see why I choose you if you allow yourself to. Maybe you aren't lying so much as too quick to demean yourself. But I forgive you. Now, I've answered your questions truthfully. Is there anything more?"

"Why didn't you tell me about your first wife?" she asked simply.

He took her unresisting, into his arms. "First,

second, third: had I as many as Bluebeard, so long as I treated them well, what purpose would it serve? Would it have made a difference?"

"I don't know," she said honestly. "Do you grieve for her?"

"I did," he said simply.

"Do you mourn her?"

"I did," he said.

"Were there children?"

"No, I'm sorry to say. I've never been fortunate enough to sire a child."

She tried to think of what else to ask him about his wife, and his life in those days. "What was her name? What did she look like? Why did she die?"

"Her name was Arabella," he said. "She was considered a great beauty. Illness took her; an illness no physician here or abroad could cure." He spoke softly, sadly. "Eve, what use is it to speak of her now, for me or for you? I'll tell you chapter and verse, but how will it matter, except perhaps to make you think I can't stop thinking of her? I have, you've seen to that.

"All that was then," he went on, "before we met. There was pain and grief enough. I nursed her through her final illness. After a long time, I came back here to find life again. And in you, I found more than I ever knew existed. I don't denigrate what went before, neither do I demean it. But it's the past. I returned to the Hall to find happiness. I did. You're my wife now. We are the future."

"Why didn't you say *something*?" was all she could think to say.

"Again. Would it have mattered? Except perhaps to make you wary of me? Still, had you asked, I would have told you."

She shook her head. Then she studied him. "So then," she said carefully, "you're saying that if I didn't ask you now I won't know? And if I don't ask about other things, I won't know?"

He shrugged. "Eve, my love, I'll never give you a direct lie. But how shall I know what you want to know if you don't ask me?"

She frowned, wondering what to ask.

And then he kissed her, and she put her hands on his radiantly warm body, and felt the heart beating in his chest, and all her doubts and fears disappeared, as always, as they made love.

"I don't want to go to London," Sherry said angrily, putting his father's letter down. "I don't know what's got into the old boy. I like it here, I want to stay here. That is, of course," he said, looking at Aubrey instead of his sister, "unless you want me gone. Then, I'm off."

"You're always welcome here," Aubrey said. "But your father worries about you. He's right. You should return to University, Sheridan. Only one more year."

"He never kicked up before," Sherry said grudgingly.

"That's because you took the time off to mature, or so at least you said," Eve said. "Lord, Sherry! You have done. You've grown a foot, at least. You walk and talk like a man now. Finish your studies, and then come live with us forever if you want. But I can't disagree with Father."

Sherry fidgeted. Eve looked away from him, afraid something in her eyes would show him the truth. She'd written to her father telling him to send for Sherry. She wanted him gone before Aubrey's sister remembered him, if she ever did.

Sheridan was becoming a handsome youth. A late growth spurt had made him tall and straight and he was growing into his size and beginning to walk like a man instead of gamboling like a sheep. He had a ready smile and quiet good looks. He was also kind, gentle, and far too gullible. It seemed sometimes to Eve that she'd inherited all the sense in the family. Unless, of course, it came to Sheridan later, as everything else seemed to be doing. As for now, he was almost twenty, and still young for his age.

"Well, I'll go see him, and listen to him, but I'm tired of University," he grumbled. "What difference does it make if I finish it now?"

"It makes a difference to Father. So go see him. And then try again. An education is important for a gentleman, and," she added pointedly, "it's important to most ladies who are looking for a husband, because they like a well-informed mind. Sherry," she said in a softer voice, "it's been a few weeks. She likely won't call on us again this season. Soon travel will be difficult. The weather is turning. There'll be snow and sleet. Christmas is coming, and a New Year. Enjoy London at holiday time, and then go to school after the celebrations are done.

"Tell you what!" she said on a sudden inspiration. "If she does call and ask for you, I promise that I'll let you know immediately. I'll forward any letters to you too."

Sherry didn't ask who "she" was. "Promise?" he asked with touching, childlike sincerity.

"Cross my heart," she said, doing so.

He nodded. "I'll pack and be gone."

"You don't have to clear out like a cat with its tail on fire," Eve said, laughing. "Take your time."

"This is the best time," Sherry said, and strode from the room.

Eve turned away from Aubrey's amused glance.

"Yes, I wrote to my father," she murmured. "I asked him to send for Sherry. It seemed the only politic thing to do. I told him Sherry was in danger of falling into the clutches of a clever, conscience-less female. And so of course he wrote right back, demanding Sherry come to London and then go back to school. Sherry will never know my part in it or that my father knows about Arianna. My father promised me that." She looked at him. "I did it for you, you know. You were so adamant about it."

He nodded. "So I was, and with good reason. Thank you, my clever girl. And I'm sure, one day, Sherry will thank you for it too. If he remembers."

Arianna was at the door, and Eve couldn't shake herself awake this time. Aubrey was gone to the village on some errand. It was a wretched day, gray and cold, and Eve felt like the lowering weather had got into her very bones. She'd been napping because she felt logy and flat, and now she yearned to go back to sleep. But her maid had said Arianna was there, and so Eve rose from bed. She shook out her gown, which had been crushed from her impromptu nap, pinched color into her cheeks, and came down the stairs to see if she was still dreaming.

But Arianna was actually there, and she was glowing, even though tiny flat balls of sleet had settled on the hood and shoulders of her cape. She had one of the most handsome gentlemen Eve had ever seen at her side. He was tall and flaxen-haired, with eyes as blue as Arianna's, which was to say they were the color of the autumn sky at noon, and blazing with intelligence. They took off their capes, and the ice pellets scattered on the marble floor of the hall. Arianna, and merry as a sunrise, looked around the house with bright eyes. The gentleman looked at Eve.

"My dear little sister," Arianna said, coming toward Eve with two outstretched hands.

"Arianna," Eve said flatly, because she still felt as though she were sleeping.

"You look wonderfully well," Arianna said. "But tired. I hope I haven't disturbed you? I ought to have sent word, but I know your husband better than anyone, and I was afraid he'd take you into the village with him if he knew I was coming. Here is my cousin, Elwyn. Shall we go into the front salon? I see there's a fire burning in the hearth there and I confess I'm chilled. Such weather as you have here. I'd forgotten. Snow that's cold, and sleet that melts!"

Eve followed her guest blindly, trying to absorb her words. One thing she'd heard concerned her:

Arianna had waited for Aubrey to leave before she came to call. That meant she was keeping watch on the house, or paying someone to do so. And so then she must also know that Sherry was gone. So why was she here, and with such an escort? For the first time since they'd met, Eve felt a shiver of fear thinking of her visitor's possible motives.

"How cheery!" Arianna exclaimed, as she stood by the hearth and rubbed her hands together. She wore a long-sleeved white velvet gown with a green ribbon beneath her high breasts, and her hair spilled like a fall of sunlight to her slender shoulders. The flames in the hearth accentuated her coloring, turning her hair to shades of gold and rose. She was, Eve thought again, beyond mere loveliness. She was entrancing, and it was a very good thing that Sherry was in London. Her escort was breathtaking too, but he had an unsettling stare and Eve wished again that Aubrey were there.

"I'll ring for tea," Eve said, as she settled in a chair near the hearth. "You will stay for dinner, and the night?" She mightn't like Arianna and suspect her motives, but Eve knew her duties as hostess.

So did Arianna. She laughed gaily. "Oh, no. And I think you know that. My bear of a brother will have a fit if he finds us here. Ours will be a brief visit, my dear." Arianna turned from the fire and circled Eve's chair. "But you interest me," she said. "He's never had anyone like you before. And neither have I. See what I meant, Elwyn? I can't put my finger on it, but it's there."

"She has innocence and knowledge about her, in equal measure," Elwyn said, watching Eve with fascination and obvious lust. "Very intriguing."

"Oh, don't look so panicked to hear a compliment, little sister," Arianna laughed. "You look like a doe seeing a crossbow aimed at her. Elwyn is only being truthful because I asked it of him. As for me? I'm neither violent nor mad. I simply go my way, and Aubrey goes his. We seldom agree. But on you, perhaps we do."

"I'm not remarkable," Eve said, forcing herself not to shrink back in her chair as they both stared. "In fact, compared to your exotic family, I'm plain as dirt."

"Are you? Then that may be it. There's much power in the earth," Arianna said seriously, taking a chair opposite her.

Elwyn nodded in agreement, and kept his unsettling, beautiful eyes on Eve.

"Do you know exactly how exotic our family is, Eve?" Arianna asked. "Has Aubrey told you?"

Eve sat still. There was much she wanted to hear, almost as much as she didn't. There was no sense in lying about it, and much sense in learning more, so long as she didn't find herself prying. So she answered honestly. "I know you and Aubrey are siblings. I know you have no mother or father and that your family has lived here, at Far Isle, or it's site, for ages."

"Yes. So she does know a bit," Arianna told Elwyn merrily. "But only a bit, methinks. Where is your charming brother, Eve?" she asked, in a quick turn of subject. "I know he left for London, but where does he stay there? With your father? Yes, so I should think."

Eve sat up straight. She said nothing as the butler and a footman came in, bearing tea and biscuits. When they had set up a little table between their mistress and her guests, and arranged it with the teapot, cups, and cakes, Eve waved them away. She'd had time to think.

There was little question that Arianna was odd. In fact, it occurred to Eve that Aubrey might well have concealed knowledge of her because he feared no woman would want to marry a fellow with such a weird sister. But Eve had heard stories of her own reclusive grandmother, and a very odd great-great-grandfather, and still, neither she nor Sherry was strange. So that didn't matter to her. But now Arianna was obviously being provocative and challenging. That did matter.

Eve didn't want to argue with her. But she wanted the woman gone. Elwyn did nothing menacing, but his whole demeanor was somehow insulting. He exuded sexual interest, his eyes weighing and judging her as a woman. Instead of being flattered that such a magnificent gentleman was so interested in her, Eve felt threatened.

But, she thought, lifting her head, she shouldn't be afraid. This was her house, and it was her brother she was concerned with.

"Oh, your face!" Arianna trilled. "You worry about Elwyn? Do not. He's merely puzzled that you don't melt for him as all females do. And me? It's clear you think me as mad and as bad as that fellow Byron. I'm neither. I am flighty, though. I admit that. I find it dull to keep my mind on one subject too long. I like to flit about in conversation as well as actions, like a bee in blossoms. You gather more that way. I tell you what, Eve, my dear, tell me nothing now. No, not a word! Come to know me better and you'll see there's no harm in me. Then tell me anything you wish, or I ask."

She leaned forward, her blue eyes suddenly keen. "Have you considered the thought that Aubrey doesn't want us to be friends because there are many more things he doesn't want you to know about?"

Eve had. She sat still. Then she tried to steady

her thoughts and her hands as she poured tea for
her visitors.

Arianna laughed. "Well, there we are, because
there are many things I could tell you, but they'd
only make you think me madder or stranger. And
I so want you to like me. You might, in time, actually find you'd like to come live with me! I know
Sheridan would. My home is so fine. You've never
seen the like. I promise you'll fall in love with it
and with my neighbors, and with the whole world
around me."

Arianna's smile was so warm and winning that
Eve began to believe her. "You don't have to like
me, dear little sister," Arianna went on, "though
I vow you would, should you come to stay with
me even a little while. But the things you'll see,
the things you'll learn. And the food! My cook is
magical. We should have such a good time. I cast
no aspersions on dear Aubrey, but this house is
so *natural*. Nature is beautiful, but even she needs
a helping hand. My gardens are fantastic. I have
roses that bloom in the snow, and honeysuckle
that perfumes the air all year. My friends are delightful, colorful, and sweet enough to match my
flowers."

She playfully swatted her cousin. "And not all
the men are as obvious as Elwyn here. At that, I

can promise you that he'll mind his manners in future. Our life is simple but grand. But you still don't trust me. So what to do? I know," Arianna said, clapping her hands together like a child. "Ask Aubrey some questions. Once you know more, you should be able to do more, and especially, you'll come to see that there's no harm to come from me to you or yours. Let me see, how to broach the subjects to him, because he's so prickly? Ah, yes. Ask my brother how old he is."

She rose from her chair, leaving her tea untouched, and stepped closer to Eve. "That's a good start. Because I'll wager you never did, or if you did, never got a real answer."

Eve frowned. She hadn't thought about that. She guessed Aubrey was her senior by some seven years, and when she'd asked him, he'd smiled and said, "you flatter me." And then she'd forgot to ask more. She scowled. How could she have forgotten to ask more? But what difference did it make?

Arianna nodded. "Insist on that answer, and much will follow. Then, if it doesn't, let me see . . . ah yes! Ask him how many wives he's had."

Elwyn chuckled as Eve's eyes widened. She'd never thought of that either. Had he married more than once? He hadn't said—but then he hadn't mentioned his first wife. She felt cold.

"Good, good," Arianna said, pacing. "And then, only one more question. Ask him that and the rest will tumble out."

"What rest?" Eve asked, growing impatient and afraid. "What are you saying?"

"Nothing and everything. You've probably asked him why he married you, and he likely answered in loverlike phrases. That's all to the good, and probably true. But ask him what it is he most wants from you. Yes. That should do it. When you ask he must tell. And in truth, I've told you nothing; you must discover everything yourself. He must tell you, so I've been fair to my brother and our code. Although, I vow I'd be more honest with Sheridan than Aubrey was with you.

"But I must leave now," Arianna said, lifting her head. "Aubrey was quick about his errands. I think he feels that I've returned. So I'll go. But know this, little sister. I'd never harm your Sheridan. It's only that he may be as useful to me as you are to my brother. And you are, never doubt it. It may be, we must see. Adieu. But remember, if ever you should need me, send word. Just ask anyone here in the house, or in the village. Or call to me. I will come. I am not your enemy. Believe me. Adieu, Adieu," she said as she danced from the room. Elwyn quickly followed her.

Arianna snatched up her cape from the footman, gave Eve a brilliant smile, and left the Hall with her cousin. They went out into the growing darkness of the snowy afternoon, and were gone into shadows even as Eve heard Aubrey's carriage hurrying back down the drive.

Chapter 14

Aubrey came in from the cold. His high cheek-bones were touched with a rosy gold flush and the breeze had mussed his hair, but his eyes were as dark as storm clouds.

"Where are they?" he asked, as he stripped off his greatcoat and handed it to a footman. "My guests? Never mind. Probably gone by now. Where's my wife?"

"Here," Eve said quietly from where she stood in the doorway of the front salon.

She looked subdued, pale, and slight as a shadow. Her usually impish grin was gone and her clear eyes looked dulled. His heart sank. Arianna had been here. He didn't know what she'd said, but he suspected it had been too much, and much too soon. He had been married to Eve for only a matter of months and had hoped to keep things to himself for a while longer. No, in all honesty, he'd wanted to keep them from her until he no longer had any choice, and that might have been decades from now. But one look at her showed him that it was already far too late.

"What did they say?" he asked.

"Nothing we can discuss here," Eve answered.

He hesitated. "The open air is best for truths, but it's snowing." He essayed a smile. It wasn't returned. "Do you want to come upstairs to our bedchamber?"

She shook her head, looking even more wary.

"I didn't mean that," he said quickly, realizing that she thought he meant to make love to her to win her over. "I don't mean to cloud the issue. I just wanted privacy. Very well then, will you come into my study so we can discuss it in comfort?"

She followed him to his study. He showed her to a chair, and waited as a footman hurriedly piled logs on the hearth and refreshed the smoldering fire until it blazed. Then Aubrey let the man out and closed the door behind him. He stood there a moment, his back to Eve, wishing he could pray. Instead he called on all his powers of persuasion. Then he turned to Eve. "My sister was here. Who did she bring with her? What did she say?" he asked again.

He realized she hadn't asked him how he knew his sister had been there at all. Her grief and confusion over whatever Arianna had said and whomever she'd brought with her was too all encompassing for those trivialities. Instead, she gazed at him with those bright, thoughtful brown eyes that had first called to him.

"She brought her cousin Elwyn," Eve said. "He didn't say much, which was as well because I didn't like him much either. But he did nothing."

"You didn't find him fascinating?" he asked in puzzlement.

She shook her head. "He tried too hard to make me think he was, I think," she said.

He was surprised, and laughed with relief. "My clever, sensible Eve, you never cease to astonish me. He sets females longing for him wherever he goes."

Eve shrugged. "I didn't."

"Well and good. He's a nasty piece of work."

"As for your sister, she said she only came to tell me I'm always welcome at her home, which sounds lovely, and to assure me she wasn't my enemy. She also asked after Sherry. Somehow, she knew he'd gone to London, but she didn't know where."

Aubrey let out a pent-up breath. Then he checked. If it wasn't so bad, then why was Eve so sad? He waited.

"She also told me there was much you hadn't

told me," Eve went on in a colorless voice. "And she told me what I must ask you if I want to know what it is. I have questions for you. And each hurts to even think about, Aubrey." Her voice broke; she looked away and took in a shuddering breath.

Before he could answer, she continued. "You say you never lied to me. But now I see that not lying isn't being truthful. Dreadful, incredible things have occurred to me. Ignorance isn't bliss, not anymore. I love you, that hasn't changed. But now I know I don't know you." Her eyes met his. "You're too handsome, too wealthy, too sophisticated, and too clever to instantly fall in love with a woman like me. In time, perhaps, it might have come to be. But you never gave it time. I always worried about that, and always said it, and you always flattered it away. But I also always knew it was true, though I chose not to. Now, I choose to. And so I've three questions for you, ones I never thought to ask before."

Arianna's questions. Aubrey strode to the window and looked out at the snow. Three questions: that had the stamp of Arianna on it. So his time of peace was over. It was a time for answers, and without trickery, deceit, or any attempt to charm Eve out of her mood or the truth. He thought about his new wife as he waited for her questions.

He'd come to care for her very much, far more

than he'd ever done for any woman. It wasn't just because of the treasure she now bore. It was the woman herself. She reached him in ways no one, not even one of his own people, had ever done. Eve touched his heart even though he'd doubted he had one, just as she inflamed senses he'd thought were long jaded. He still hadn't sorted them all out, except he knew he was happy with her.

He cared about what she thought of him, which was why he'd never tried to influence her feelings for him except by common, human means. And now she wanted the truth, years too soon, and so now he might lose her, forever. Or at least lose her love. He knew, in his bones, that she'd never love another as she had loved him. And that she'd never leave the child she didn't even know that she now bore. But she might refuse to let herself love him from now on. That was a loss he couldn't begin to contemplate. But he had no choice.

"Fire away," he said, clasping his hands behind his back as he stared out the window into the storm.

"How old are you, Aubrey?" she asked quietly.

"Ah!" he said, as though she'd struck him. "Good, very good, Arianna got right to the heart of it, didn't she? I'll answer you, Eve. But I think it's best that I know all three questions now, because they're all of a piece, and may be best answered together."

"How many wives have you had, Aubrey?" Eve asked softly.

He nodded, his chest growing tight. "Ah, yes, to be expected. And the third question?"

"That," Eve said, "I now see must come last of all."

"Very well," he said.

"No!" she said. "Please, turn and face me so that I can see you when you answer me."

"That will be harder for me," he said quietly, but he turned to face her. In truth, were she just any woman, it would be easier for him, but he refused to try to influence her by anything but facts. He realized he'd said that out loud when she took in a deep breath, folded her hands in front of her, and waited for him to say more.

"And it's also rare for me. All of this is, Eve," he said. He shook his head, and walked close to her. He dragged a chair from behind his desk and placed it next to hers. There he sat, and looked at her, his eyes searching her expression for every nuance of change as he spoke.

"You will not choose to believe me at first," he said. "And then you'll think about it. And then?" He shrugged, an ineffably sad expression on his own face. "You will decide. My age, Eve? I'm old, older than any man you've ever known. But then, that makes sense, because I am not a mortal, human man."

She sat wide-eyed and still.

"Shall I go on?"

She nodded.

"At least you're not laughing," he sighed. "My people, my folk, my troop, have lived here at Far Isle or what came before it, from time out of mind. It could be argued that we're more British than any of you latecomers: you Celts, Angles, Romans, Vikings, Francs—all you latecomers. We were born on and of this very earth that is Britain. But we're not precisely humankind. We're an older race. We look the same. We feel many of the same things. Three things differentiate us. We live for ages more than you do. Maybe that's why we're not bothered with religion, or the other superstitious emotions that you have in plenty. We don't care about our souls, if we have them, because we've never seen them. Nor do we worship any higher powers. We can think of no one higher than ourselves.

"We can also cast spells, which are only light enchantments, over humankind. That's also partially why we were, in our racial youth, amused by your kind and treated you with no respect. We were callous and thought you inferior, and used you only for our own pleasures, which were self-serving and chiefly mischievous.

"As time went on, we began to see your qualities. You were capable of being fully as wicked as we, equally as intelligent, and quite as conceited. The problem was that your kind are mayflies compared to us. We no sooner came to know you than we lost you, so we considered you of no account. But your race was intelligent enough to accumulate wisdom and pass it on. And mankind is ambitious, far more than we are. Is it your fear of extinction that makes you so? We don't know. But you began to grow wiser as a race, and as you did, to distrust us, and with good reason. So we began to keep to ourselves more. In fact, were it not for one thing, we would retreat to our own realm, which is really exquisite, and you would see us no more."

He waited for her to ask. She wasn't dull. She'd put it together. He watched her eyes, those sincere earth brown eyes, and he vowed that if humans did indeed have souls, he could see hers there.

"You're not joking," she said flatly.

"No."

"But you must be."

"No," he said.

"It isn't a game?"

"No."

You believe what you're saying?"

"Yes."

"Ah," she said, and sat and thought a moment. "Nor are you mad," she whispered, as though to herself. "At least I don't think so. So what could be your reason for telling me such a tale? Ah, it's a jest between you and your sister? Some sort of test for me? Or is Sherry in on it? I don't think it's amusing. Please stop it. I don't find it funny; it's frightening me, and it's cruel of you all to tease me so."

"It's neither a joke nor a test, nor am I teasing you."

"Of course, no human male could be as beautiful as you are," she mused. "And you never do have a blemish or a skin problem; you wake as handsome at dawn as you are at night, and however much I look at you, one glance at you and you always take my breath away. It's more than infatuation. I feel it here," she said, her fist to her chest. She cocked her head to the side "Have you truly enchanted me then?"

He smiled. "No, I have not."

"Never?"

"Once," he said. "The first time we made love. I didn't want to hurt you. I did, but I didn't. It was only for a moment. Never before that, and never again."

She laughed and put both hands to her head. "Oh, I must have run mad then. Or you have. This is the most peculiar conversation." She lowered her hands. "But ours always was a peculiar relationship, wasn't it? Why should a little brown girl like me attract a man such as you? Very well, finish it. Tell me, Aubrey, all of it. How old are you? How many wives have you had? I may even believe it's true as you speak to me. I'll doubt it the minute you step away. I'll wonder back and forth through a week of nights or more, but you know? In the end, I'll think less of you, or of myself, for not seeing the cruelty, or the madness in you before this.

"If it is madness, Aubrey," she said, leaning forward, her eyes huge and sincere, "we'll seek physicians for you, I promise. But you've never shown any hint of it. Oh, damnation. Have done. Now, will you share the jest? Or do you still intend to continue with this story of yours?"

"I'll continue with the truth," he said. "I have lived three centuries."

"Ah! And so you knew good Will Shakespeare?"

"You're joking now," he said. "You're shocked, and with good reason. Say then, I've known many men and women."

"Why are you here then?" she asked patiently,

watching him closely. "When your own country is so much more beautiful and your own people, to judge by you and Arianna, so much more beautiful too?"

"We like diversity," he said. "This land was all ours once. Now it's becoming too crowded and too different. Your people discovered iron centuries ago. We've never liked it. It stings to the touch, it jangles our nerves, and it's the antithesis of trees, leaves, and grass, even of living rock. Your people used it only for hunting once, and to put on horse's hooves. Now you build gates and towers of it. They're talking about laying down iron tracks across the land, for iron beasts to travel on." He shuddered. "Our own land becomes more pleasant by the day to us. And yet, and still, there's no question that you still fascinate us."

"Oh, and so what exactly are you, Aubrey?" she asked, as though she were asking if he wanted some tea.

"We are called by many names. Elves, faerie folk . . ."

But she was laughing. "Oh, I see. "Where the bee sucks there suck I?'" she quoted. "You must have known Mr. Shakespeare. But it's not midsummer, and where are your wings? And shouldn't you be much smaller? Come, what's the jest, Aubrey? I've had enough."

"No jest," he said quietly. "Humans have depicted us as they need to see us, but we are as you see."

"How many wives?" she asked so conversationally that he realized she disbelieved him entirely.

"Three," he said. "I was faithful to each of them in turn. I nursed them until their deaths. I took them away from here as they aged. I don't age, you see. The differences between us became too much for them to have their friends see, and for me to risk being seen. One lady I took abroad. I couldn't stay long because I can't leave my own spot of earth for too long. But she was ill, and died soon after we left, and was peaceful at the end, looking out at the sea." He turned his head and avoided Eve's eyes. "She couldn't bear to look at me at the last. She was vain. It made her ill to see her face in the glass and then mine. That, I couldn't help.

"When the other two grew old and sick, we said we were going abroad as well. But I took each in turn back with me to my country. The gateway to it is down at the end of the lane, in the wood, beneath a burrow, under a tree and in a hillock. The Hall has its reputation for a good reason. Worlds intersect here and always have done.

"My land didn't make the poor ladies any happier, not for long. Even if one isn't vain, it's not a joyful thing to grow old while those about one stay forever young. Then, when my wives died of advanced years, each time, after a decent absence from human sight, I returned to your land again, impersonating my own son. Those who had known me before remarked on how much I resembled my father. But they were usually too old themselves, and their vision too fogged, to note that I hadn't changed at all, except for my hair and eye color. For some reason, coloring always deceives mortals.

"For what it's worth," he said bleakly, turning to Eve again, "I respected each of my wives, but I never loved. I'm not sure that I can. Not in the way you mean. But with you, I try, and sometimes, I think I know what it is."

"Ah!" she said. Her hands were clenched. "And so, the last question. Arianna was right. I never asked it correctly. Why did you marry me? And by that I mean, what do you want of me? I think it was what you wanted of the others as well. Good lord! You have me repeating that nonsense. Never mind that. If you didn't marry me for love, then what is it that you want of me?"

"We are a small nation and we grow smaller each year," he said bluntly. "We need children. We stopped producing them centuries ago. When we were young, we stole yours. They aged more slowly with us, but they aged and eventually died, to our great sorrow. We haven't had a new child of our own kind since my own birth."

"And you want one from me? But why? I'm not of your kind."

"Your great-grandmother's mother's mother mated with one of our kind. Though she had children, none were of our kind. Nevertheless there is more in your blood than you know."

Eve arose. "And you knew her, I suppose? Of course. Enough. Have done. Yes, this is, I think, an elaborate trick. Or I have run mad, or you have. It may be that you and your sister are toying with me. Or Sherry has thought up a new game. And I think very badly of you, Aubrey, for taking part in it. Everything you say makes sense and no sense."

She hugged herself against a chill, though the room was warm. "You're toying with me, and that's unlike you. Or maybe it is like you. We haven't known each other that long, have we? I should never have married in haste. But I don't intend to repent at leisure. Whatever it is, this is either so cruel I can't grasp it, or so bizarre it's true. I can't tell truth from lies anymore. One thing I do know: I can't believe it of you. Obviously, I don't *know* you. I want to go home." She raised her head, turned on her heel, and left the room.

He stood there, watching her leave. He couldn't

follow. She had to come to him. She believed and disbelieved. He'd seen it before. He'd wait. She would or would not believe him. Too bad Arianna hadn't given her a fourth question, because he was bound to answer all she asked.

Eve had already conceived. And the babe was as much his as hers. She'd know that soon enough. In the meanwhile, she wouldn't leave him yet, she'd think about it, and take her time deciding. He was sorry he'd hurt her, sorrier still that he'd had to tell her so soon. Whatever happened, he was her husband. He'd stay with her. After she thought it over, she would stay with him.

Divorce was rare, scandalous, and shameful, as well as a long tedious process. She wouldn't risk it. She might be embarrassed to repeat his story to anyone else anyway. But even if she did, he was a charming and fabulously wealthy gentleman. They'd say he was an eccentric, and eccentrics were well known to Society. At a time when ladies and gentlemen of the *ton* cultivated eccentricities as their ancestors used to propagate exotic flowers, when the King of England himself walked about his palace in his nightshirt curtsying to ghosts, and the prince squandered state money during a war to erect a vast Chinese palace for his seaside pleasures, peculiarities were well tolerated.

But she mightn't talk to him again.

Still, he wouldn't leave her, not until he looked into the eyes of the child and saw if he'd accomplished what he'd set out to do all those many long and lonely years ago. He had to know if he'd succeeded, if he'd saved his troop and his clan. If he had, he'd take the child to it's proper home. If not, he'd try again. And at the last, he'd have to see if he could save her love for him. Because he realized that for the first time, that it mattered too.

Chapter 15

Eve didn't know what to say, or if she should say anything at all, but she hated silence. When Aubrey came into their bedchamber much later that night, she put a trembling finger in the book to mark the place where she'd pretended to be reading and looked up with hope. "You've thought better of it? It was a distemper of the spirit, wasn't it?" she asked him. "Too much wine?"

"No," he said wearily.

"And so," she asked carefully, "You have always believed this? Or was it something that just came to you suddenly in a blinding flash and you knew it was right?"

"Always. It wasn't a brain spasm or seizure."

"And have you told anyone else?" she asked. She sat up in their bed, but had never looked less sleepy. She wore a robe over her nightshift, and hadn't even undone her hair. She'd been reading, but now she held the book in a white knuckled grasp, as though it anchored her.

He paused. "I told my past wives, in turn. Everyone who has worked at this house for more than thirty years knows the truth, or aspects of it, and many others suspect it."

"You told your wives at once?" she asked, "Or only when you thought you could no longer avoid it?"

"Only then," he said.

She stared at him. "So where are the pointed ears? The wings and the wand and the like? There's no way you could dance under a toadstool in the moonlight."

"Of course not," he said. "We never looked different from your people. That's folklore. We're not immortal either. We do live for longer than you do, much longer. But when our time comes, we do cease to be. We can be killed before times, as well. When we die in natural course of things, we simply become less solid. We stretch out on the wind and flow away. I hear it's not painful, but only very sad. We aren't human, but we can become much more mortal if we stay with you too long. The longer we stay, the less we become, and if we stayed all our lives we would lose our lives quickly, or at least as quickly as you mortals do. Our own land gives us substance and years."

She nodded. "So that's why you're leaving me?"

"Leaving you?"

"Well, one sort of announcement such as you have made usually precedes another," she said with an attempt at her usual tone of voice. "And if a person's husband comes to his wife with a wild tale it's either because he's run mad, or he's trying to lightly but firmly let her think he has, so he can leave her, or be left alone."

Aubrey sat on the side of the bed. "I told you the truth. It takes some getting used to, but it is so. That is what I am. Many things in your world are fantastical but true, Eve," he said gently, his expression gentled and sympathetic. "Who would think spring could rise from cold dead earth every year if they hadn't seen it and gotten used to it? The ancients didn't believe it. They sacrificed their own blood to ensure the marvel kept happening. Only when spring came without their sacrifice did they believe it wasn't a miracle and began to take it as a matter of course.

"But think of the other fantastic things you take for granted: birds flying through the air, an ugly worm weaving a crypt for itself and emerging as a beautiful butterfly, fish popping out of eggs: it's all fantastical. Life itself is fantastic. Two humans make love. They either give each other pleasure, or one is bored, or one is terrified, it makes no difference. If the time is right, another human comes into being from the act. Is that not magical? And oysters and whelks and cold creatures from beneath the seas need not even meet another of their kind to produce young. Which is more fantastic?

"There are many more kinds of life on this earth than you know of, Eve," he said softly, reaching out to touch a lock of her hair. "You've read the old legends, heard the stories, even seen the pictures the ancients drew and carved. Those depict real things too."

"Dragons and mermaids?" she asked. "Brownies and ogres and trolls? Giants, and dwarfs with pots of gold? Werewolves and great worms rising out of Scottish lochs? All the creatures from fairy stories I heard as a girl? I suppose I could believe that there was once some foundation for those tales. Deformed humans and animals could have been seen as strange and new creatures. Tales told around a fire with wolves prowling outside the light take on lives of their own, just as fire shadows from the hearth seem to do. Primitive people are afraid of the dark, and they see enemies everywhere."

"Possibly because they have them," he murmured.

"Well, I suppose," she said. "But elves? An old

race still living and weaving magics today, and I married one of them? And he's one of the last of his kind and only here because he wants an elf child from me? No," she shook her head sadly. "That, Aubrey, I can't believe."

"Others still live here," he said. "Not everyone went away. Many more visit."

She gazed at him long and hard. "Aubrey," she finally said with infinite sadness, "I can't help loving you. Although it feels like my heart is breaking, it's made of sterner stuff. It would take a great deal more to make me stop loving you. But that love has changed. You'll have to give me days, weeks, months, I don't know, perhaps years to absorb all this. And I don't know if I'll ever believe it. In the meanwhile, if we go to London, will you go to see a physician, and tell him all this too?"

He nodded. "Dr. Frost in Marble Arch, or Dr. Jennings in Harley Street? They already know, because they have their own powers and reasons for being here. We aren't the only race to live in secret, as I said. But that is their story to tell."

"I see," she said slowly. "Aubrey, I don't want to leave you, but I don't know what else to do. For now, this seems to me to be for the best." Her eyes filled with sudden hot tears. It had all been too wonderful to be true. She should have known.

She *had* known but he'd denied it, and if there was magic, it was in his convincing her he was marrying her because she was so wonderful to him.

They were speaking of fairy tales. How could she have believed, for a moment, that a man like Aubrey would have fallen in love with someone like her, and on first sight? Though his story about his old race was bizarre, it made more sense than the romantic dreams about their marriage that she'd woven for herself.

He sat beside her now, outlined by lamplight, as perfectly beautiful as a dream that came to a maiden lady in the depths of night. Commanding as the mature Apollo, as lithe and languidly beautiful as a statue she'd seen of the young Perseus: supple and easy and certain in his masculinity. He radiated warmth and desire, and he was knowing, knowledgeable, and kind. And he was mad, utterly mad, from a mad family. And he was her husband.

She bowed her head and wept.

"Ah, no," he said, gathering her in his arms.

She clung to him, absorbing the heat of the strong firm body next to hers, wondering how she could take comfort from the one who had so grievously wounded her. He wore a soft linen shirt, and she heard his heart beating against her ear. He was the most wonderful man she'd ever met, and he believed he was a creature out of a fairy story.

"Do the people of your race have hearts as we do?" she asked softly.

"Yes," he said.

"And those hearts beat red blood throughout your veins? Or is it green, or blue?"

"Red," he said, with laughter in his voice.

"And your women bear children as we do?"

"They used to," he said with sorrow.

"Had you not known my great-great however great grandmother, would you have loved me?" she asked very quietly, and waited for the count of three heartbeats before he answered her.

"I didn't know her," he said. "I heard of her. I saw her once too. And I don't know because I wouldn't have sought you had I not known about her, and had our situation not grown so desperate. But once having found you, I would love you as I do . . . insofar as I am capable of doing."

"Ah," she said.

"Please don't weep," he said, his lips on her hair. "I am what I say I am, and all the tears in the universe can't change that. But for what it's worth, however long I've lived, I've never before felt as I feel for you, not for any other being in the universe. And remember, I've never lied to you."

"Yes," she said, lifting her tearstained face and looking into his. "You've always told me only what I asked of you, *if* I knew how to ask it. You break my heart, Aubrey, that you truly do."

He stayed still. "What else can I tell you?"

"But why do I feel this way? Tell me honestly, Aubrey. Do you believe you can enchant mortal women? Do I feel this way because you've bespelled me?"

"You've asked me that before. No, or only the once as I told you. Never again. Because I wanted you to want me as only free will could make you do."

She sat quietly, her tears subsiding, feeling desperate, feeling alone, and needing him although she no longer knew who he was. "Aubrey?" she said. "Can you show me? Nothing mad or strange, but can you do something to show me that you are what you say?"

His arms tightened around her. "What would you of me?" he asked. "I can't show you how to weave straw into gold. I can't make myself vanish, or walk into the air. Not here. I can at my true home, but while my jealous sister hunts for a mate it's not yet time to take you there. Here our magics are subtle things: spells and seemings, all of it. Shall I make you love me, Eve? But you say you already do."

"I do," she said, looking up into his eyes as best she could through the mist in her own eyes. "So then, can you make love to me now, and cast a spell as you said you did once before so I wouldn't feel pain? Can you make me forget all this and only revel in you, as though I never knew any doubt or fear or regret? Can you enchant me, Aubrey?"

His eyes narrowed. "You want me to cast a spell on you, to make you enjoy my lovemaking?"

"No, I do that already. I want to know if a spell would make a difference." There, she thought. I didn't ask for any great feat of magic that would belittle him, just something I would notice, and not anything to shame him. "I just want to know the difference between what is," she said carefully, "and what you can make me feel, without my knowing it."

His smile was sad. But he stripped off his jacket and his shirt, and cast off his other clothing. Then he came into bed with her and held her in his arms. He bent his head to kiss her.

She hesitated. "Don't you have to wave your arms, or whisper an incantation or something?" she asked in a small voice.

"That's a magician," he breathed in her ear. "That's a conjurer. Or a wizard. They try to make magic. I *am* magic."

Then he kissed her. His lips were warm, so

sweet and warm that her senses heated, and she struggled to remove her nightshift because she couldn't bear to have a thing stand between him and herself. When she'd cast it off, she came back to him, and clung to him. This time his kiss was sweet as a sigh and hot as the sun, and the touch of his tongue on hers made her tingle and splinter and soar until she almost couldn't bear the thrill of it.

She felt streamers of electricity through her; she felt scalding chills. She shook and shivered, wanting more of the delicious freezing heat. She closed her eyes and saw motes of light sparkling and shifting, as she floated in a sensual haze, and yet at the same time every sensitive bit of her body was jangling. She smelled flowers and amber and everywhere her body puckered and pouted and yearned.

But something was missing, something vital, something was wrong. In the midst of all this incredible bliss, she was utterly alone. Where was he? "No!" she said.

She opened her eyes and saw his eyes clear and cool and measuring on her. She pulled away from him with great effort. He opened his arms to let her go, and the further away she got, the easier it became for her to leave his embrace.

She sat up. "No," she said breathlessly, holding

up a trembling hand. "If that's what you mean by casting a spell over me, then no."

"Why not?" he asked, frowning.

"Because once we began I couldn't feel *you* anymore. Not your reaction or your presence. I couldn't feel your lips, your tongue; I couldn't even feel the strength in you." She took some deep breaths, and then moved closer, and leaned against him. She kissed his neck. "Your skin tastes salty, did you know?" she murmured. "Sun warmed and salty, always. You make sounds when you make love. I love it because it means I'm giving you satisfaction and that makes me feel powerful. You smell of ferns but also like a man."

She lowered her voice and her head and spoke against his heart, "I love how I feel when we join. But just now, whatever you did before, I felt that I was alone. If that's enchantment, I don't want it. Be Aubrey, just Aubrey, for me, please."

He looked surprised.

"It was interesting," she said, "and I'd be lying if I said it wasn't nice. But it wasn't you. I want you."

He smiled, bent his head, and kissed her. She felt his lips, warm and questing, against her own; his hands, gentle and coaxing, on her body. She relaxed. He made love to her with his usual fire, but also with the tempered gentility she had come to expect from him, and with the desire that she always loved. When he came to her at last, she arched her back to help him, and when he came to his moment, she reveled in it before she felt herself shiver and shatter in release as well.

They lay still a while.

"Better?" he finally asked.

"Yes," she breathed. "Before, all I felt was my own pleasure. Nice, but lonely. I don't know if that was enchantment, but if it was, I think it lacks something. Lovemaking is meant for two people."

He lay back on his pillow, put a hand on his stomach, and laughed. "You don't like enchantment?" he asked.

"If that's what it is, then, no, not really. So," she said with a great effort to sound casual, tracing her name on his chest with the tip of one finger, "you don't need to use it with me. In fact, I think if you tested yourself you'd find there was no reason to use spells at all, on anyone, and so there'd be no reason to claim you were different from other men, either. I love you just as you are. Most people would, you know. As for the others? Who needs them?"

He rolled over on his side, and lay still, regarding her. "Eve," he said quietly, "I don't use enchantments anymore. And I have never done with you, except that once and now for the second time. But I am what I claim to be. Only time will prove it to you, though."

"You sister said she could."

"My sister," he said flatly, "has her own reasons for everything she does, and none of them to profit you, or me. If you give me the time, in the fullness of it you will come to understand who and what I am. Can you wait, trust me, and continue to stay with me?"

"Will you tell other people what you are?" she asked. "I mean, like my father and brother, and our relatives, and such?"

"No," he said sincerely. "I never planned to do that."

"And you won't mention how old you are?" she asked anxiously. "I mean, I wouldn't mind if you claimed to be any age at your next birthday so long as it wasn't three hundred years. That's bound to cause talk that we don't need."

"I understand and quite agree," he said. "Consider it forgotten."

"And you won't discuss your previous wives, except," she added quickly, "with me?"

"Of course. If you wish me to talk about them, I

will," he said. "But I can't see the point in it."

She sighed. So did he.

"I understand," he said again, gently. "I honestly do. No one else will know, and that's a vow."

"Thank you," she said. "It's not that I'm unfeeling or uncaring, and believe me, I more than anyone else know that you're a very unique person. But you know how people are. They're bound to find it odd."

"I know. Don't worry. I told you only because you asked. And I will never lie to you."

"Good," she said, suppressing a sudden urge to yawn.

"Good night then," he said, and she heard the smile in his voice.

She curled up against him. He could work enchantment with her just by being himself. When he withheld his love while making love it hurt her. That was natural, and no spell, unless love itself could be called such. Having a husband who thought he was immortal, an elf or an Old Person, a creature out of legend and folklore, wasn't wonderful. But if you loved him desperately and you were the only one to know about his conviction that he was that, and in all other respects he *was* wonderful, you could deal with it. She could, and would. It wasn't what she had wanted or expected in a husband, but she supposed there were far worse things he could be.

And if he were discovered, well, eccentrics were all the rage. The greatest fops and fashion setters outdid each other trying to be even more peculiar, dressing in bizarre fashions and taking up outlandish hobbies to call attention to themselves. Collecting dogs, or wearing only green clothing, or such. Her husband's strange conviction hardly approached such folly. And he'd promised to keep it to himself.

One day, perhaps, she'd find the reason for this illusion of his, and maybe somehow deal with it, so that he wouldn't need it anymore.

"Eve," he said as she drifted to sleep, nestled against him, his voice vibrating through her own body, "you amaze me. No human has ever disliked sensual enchantments or understood the difference between getting satisfaction, and giving it as well as taking it. You're right, of course. That does make even the finest spell seem somehow lacking. Humans never notice it. You did. I sought you because you were different, but you continue to amaze me. And if I knew exactly what it was, or if I was at all capable of it, I could believe I was falling in love with you."

She froze.

"No," he said, taking her hand and holding it

to his heart. "That's a compliment. I never felt this way before, and didn't know that I could."

She sighed. That, she thought, wasn't much. But perhaps it was, coming from him. It gave her hope, because she wanted and needed it to.

Chapter 16

If he was any mythical character, Eve thought sleepily, then Aubrey was Cupid to her Psyche: a dream lover who was gone from her bed every morning when she awoke. But lately, she was so loathe to wake up early that she wasn't really surprised to find him gone. When she opened her eyes this morning she saw the sun was already well up.

"Am I become like one of those elegant London ladies?" Eve asked her maid when she came in. Eve yawned and stretched and then accepted her morning cup of hot, bitter chocolate in bed. This was a wealthy married lady's luxury she really enjoyed.

"No, ma'am," her maid said, as she pulled back all the bedchamber curtains to let the sun stream in. "Those ladies don't wake until noon. It's only just ten in the morning."

"Well, I'm used to being up with the chickens,"

Eve said on another huge yawn. "It must be all this fresh air." She secretly wondered if it was all the lovely lovemaking that was making her so deliciously exhausted, but couldn't mention that to anyone. That reminded her that not everything about her husband was lovely.

"Betty," she said more seriously, sitting up, "You're from London. Have you heard any strange stories about Far Isle since you've gotten here?"

"Oh, many!" Betty said cheerfully. "But, begging your pardon, ma'am, there's stories about all old houses, what with ghosts and specters and strange doings in the night. There's lots of that but I don't hold with any of it. What I did hear about what's dodgy, and kindly tell me to stop if I give offense, but they say that the master's sister is a piece of work, a female to be reckoned with, and no one's favorite. And that the master is as good as he's kind, and that's as much as he's handsome, so you can imagine how much everyone likes him. And you too, ma'am, they like you too, that's sure. Will there be anything else?"

"No, thank you," Eve said, looking down at her tray, embarrassed and annoyed with herself for asking about gossip from a maid, because now for certain, that would be the new gossip of the day.

She hardly touched her light repast: the chocolate tasted off, and the little biscuits she usually enjoyed were too rich. Her stomach, her taste buds, or her cook was obviously not in good spirits this morning. So Eve arose, feeling hollow and slightly rancid. After much yawning and stretching, she dressed by herself, in order to avoid Betty's conversation. She didn't want any more gossip, after all. Eve threw on a salmon-colored, light wool long-sleeved gown. She brushed out and tied up her hair herself, and wandered downstairs, feeling restless.

She put on a light shawl and went out into the daylight, hoping that the fresh air would wake her thoroughly. It was deep autumn but the day was mild. The leaves that remained on the trees were ragged and brown, the sun was warm on her upturned face, acorns and dead leaves snapped and crunched under her feet as she trailed down a long path into the little wood nearby. A rambling stream melodically chuckled over smooth stones at the side of the path; the air was cool here and smelled of earth and leaves, and she began to breathe more easily.

"Good morning, dear little sister," Arianna said, appearing before her.

Eve halted, a hand on her heart. "I didn't hear you coming."

"Of course not," Arianna said merrily. "Tell me, did you ask Aubrey those three questions?"

Eve was a reasonable woman and prided herself on being an even-tempered soul. But now as she looked at Arianna's smiling face, she felt rage bubbling up inside her. She put her hands on her hips and glowered at her sister-in-law.

"How dare you!" she said, her voice low and aggrieved. "You knew about Aubrey's problem, and the full extent of it too. And yet, under the guise of friendship, you told me to ask the very things that exacerbated it. Poor man! Most of the time he forgets his illusions, but you went and deliberately had me stir things up, didn't you? You made sure that I saw every facet of his delusion. Well, I did, I have, and guess what, *my dear sister*?" she added in scornful mockery. "It makes no matter to me."

Eve snapped her fingers. "I love him still, so if your goal was to chase me away, I'm afraid it didn't work. Just never call yourself my 'sister,' or my friend again, thank you very much. Now, if you'll excuse me? I have things to do."

But Arianna didn't stir from where she stood in front of Eve. Nor did she stop smiling, though she cocked her head to the side. "And what you have to do now is think things through, right? But there's no need. It's you who labor under an illusion, poor Eve. Aubrey is what he says he is, as am I."

"Oh," Eve said on a sneer, "I see. How dim of me. You're one of the Old People too? I suppose you can fly and cast spells? Oh bother! Arianna, I'll thank you to mock me no more. I know this delusion isn't a game for Aubrey, but I think that it is with you."

"Oh, all my life is a game, I never take things as seriously as Aubrey does, or rather, has begun to do. But hear me out, Eve. What he says, what I say, what we are, is true. Should you like to see for yourself?" Arianna cocked her fair head to the side, for once not smiling, only looking curious. She was wearing a green cape this morning; her hair was unbound, and the sunlight made a golden nimbus around her.

Eve was tempted, though she knew it wasn't what Aubrey wanted. But if his sister claimed to be supernatural as well, it might be she was part of some sinister plot to cloud his mind. Or it might be that both children had been brought up to entertain such fancies. Aubrey seldom spoke about his parents. This might be the reason for the delusion, and this was her chance to perhaps know why.

She stared at Arianna, and suddenly decided that just this once, she might go against Aubrey's wishes. His reasoning was obviously unbalanced when it came to his personal life and his illusions.

If she could see for herself she might be able to help him, or at least help herself to deal with him. She nodded. "Maybe." She waited, standing firm, but poised to run. No telling what Arianna might do to prove herself.

Arianna laughed at her stance and her expression. "Oh no. I'll do nothing right here, and there are no magic tricks. Instead, I'll let you see my home, our home, your husband's true home. I'll take you there and then you'll doubt us nevermore."

"Is it far?" Eve asked, babbling the first thing she could think of to fill the time as she backed away. Nothing could induce her to walk a step further into a dark wood with this strange woman.

"Not at all. It's here," Arianna said. "In the same place as Far Isle, but in a different world, a different and better place. There's a border, a boundary that only we know. Just follow me." She held out her hand.

Eve didn't take it.

"Oh, come along, do," Arianna said impatiently. "What would be the point of my harming you? I want to be your sister, Eve, perhaps in every way. Because your brother Sheridan interests me. He is of your blood, and so he has great potential, for me, I think."

Eve felt cold.

"But for now," Arianna went on, "it will be just you. Don't look so alarmed. You're safe with me; we can come back any time you wish. The thing is," she laughed, "you may not want to go home again."

"No!" Eve exclaimed. "On second thought, no, thank you. I haven't the time today." She took a deep breath. She couldn't be such a coward. She had to find out something, anything more, before she walked away. "But tell me, Arianna, did your parents tell you about this place, you and Aubrey?"

Arianna laughed. It was such pretty laughter, Eve thought sadly. It sounded like bells. But the lady was obviously mad as a hatter. It must run in the family, she realized, backing away. Aubrey was kind. But who knew if Arianna wasn't violent? That might be why Aubrey wanted her to stay away from his sister. Eve put a hand over her abdomen as if she had something there to protect. She did, she realized. Her fertility, her legacy, her as yet unborn children. Her heart felt leaden when she thought about it. Because though she could perhaps tolerate Aubrey's obsession and ignore his sister's illusions, she realized she never wanted to deal with a weak-minded child as well.

Arianna's eyes widened. Her smile was the broadest Eve had ever seen, so wide and white it was almost lupine. "Ah, I see! Oh wonderful! It's true! Joy upon you, little sister. And I see you know already."

"Know what?"

Arianna nodded to where Eve had placed her hand. "That you carry my brother's child, of course. Early days for you to know, but I suppose you must have some powers or he wouldn't have chosen you in the first place. This is more than exciting. Last time we met I thought perhaps, but it was too soon to know for certain, or even if the babe would take a tight hold. But it has. It grows and prospers." She clapped her hands together and whirled around. "Such a special child too. The first one Aubrey has ever conceived. The first one any of us has conceived in generations. And if it's born with the power, then it will be the first new one of our kind in generations. It gives us hope. It will mean that our long day is not yet ended."

"I am with child?" Eve asked, astonished and yet suddenly convinced of this truth.

"Didn't you know? Well, you should. Count your days, count the moon cycles, and you'll see it's true." Arianna closed her brilliant blue eyes for a second, opened them, and smiled. "You will certainly know within the week, little sister. And to relieve your mind, it is a male child."

Eve stood still. She had been feeling ill in the

mornings, and weary in the day, when she ought not to be. She hadn't dared hope, but now she believed what Arianna said. Not that she was having a boy, but that she was with child. It was possible.

"What fortune, what luck; what a clever fellow my brother is after all," Arianna crowed. "Because luck had little to do with it. How did he know he'd find such welcome in you? Who could have guessed it? Such a simple earth-bound female as you are, and yet with an interesting heritage, and above all else, the ability to continue our own heritage. He followed your line and found gold in plain earth. His powers are wider than even I knew, and I salute him."

"That's all you think he married me for?" Eve asked.

"Of course," Arianna said. "Why else? Don't look so unhappy, it's a great honor to bear one of our kind. You'll be awarded great riches and tribute. And never fear, we'll bring the child up to appreciate you as well as his own legacy."

"You?" Eve asked in shock. "*You* will raise my child?"

Arianna laughed again. "Who else should rear such a miraculous child? You? I can't wait to tell the others! I'll see you again, little sister. I salute you, and don't worry; I'll see no harm comes to you. What joy!" she said, twirling in place again, creating a swirl of gold and green. "Good day, Eve. Until we meet again, adieu!"

Arianna vanished as quickly as she'd arrived.

Eve walked on slowly. She had much to think about. Was she really pregnant? It would explain the wretched feeling she'd had this morning. Arianna's guess was right at least in that she wouldn't know for another week. But there was no magic in that. Arianna could have found out her moon cycles from maidservants and the laundress at the Hall.

If she were really going to have a child she was thrilled. But also now very worried. Arianna was certainly mad. Aubrey was . . . confused or deluded, at times, about his identity. But if this unborn child bore any such tendencies, then being exposed to his aunt would be dreadful. Eve stopped in her tracks. And being exposed to his father would be just as bad.

But she loved Aubrey so much. He was wise and kind, gentle and loving. He was her soul mate. He made her laugh and cry, and she didn't know how she'd lived her life so far without him.

And he believed that he was more than three hundred years old, not mortal as humans were, and had supernatural powers. Not even love could overleap such an obstacle. It could, she supposed, because it had done in her case. But only because she hadn't known when she'd married him. And now the love for her own unborn child began to preoccupy her.

Eve walked on slowly, thinking, arguing with herself, worrying and planning. At last, she stopped. She came to a decision. She turned around, retracing her steps, and walked back to the Hall. First, she'd wait and see if it was true that she bore a child at all. Then, if she did, she'd do whatever she had to do to ensure its safety now, and forever. She could do no more, and certainly no less.

Eve strolled into Aubrey's study when he returned after doing his errands around the manor. "I saw your sister today," she said.

He was rumpled, his dark hair tousled. He was in his shirtsleeves, his neckcloth gone as he went through the post he was sorting on his desk. He looked up at her comment, his eyes bright and concerned. "Where?"

"I walked down a path near the wood, and suddenly, she was there."

He frowned. "And what did she say this time? You seem a little disturbed."

Again, she wondered if she could ever hide anything from those perceptive eyes of his. "The usual," she said as casually as she could, waving a hand. But she also felt relief. Obviously he hadn't seen his sister, because he hadn't known.

"You see her more than I do, you poor girl," he said, shuffling through the letters once again.

Eve breathed a relieved sigh as she took a chair near his desk. So he wouldn't know what had been discussed. She wanted to keep it that way. "You two don't get together often?" she asked.

He shook his head. "We don't get along. We have different views of the world. And we both have tempers."

"I've never seen yours," she commented.

"Nor will you," he said, looking up again with a brilliant smile.

"Nor hers," she said idly, while watching him closely.

His expression changed. "Nor should you." He stood and put both hands flat on the desk as he stared at her. "As I've said before, I'd prefer if you had as little to do with her as possible. She seems charming, but her intentions are always self-serving and seldom to anyone's benefit but her own. So ignore her, and never worry about insulting me because you do, because so do I."

Eve smiled. That suited her perfectly.

"I care about our people too," he went on. "And I too try to help them. But I don't have as much—I shouldn't call it malice, but I must—in my heart. She can be unkind, even cruel, to those she thinks inferior, and however pleasant she seems when she's with you, you're mortal, so she believes you to be inferior."

Eve stiffened. There it was again. He was as deluded as his sister. "And you?" she asked.

He stared at her.

"Do you believe me to be inferior?"

"Would I have married you if I did?" he asked in return. His eyes blazed. "Damnation, Eve, what did she say to you to get you to doubt yourself and me again?"

"She was talking about our future," Eve said, telling half a truth to buy the whole of it. "About the possibility of our having children."

He stood straight. He frowned again. "I've hopes, I confess, that with you I will, *we* will do just that. Why? Have you any indications?" he asked eagerly.

"No, no," she said, hating herself for the lie. "I thought . . . but I was wrong. Still, it's early days yet. Aubrey," she said seriously, "what bothered me was that Arianna said that if we *did* have a child, she'd have the raising of it. She, and you, and your people. Not me." She watched his expression. "You said you'd never lie to me," she prompted gently.

"Early days yet, as you said," he said.

"Yes, but, if those days ever come?"

"You would, of course, come with me wherever I went," he said. "If the child was like me, and my sister, it would only make sense to acquaint him with his birthright. But come, its foolishness discussing this now. Obviously my sister upset you more than you know. I tell you what," he said, as he came out from behind the desk, came to her and put his arms around her. "Why don't we try to see if we can make the question arise . . ." he whispered against her ear, "among other things."

She forced a laugh. "Not now. I'm still a bit disconcerted. Let me take a nice warm bath, and then, we shall see what . . . comes up." She laughed again.

She wanted to buy herself time to think. The longer she stayed here with Aubrey, the more confused she became. He mightn't have bespelled her, as he believed he could. But she'd fallen so much in love with him that she was afraid that the longer she remained with him, the weaker her own hold on sanity would become. She needed to see things in perspective and that was unbearable to think about when she so much as looked at him. When he touched her, it was impossible. Right now the thought of leaving him was like a stabbing pain in her chest. Soon she believed it might cut her to the heart, and she'd surely die if she left him.

But now he didn't leave her side and his warm breath on her ear made her shiver. "It's still light, is that what bothers you?" he asked gently. "There's no shame in love by day or night, my love."

She leaned against him, one hand on his chest, fighting her desire and her resolve. "I know," she whispered. "But the servants . . ."

"Think we are holy married monk and nun? I don't think so," he murmured, as he trailed kisses along her neck. "We don't even have to go up- stairs. Look at the rug, the deep chairs, the lovely couch I have here. There's even a floor and a wall or two." He chuckled. "But that's more advanced, for other times, when there's no question but haste, and no time for questions. The couch? Yes, so I think too."

He walked her to the leather couch and sat her down. He smiled down at her. "Three steps more," he said. "One," he said as he walked to the door, closed it, and turned back to her.

"Two," he said as he pulled off his shirt. Then he sat beside her and took her in his arms again. "Three," he said. "We're alone, no need to count any higher or wait a moment longer. Are you fear- ful of coming to me in the broad light of day? Or of being here, where we never make love? Please don't be. Even the thought displeases me."

Poetry, she thought with despair. When he is impassioned he speaks in rhyme, his wild fancy is with him all the time. Ah, it's catching, she thought with humorous despair. But she loved him more each day, even with what she now knew. She found herself wanting him as much as she wanted to comfort him for reasons he wouldn't understand. She shivered as she removed her gown.

He sat back and looked at her for a long moment. Her mind might shy from his intent inspection, but her body responded to his direct brown gaze as it traveled across her like a caress. Her nipples peaked, her color rose, her breathing became rapid.

He smiled as he bent to pull off his boots, and divested himself of his breeches. Then he lay down next to her on the narrow couch until they were skin to skin, heart to heart. She ran her hands through his clean smooth hair, it felt silken cool as it streamed through her fingers. She felt his hard chest against her breasts, and his arousal against her abdomen. It pulsed like her own heart's irregular beat. There was no need for further kisses or caresses, she was astonished at how ready she was, how much she wanted him.

"Come to me," she whispered, holding him closer. "Here, now, just like this, and now please."

"Yes," he whispered to her. "Whether we prove successful or only appease ourselves. Whether we continue my line, or yours, or only spend joyous time, you are mine, and I am yours, and nothing can change that."

He put his arm around her waist and raised her bottom from the couch. She clung to his shoulders and opened to him, wrapping her legs around his waist, offering her body to his. As he came to her, she closed her eyes and forgot the future and the past, forgot even to think as she became one with him.

Sometime in the night, he carried her up to their bedchamber, and they made love again on their soft broad bed, slowly, beautifully, and as exquisitely as if they both were dreaming of love.

And when he woke in the morning, this time it was she who was gone before the sun had fully risen.

Chapter 17

The note she left for him, on her pillow, was simple and concise.

Dear Aubrey,
I must have time to think. Your sister said some disturbing things to me. And without knowing it, so did you. So I am leaving you for a little while—only a little while—just enough time to think. And then I'll be back, I promise. Please don't be angry that I left with only a note and didn't tell you myself. It was because whatever else you do, or think you do, you do bespell me when I look into your eyes.

I needed to think for myself for a while. To be by myself as well. You always said I was level-headed and I wish to remain so. I love you so very much. I do this for the both of us, and will return soon. Please forgive me. Yr. Eve.

It was a fearsome thing to leave one's husband, Eve thought as the mail coach carried her through the countryside to London. It was wrong and deceitful, and if he'd left her the same way, she wasn't sure she'd forgive him for it. But she had to. Her marriage was becoming too strange, and now she was convinced she was carrying Aubrey's child. Before she went any further, she had to go forth with a clear head. She'd had to act quickly. Soon travel wouldn't be as easy for her as it was now. She didn't want to endanger this babe she carried.

And yet so much as she loved Aubrey, and that was as much as her own life itself, still, under no circumstances did she want that child being brought up by people who shared Aubrey's strange fantasies.

She'd talk to her father. He was not a fanciful man. If she had to, she'd go anonymously to talk with a physician who dealt with weird fantasies people succumbed to, and see if he had any ideas of how to deal with this problem. And she'd also take the time to warn Sherry about Arianna's obsession with him. He was too young and callow to get involved with such a female. However old he was, she didn't want her brother to have to deal with the same kind of problems she now had.

She'd only been gone from Far Isle for a matter of hours, and yet the pain of leaving Aubrey was intense and growing even more so with every milestone she passed on the road. Would he forgive her? Would he come thundering down the road behind her, and tear her from the coach and take her back to the Hall? She half feared that he would, and she half wanted him to do it.

Or would he desert her, as he may have done with other wives before? She hadn't known he'd had three wives when she'd married him. She still couldn't believe it. He may well have had them; a man didn't need to be three hundred years old to have been widowed that often. But had he even *been* married? The things that had sent her flying from him were the things she hadn't known when she'd accepted his hand, his heart, and his body. Or at least, they were the things he hadn't told her.

Even so, she felt guilt and shame. What sort of a person was she, to leave her lawfully wedded husband? Especially if he were ill and suffering delusions? Still and all, what sort of a husband had she, who believed he was an almost immortal magical creature, and who would take her child from her and bring it up to believe that it was magical too?

She raised her chin. She'd go to London and reason out what to do. She'd taken the Royal Mail coach because it went faster than any other, and she felt more secure in it. The coach would travel onward without stopping for more than changes of horses, all the way to London. She'd sleep sitting up, when she could, and then go straight to her father's house. It had been her home too.

Her father had been in London with Sheridan when she'd last had a letter from him. But he loved his country house too. If he weren't in London now because he'd gone there, she'd stay in London and send for him to come and meet her.

Aubrey doubtless guessed where she was going. Where else should she go for comfort and advice? But if he wasn't pursuing her now, she'd have time to do what she needed.

Eve drew herself as far away as she could from the old lady who dozed on the carriage seat on her right, and the rotund gentleman who sat snoring on her left. She closed her eyes to ignore the two gentlemen sitting opposite her. She couldn't sleep and didn't expect to. Instead she thought of her husband, and grieved for him, for herself, and for their child to be. Because she feared that this short leave from Aubrey might become the end of her marriage. But whatever she did, she couldn't just think of herself anymore. She had other lives to protect. Not just Aubrey's. But his child's as well.

• The journey took a day and a night. Eve was weary and aching in every limb when the Mail stopped at the Bull and Mouth, the famous coaching inn just inside London's ancient wall. She left the coach on stiffened legs, took her hastily loaded cases, summoned a hackney, and directed him to her father's town house. Only when she looked out the window as the hackney finally slowed, and saw the familiar house, did she breathe easier. The knocker was still on the door; her father still lived there.

She was home. Eve longed for her own home, Far Isle, as she stepped out of the hackney. But at least here she could think her own way through this tangle without the distractions of duty and honor and the only man she'd ever loved.

Her father was shocked. She'd expected that and was prepared.

"No," Eve said, stripping off her gloves as she sat down in his study with him. "I am not hurt. I was not brutalized. I still love my husband." She leaned forward and looked at him earnestly. "But I *am* alone. And I came without his knowledge. Because I need advice."

Her father winced.

"I won't discuss anything intimate," she reassured him. "I just need some counsel."

Malcolm Faraday sat back in his chair and tried

to look competent by taking off his spectacles, and polishing them.

"By the way, before I say another thing," Eve said. "Where's Sherry? I don't want him hearing this."

"No fear of that. He just left. Off to Tattersalls to see a horse, or off to a friend to talk about a horse, I can't keep track of him. He should be preparing to go back to University, but he isn't. I'm glad you're here, you can try to talk some sense into him."

"I'll try, I promise you that," she said. She looked at her father, and then away from him. The poor man was worried about why she was here. So was she. But it was hard to tell him about it.

She didn't want to betray Aubrey's secret obsession yet, and had tried all the way here to think of a way to creep up on it, so that it sounded less terrible. Her father wasn't a dictatorial fellow. But there was every chance he'd try to keep her away from Aubrey forever if he felt she was in any danger from him. There were such things as madhouses. And her father had friends in high places. For all his wealth Aubrey seemed to know no one, and certainly no one with any kind of judicial power in London. She wouldn't tell her father about her condition for the same reason. At any rate, it was far too early in the day for that information. Nobody would guess it except for Aubrey's weird sister, Arianna.

And too, once this was resolved, if she did go back to Aubrey and learn to live with him, Eve didn't want her father prejudiced against him forever. It might just be a strange turn of mind that sometimes happened with brilliant people, an idiosyncrasy she could live with. She could live with it more easily if no one else knew about it.

"Aubrey is a fine man," she said as preface. "He makes me very happy. But some things I've learned since we married confuse me." Her expression brightened. "Mind, these were things that Aubrey's sister hinted at. You never met her. She's lovely. She lives somewhere nearby, and I've discovered that she's a very strange woman."

"Ah!" her father said. "A strange sister. Every family has one of those. Why, my own Aunt Elizabeth collected cats. Dozens of them. Her husband, Uncle Roland, moved out of the house because of the stench." He grew thoughtful. "Now I think back, perhaps she wasn't so strange. Fifty stinking cats were actually a deal better than one Uncle Roland."

"She's not that sort of strange," Eve said quickly. "She's charming. Sherry met her and was mad for her. But she's told me some tales about Aubrey that he doesn't deny, and they upset me."

"Aha!" her father said wisely, laying a finger aside his nose. "Now that's something I know something about. She's possessive of her brother and worried about your stealing his affections away from her. A common thing, child. It happens all the time. Aren't you possessive of Sheridan? You're always giving him advice and looking out for him."

"This is different," Eve said. "She told me to ask Aubrey some questions, and I did. I didn't like the answers. Did he tell you that he'd been widowed three times before he met me?"

Her father's eyes widened. "No. Never. Did his wives die from some misadventure?" he asked at once.

"I don't think so, or she'd surely have asked me to ask him about that. He doesn't lie to me. Perhaps it would be better if he did," she murmured.

"Then his being so often a widower is solely misfortune," her father commented. "I don't like his secrecy in the matter, I can tell you that. But what is the problem? Is it that he grieves for his late wives? Or compares you to them? Is he too possessive because he fears for your life? Is that what bothers you? The longer you're married, the less that will happen," he added helpfully.

She shook her head. "No, he never mentions them. He says he loves and has loved only me."

"Well, there you are. And, come to think on, it does explain why he was so eager to marry you. You're a fine, healthy young woman, Eve. Anyone can see that. And you're sensible. Perhaps his other wives were slaves to fashion, always denying themselves good food and dosing themselves with medicines to improve their looks. I hear that some cosmetics are decidedly harmful, and anyone can see you don't use a pinch of them."

"But I wish he'd told me before we wed," she said.

He nodded. "As do I. He should have at least told me, you know. But that's done and past. Tell me, if you'd known, would you have broken off, would you not have married him?"

She looked down at her fingers. "No," she said. "But it would have given me pause, and made me more indecisive."

"As it would have given me pause," he agreed. "Yet since it's a sad thing, but a done thing, I suppose I can't blame him for not mentioning it. It might have presented obstacles, and he didn't want to put himself in a bad light. You're sure they died naturally?"

"Yes," she said, looking up. "I believe him in that. I suppose I could have dealt with his lack of honesty and the fact that he was thrice widowed, in time. The thing is that he also said that he sought me out because of my family history."

Her father frowned. "A devotee of genealogy, is he? Our family has no stain on our name, but no honors. I can't see what attracted a man like him particularly. He must have been jesting, Eve."

"He said it was my mother's family, and something that happened with them, ages and ages ago," she said evasively. "Can you tell me anything about them?"

Her father shocked her by leaning back and roaring with laughter. When he stopped, he looked at her, smiling. "That old chestnut!" he said, wiping his eyes. "And he heard about it? I'm not surprised. Your mother told everyone within earshot. Well, life is strange, after all. I wish she were here to hear this. She'd have been very proud. She and her family told the wildest tales about their origins. They were a good solid family from the West Country, mind you. No titles, no honors, but proud of the fact that they'd been here forever. And she did mean that. She said her family had been here in Britain before the Druids. Before the Saxons too! Backbone of Britain, she said. She said that when more and more foreigners, like Angles and Celts and such, came here, her people avoided them, then moved west, and then slowly disappeared. All but for her branch of the family, that is."

He looked sad. "Their luck did run out. I'm sorry to say there aren't many left of them now. But if Aubrey sought you out for that reason, it only means that he's heritage mad and family proud. It's a common trait. And so you should be proud of them too."

"I don't think that's what he meant," Eve said slowly. How could she ask him more and yet not betray her husband? She'd have to be oblique. "Father, did my mother ever tell you strange tales about any magical abilities in her family?"

He shook his head. "No, never. The reverse, in fact. She said her folk were the most commonsensical in the whole of England, and that they didn't hold with such nonsense."

"I see. But did she ever mention any woman in her family, once upon a long time ago, marrying into an even older family?" she asked desperately, thinking he may have forgotten something. "Perhaps one that knew the old magic that folklore tells about? Herb lore and healing or such," she added quickly.

"Never heard that. Not likely either. Heard about how clever her family had been: plain, practical, resourceful, and inventive folk. They were hardworking and honest, she'd say, not a poseur, or a blustering fop, or a climber in the lot. 'Much done and little noted,' she said was their motto, although on no coat of arms. They were proud people, but mainly artisans, leatherworkers, smiths and such. They didn't hold with nobility or royalty. She'd sometimes tell me that they'd be ashamed of her for marrying someone so English as I am."

He sighed. "That was when she was vexed with me. But, Eve, my girl, you didn't leave Aubrey and come all the way to London to ask me that, did you?"

"No, not entirely," she said, rising from her chair. "I might go to see some people here in Town, I might do some shopping too. Mostly I need to be alone. Aubrey can be quite overpowering. He's gentle and kind, but it's hard for me to even think when I look into his eyes."

"Ah!" her father said with vast relief. "Just as I thought. A spat between lovers. Well, feel free to stay on here with me, but not too long, mind," he said, wagging a finger at her. "The silliest quarrel gains seriousness the longer the silence lasts. Sometimes just a word heals all. You might try it."

"True, true," Eve said. "I know. I won't. I will."

It was late that night when Eve heard Sherry coming home. He made heavy going of it, humming a little tune as he clumped up the stairs. He bid a cheerful good night to the footman who'd let him in, and from his voice, Eve could tell he was a few sheets to the wind. She'd been waiting for him with her bedchamber door half open. This was a good time for her to talk with him; no one else was awake or about. She stole out of her bedchamber and down the hallway, and accosted him as he reached the second floor.

"Sherry!" she whispered.

He leapt back. She reached for him, but he regained his balance by grabbing on to the banister. "Lord! You frightened me," he said, one hand on his immaculate shirtfront.

She sniffed. "You're too drunk to be frightened. Come away, I don't want you to fall down the stairs."

"Then don't leap out at a fellow when he's on the top step. What are you doing here anyway? Is Aubrey here?" he asked eagerly.

"Aubrey is not here. I am. Are you in any condition for rational speech?"

"I can hold my spirits," he said proudly. Then he added, "I'm a trifle foxed, but by no means insensible. What did you want to talk about?"

"Come," she said, and led him to her room. When he'd seated himself in a chair by her hearth and stretched out his long legs, she sat at her dressing table and stared at him. It was true: he was a little well to live, but not terribly drunk. But he was overeager, leaning forward to listen to her. Her heart sank at his first question.

"Is this about Arianna?" he asked. "I've written to her, but she hasn't answered yet. Did she send you with a message for me?"

"I don't have a message from her," Eve said blightingly.

"Have you seen her? How is she?"

"I have, and she's fine. In fact, that's what I came to talk to you about. I know you're a bit infatuated with her, but I've gotten to know her better, and I just wanted to warn— ah, uhm, talk to you. She's much older than you are, Sherry. And she . . ." Eve paused.

She still didn't know how to tell him the dangers and extent of the family obsession, without telling him about Aubrey's part in it. She didn't want to hint at any of Arianna's possible motives either. Nor did she want to say anything terrible about the woman, because nothing could make a young man like Sherry want to defend her more.

So she compromised, with half-truths. "She's passionate about genealogy and family, and I think that since her brother found me such a good match, she's beginning to wonder if you'd be one for her too."

He grinned. "Capital!" he said.

"Sherry! You're just a boy, really. Not even at your age of majority yet. A flirtation is one thing. I meant for marriage. You can't be contemplating that? At your age? At her age? Anyhow, you're supposed to be going back to University next term."

He got up from his chair and looked down at his sister, his expression as cold and serious as a half-drunk young man's could be. "I'm more mature than you realize, Eve," he said in a hurt voice. "I can decide what to do by myself, for myself, thank you very much indeed."

He walked to the door with stiff correctness. "So as for your advice, thank you, but no thank you," he said, and bowed. He swayed, regained his balance, and left her.

Eve lay awake a long time that night. Not because of Sherry. However infatuated he was, he was a long way from Arianna. And time might disenchant him.

But Eve's body ached all over. It might have been from the constant traveling she'd done, but she knew better. She missed Aubrey so much it was paining her, heart, mind, and body. She lay on her back and put her hand across her flat abdomen, thinking of what might come. She turned over, pounded a pillow, and laid her aching head on it, trying to think of what she could or should do. She missed her husband. She missed his voice, his scent, the solid warmth of his strong body next to hers. How could she sleep in peace without him, wherever she was?

How could she ever rest easy if he took it into his head to let his daft sister help bring up their child? And how could she remain married to a man with such strange fancies?

How could she not?

She turned over in bed again, and closed her weary eyes. They felt sandy, gritty from lack of sleep. She couldn't go on as things were. This was no way to live, longing for her lover and afraid to go to him. She had to return to see him soon, and not just so she could hold him close and feast her eyes on him once again. She had to go back to tell him what she'd decided. Whatever that was.

The wind blew Aubrey's black hair and spread his black driving cape streaming out behind him until he looked like an avenging specter. But he only stood still, alone in the night, facing the coming storm. He couldn't sleep. He'd gone out to the stables to get a horse and ride like this freshening autumn wind to join Eve. Then, once out into the night, he'd decided it was better to take a coach so he could bring her back with him straightaway. But now he couldn't move from where he stood in the drive. Because he knew there was nothing for him to do. Or rather, nothing he could do.

He knew where she was. She didn't know that there was no place on earth she could go where he couldn't find her. She might not yet realize that she carried his child. And though he could easily pursue her, persuade her, bring her home and keep her at his side, it wouldn't be fair or honest of him. She had to decide without any enchantment or coercion of any kind on his part. Of course, if she stayed from him until she bore the child, he'd have no choice. The baby was his. But he wanted Eve too. And she had to choose him, his life and his decisions, all on her own. His sister might laugh, his cousins might think him mad, but it was, after all, how he'd decided to live his life, long ago.

So now he had to wait, and waiting was never easy for him. He missed her fiercely, he'd never missed a female more—or a male, come to think on it. He worried about her and for her. He wanted her for more than her bright conversation, her warm and willing body, and the delightful workings of a mind that so strangely dovetailed with his own. She also held in her possession two wonderful, incredible things he'd never thought to have in his long lifetime: not only his child, but his heart.

Chapter 18

The physician was well known for his treatment of the insane. He headed a famous and famously expensive private madhouse for the incarceration of the infirm of mind and the hopelessly insane. That was why Eve had hesitated to consult him. But he was everywhere recommended, and he was elderly and seemed wise and understanding. He pretended to believe it was a friend she was consulting him about. She was grateful for that, and for the advice he gave her.

"Do you think this deluded fellow could do your friend, or you, or anyone, any physical harm?" he'd finally asked.

"Never," she'd said.

"Or harm himself?"

"No, there's nothing to indicate that."

"So, in other words, he's a kind, intelligent, well-bred and wealthy gentleman, who happens to believe he's nearly immortal, is of an ancient race, and has got magical powers of some sort, but he never presses them on anyone?"

"Just so," she'd said, tight-lipped now, her color rising.

"And your friend has never seen him try to cast a spell or do magic?"

"Never," she said, shaking her head. Then she blushed, remembering. "Unless you call the way he charms her, and everyone he meets, magical."

"I don't," he said. "Does he brag about his powers all the time, and bring them up frequently?"

"No," she answered. "In fact he only told his wife when his sister gave her the questions to ask him, possibly to make trouble. And at that, he was only trying to be honest about his past and his family, he said. He is otherwise closemouthed about it."

"I see," the doctor had mused. "And so, apart from the fact that he seems to be a thoroughly likeable fellow, I can't see how he's different from many people who have delusions of glory, except that he tells his wife about them. He harms no one, makes no disturbances, doesn't frighten the neighbors or alarm his relatives. Even his sister seems to accept his nonsense. My dear lady, if you only knew the sort of things I hear and see each day! Half my patients are in my institution, the other half only steps away. From what you say this gentleman seems perfectly normal to me. Well, perhaps not perfectly so. But who is? He hurts no one and nothing, and keeps his secret to himself most of the time."

"He also says he's had three wives. But there's no proof of that and my friend has never attempted to prove it."

"Nor should she. He may well have done. Life is short, and many husbands and wives are left alone after illness or accident befalls their partners. If he has not been married before, but only says so, then again, whom does he harm? Marriage is a sacred bond. He treats his present wife well, from what you say. She has no other complaint about him?"

"No, none," Eve said.

"Then she is a fortunate woman. I suggest your friend return to her husband and only leave him if she feels his temperament is changing in any way to her danger or displeasure."

"And their children?" she asked, leaning forward, clutching her hands together. "If she has them, that is to say. He wants to educate them in his ways."

"A child's education is the father's choice," he said gently. "You know that. Most children are sent away to be schooled by the age of eight anyway, so your friend can always campaign that he wait for that, or even ask if they can send the children to a place of her choice earlier. No one would think her presumptuous or incorrect, because it is the general practice among those of her class. But if she ever feels that her child is being wrongly tutored, it is her right to protest. If her husband loves her, he may see her reasons for it. If not, she may attempt to hire another tutor, more to her own liking. Many children have several tutors."

"And what of his sister, who suffers from the same delusions?"

"Does she? Or is she merely trying to make trouble?"

"I don't know," Eve admitted.

"Keeping them apart would be a good thing, whichever it is," the doctor said. "Introducing him to new friends and relatives would be beneficial too. In fact, I believe that the longer your friend is married to this gentleman, the more his delusions may fade away. Leaving him at this juncture is not a good solution. It might even exacerbate his problem by causing him to turn to his sister for comfort and friendship, and she, as you say, isn't good for his state of mind."

"Thank you, Doctor," she said, rising, and smiling brilliantly. "You said just what I wanted to hear. I mean, just exactly what I want to tell my friend."

That was why Eve was now standing with her bags in the hallway of her father's town house, waiting for a carriage to come out of the stables to return to her home, and her love.

"I'm glad you're doing this," her father said, lacing his hands behind his back as he watched her preparing to go. "Lover's spats are best mended with a kiss. That's difficult by letter." His smile faded. "But you came alone. That was dangerous. You must take a maid back with you."

"No need," she said. "I came with the Royal Mail, and I'll be safe enough in your carriage with an outrider and the strong footman sitting with the driver on the way home. They've said you've already sent word ahead to a fine inn where we can stop for the night. Thank you for thinking of it. That's far better than sitting awake through the night. All's prepared. But I did think to ask Sherry if he wanted to come along. He seemed eager to speak with Aubrey again. I can't find him. Where in the world is he?"

"I've no idea. I hear he was gone at dawn. Or he came in at dawn, and left soon after, I'm not quite sure. The boy is a whirlwind; he hardly ever touches down here for long these days. Here and there, here and gone again. I suppose he's thinking of all the friends he'll miss when he returns to University, and is trying to see them all before he goes. Do you want to wait for him?"

"I dare not," she said. "The weather is cold and the ground is hard, perfect for travel, John Coachman says. So I must go straight away before rain or snow makes it a chore. Come visit me soon, Father. Come visit *us* soon, I mean. And again, thank you for all your help."

"I didn't do a thing," he said, as he watched a footman carry out the last of her bags. "And you may come to visit with me, or stay with me, or live with me, anytime you wish. I only pray that you don't feel the need to do the latter, but know that you're always welcome to."

She kissed his cheek. "I know, and I thank you. I'll send a note back with the coach when I get safely home. Don't worry about me. I think all will soon be mended. And if that whirlwind of a brother of mine returns anytime soon, tell him he's always welcome to join us at Far Isle. As are you, Father. As are you."

She sniffled back a tear, smiled at him, and hurried out and down the front stair to the coach, so she could start her journey home again.

* * *

Eve thought of all the ways she could explain her absence to Aubrey, all the way home to Far Isle. But when the door to the manor house opened, and she saw him standing there: unsmiling, sober, somber; looking like a demon, looking like a dark angel, looking like a deserted lover, she couldn't think of a thing to say. It didn't matter. He opened his arms wide, and seconds later she was in them. They looked at each other and kissed. And kissed again. And then it was Aubrey who spoke.

"Welcome home," he said.

And then she wept.

"Don't," he said, holding her close and whispering in her ear. He drew back so he could look at her face. "Unless you're ill, or hurting?"

She shook her head. "I'm sick thinking of how I left you, and ill at the thought of how I may have hurt your feelings." She raised her head and looked into his eyes. "I don't know why you so readily forgive me. If I were you I'd be very angry at me and very hurt to boot."

"I was," he said in a low voice. "And then I realized that I'd told you some things that made you doubt me. They would have made anyone doubt, and be perhaps a little afraid. I should have thought of that, but I never told any other mortal before."

She tried to conceal her wince as he said that.

"How can I blame you then? At least, you came home again. You trust me now, don't you?

"I do," she said, tears starting in her eyes, "with my heart and with my life. I wouldn't have come back to you otherwise."

"Welcome home again, and thank you," he said, taking her hand tightly in his own. "So now come upstairs, bathe and change and then talk to me. Or talk to me while I help you bathe and change."

She smiled, wiping her eyes with the back of her hand.

"Getting your nice new kid gloves all wet," he said, watching her. "I see you bought new ones. And that's a new bonnet. Very attractive."

"I bought a few new things," she explained.

"Good," he whispered, bending to put his lips at her ear again. "We'll just idly mention that you went to London to buy some new clothing that you needed. That will stop the servant's gossiping, as well as anyone else. I'm used to it. But I don't want you plagued by so much as an inquiring look. Now, come. You must be chilled and travel weary, whatever you say."

"I am, a bit," she said, as she went up the stair with him.

He was as good as his word. Within moments, he had footmen bring a steaming tub to her dressing chamber. Eve's maid had hurriedly helped her take off her gown. When she'd left, as had the footmen, Eve, wrapped in a towel, came into the dressing room. She saw the steaming tub of scented water, let out a long, satisfied sigh, and took Aubrey's hand so she could step into it.

"I've made some modernizations here, but we must put in a proper bath now," he grumbled as he watched her. "One with the sort of new plumbing they have in London. With water piped into the house, and out of it as well. This must seem primitive to you."

"It seems delicious," she said, sinking into the warm water, laying her head back on the rim of the tub, and closing her eyes.

He knelt at her side, and smiled at her. "You must be exhausted," he said. "I'll just stay until you've bathed, and then help you into bed."

She opened her eyes and grinned at him. "You'd better help me more than that. It's been a fortnight since I've seen you. I don't know how much more deprivation I can take."

He laughed, and reached for a sponge. "Then let me assist you now, so we can get to bed sooner. It's seemed like a much longer time than that to me."

He rolled up his sleeves, dipped the sponge into the water, lathered it with soap, and then slowly washed Eve's arm. She offered him her other arm, and then her throat. She stretched like a cat under his hands. He laughed. "I can do better," he purred. "But it wouldn't do for me to get soaked, it's you taking the bath." He stopped, pulled off his shirt, and turned to her again.

He rubbed soap on the sponge and pumped it until it frothed with scented lather. Then he let the sponge drift over her body, gentle and lingeringly on her breasts, carefully moving over her stomach, asking her to move this way and that as he thoroughly caressed every other part of her. Soon, Eve's eyes were half lidded, slumberous, but not with weariness, and Aubrey's chest was as drenched as her body was.

"I think the water's cooling," he said in a husky voice, "so it's time for you to get dry. Wouldn't do for you to catch a chill."

"No," she agreed as she rose and stepped into the toweling he held out for her. "Yes," she said as she came into his embrace. The towel served a dual purpose, drying them both as they stood and kissed.

He lifted her and carried her to their bed.

"I've missed you so much," she whispered as they sank to the downy featherbed together. "I've yearned for this as well."

He didn't tell her again how much he'd missed

her. He showed her until she was thoroughly convinced.

They lay together afterward, close and sated, and still not speaking. There was too much to say, and nothing at all to tell each other now.

They woke early, at sunrise. Eve turned to Aubrey, reveling in the sight of his inky hair on the white pillow, his long lashes closed over those sparkling mirrors of his eyes. It was as though he felt her stare. His eyes opened and he smiled. But he only kissed her lightly, and tucked her close to him again.

"Oh-o," she said, wriggling against him, laughter in her voice. "Now that you're an old married man, you don't believe in greeting the dawn the way we used to do?"

"I thought that females in your condition didn't feel well in the mornings," he said.

She sat up abruptly. She stared down at him. "How did you know? I barely knew myself. Does it already show?" she asked with worry, looking down at her belly.

He laughed. "Nothing shows. But I know. I told you that there were things I could do that men couldn't. That was one of the things I worried about when you left me. I knew you were safe, but I longed to be there to ensure it. I couldn't be happier, Eve. I just could not be more pleased and grateful to you."

But she didn't relax. "Arianna told you," she said flatly.

"Arianna?" he said, sitting up to face her. "I haven't seen her since you left. I went to her at first, wondering if you'd gone with her as she asked you to do. That would have been disastrous. It terrified me. She means you no good, Eve. Not that she'd dare hurt you. But she'd confuse you if she could, and get you to desert me if you would."

She knew he was upset by the way he was rhyming his words, and her stomach clenched. The doctor was right. The less he had to do with his sister, the less they so much as spoke of her, the better off he would be.

"She guessed about my condition," Eve said, forcing herself to sound light-hearted. "Now, I know it's true. Isn't it wonderful?"

"More than that," he said soberly. "Our son will be everything I ever wanted. My line will continue. In all my long life, I've never wanted anything so much."

Her skin felt cold. She drew the coverlet up around her. "And that's why you wanted me so much?"

His eyes were unreadable. Cold and bright,

they surveyed her, and seemed again to stare into her soul. "I won't lie to you. I never have done. Yes, that's why I wanted you at first; you know that, in the hopes that you could bear me a son. But no, that's not why I began to want you so very much more. Nor why I want you so much now. You know that too."

"Do I?" she asked.

"You should."

"Should I? What if our child is a girl? Or . . . not like you?"

"The child is a male. And I don't know if he's exactly like me, or you. It's too soon to tell how much magic he possesses. But you conceived with me. And that means that you can do so again. I *will* have a child to carry on my line. My people will not be extinguished. So much as I love you, and that's with my whole heart, this news is not just a miracle for me. It's the answer to my people's greatest desire. It means we will go on."

"So I am to be a brood mare, after all? And I suppose Arianna was right?" she said recklessly, too upset to keep to her plans, mentioning his sister again. "And you intend to take him away when he's old enough to be tutored in ways you think proper for a . . . a creature of your race?"

"All boys of your class are sent away to be tutored," he said softly. "Whether their fathers be
mortal or of the otherworld."

"Not all boys," she snapped, rising from the
bed. "And certainly few whose fathers believe
they are immortal."

"We aren't immortal," he said patiently. "We
live longer than you do. But we eventually die,
and so we value life too. And the longer we stay
in your world, the shorter our lives become."

She frowned.

"That's true. If we stay away from our world,
we age as quickly as you do. That's why I return
again, and again."

"You'll leave me?"

"In time. Only for a time, each time. I must,
Eve, or I'll become mortal. That's why our race is
in such a perilous state. The temptations of your
world are strong, and always have been. And the
dangers grow stronger for us the longer we stay
with you. These days we find that our lifetimes
grow shorter because each century you invent
more and more things that are toxic for us."

She dragged in a deep painful breath. "So," she
said. "There is more I didn't understand. I know
you married me so I could bear you a son of your
blood. And you said you intended to educate him

in your world. And now it appears that you will leave me one day."

"Or you can come with me and our son each time," he said, rising from the bed, standing on the other side of it, and facing her. "You won't gain years. But you won't lose them, as I would in this world. And I'd see to it that you were happy."

"With spells, and kisses, and lovemaking, and lies, and nonsense," she said, head high. "I should have stayed in London. I should have stayed away. Why didn't you tell me everything before this?"

"Would you have married me?"

She took in a harsh breath. "That," she said, "doesn't deserve an answer."

She went into her dressing room, and didn't leave until she heard that he'd left the bedchamber. And then she wept, and then she finally controlled herself. She rang for her maid and dressed. She had thinking to do. The tears could come again later. She knew they would.

When Eve came down to the breakfast parlor, she found Aubrey sitting there, scowling. He looked up at her.

"I've a note," he said without preface, "from your father, by special messenger. Sherry, it appears, is missing. None of his friends have seen him for days. Your father wants to know if he's here with us. I would have said no. Now I discover that he was seen here, on the road, just the other day. But he never came to visit, so the servants never mentioned it to me. He had a woman riding with him, one that they did recognize. But they see her so often they didn't think it important to tell me."

They stared at each other.

"Arianna," Eve breathed.

He nodded. "So it would seem."

"Then we must go to her, and find him," Eve said, her hands clenching at her sides. "He can't stay with her. He's got to get back to school. I don't trust her."

"Nor I," he said.

"Why does she want him?" Eve asked. "Only to distress me?"

He shook his head. "No." He rose and walked to her. He took her cold, clenched fists in his hands. His gaze was both sad and wise. "Think on, Eve. I know how she thinks, and if you consider it, so will you. It takes no special powers to realize what she's after, what she wants from Sheridan."

Eve's eyes widened.

"Yes," he said. "It only makes common sense. If I can get you with child, as I have been unable to do with any female of your people or my own for all these many years, then she must believe that Sheridan can provide her with a son too."

"But he's a boy," she whispered.

"Man enough to father a babe. And he will grow older."

"With her?" she asked in horror. "No, I won't have it."

"Nor I," he said. "And yet . . ."

She snatched her hands from his clasp. "And yet you'd love it if she could have a child too? Even if it means ruining my brother's life? He's still a boy, but he's constant, and highly moral. If he thinks he loves her, and even if he didn't, he's a man of honor. If he had a child with her, he'd stay with her forever. Now is not the time for that. He needs to grow up, get an education, and take his place in life. Not spend it with a madwoman, living in a mad fantasy."

Aubrey stood still. "And so you believe everything I've said is fantasy?" he asked slowly. "I never considered that. By gods!" he said, staring at her, his eyes glittering. "You think I'm mad."

"It doesn't matter," she said through gritted teeth. "I've made my bed. I won't let my brother make the same mistake. Take me to him please, now!"

"You think you can talk him into going home?"

"I must try," she said. She looked up at him. "Aubrey, if you ever loved me, you must help me now."

"If I ever loved you?" he asked in a peculiar voice.

"If you love me, or love your mission to your 'people' more," she said, standing tall as she could, keeping her voice level and strong as she stared him in the eye. "Aubrey. Now is the time you must decide."

Chapter 19

"**I** had planned to take you when my sister lost interest in you and your family. I meant to when you knew me better," Aubrey told Eve. "I'd expected to take you when you trusted me, or at the very least, when you loved me."

Eve almost stumbled as she walked beside him. What could she say? That she loved him but wished she didn't, at least not so much that her heart hurt as she followed him into his fantasy?

"You look as frightened as Persephone must have done at the gates of the underworld," he said, glancing at her. "Don't be afraid. You may leave anytime you wish. Don't be dazzled either. Half of what you'll see will be real and half will be illusion. That's for our sake as well as yours and your brother's, and those mortals who have been chosen to live with us. But mostly for our sake. We don't much care for reality, or boredom. We live for laughter and music, love and pleasure."

"The folklore also said mischief," she commented, clutching her cloak close around her as they tramped through the dead leaves and into the dark wood behind Far Isle.

"Yes," he said flatly. "That too."

It was a cool, dim, damp day. Autumn was gone but it was not yet winter. The day didn't possess the charm of either season. There was no more bright autumn foliage overhead or underfoot, and still no snow to grace the paths or cover the naked branches on the trees or the brown tangled thickets by the side of the path. And here she was, Eve thought, tramping through a dank wood with her mad husband trying to find his mad sister and her errant brother; her seduced, errant brother, she corrected herself.

They finally neared a hole in a hillock; a suggestion of a cave half hidden by a tangle of wicked-looking thorn bushes. Aubrey stopped, turned, and looked at her. He held out his hand. She hesitated.

What should she say when she ducked into the cave and found the place alight with candles, and her besotted brother believing he was in some sort of enchanted land? Did Arianna know herb lore? Had she bemused him, and then drugged him? Because so much as Eve loved Aubrey, when she'd first met him she wouldn't have followed him into a cave and pretended to believe it was some sort of unearthly paradise. At least, so she thought now that her enchantment with him was wearing thin, leaving only sympathy and pity, and the ever-present lure of his charm and personality, and warm, delicious body.

But because he was her husband, and because she had to find her brother, Eve took Aubrey's hand, picked up the hem of her cloak and skirt, ducked her head, and followed him into the dark cave. It was more spacious than it had seemed from the outside. They walked a long while, bent double down a long, low and narrow corridor toward the back of it. Eve's eyes grew accustomed to the dark, but she still didn't like it. She felt the weight of the world pressing down on her, and the air, while still flowing, was cool, and smelled of mushrooms and roots. Eve wasn't frightened now so much as appalled, for Aubrey's sake.

She was dismayed at the sight of a grown man going to such lengths to follow his mad pursuit of the inexplicable. Who had started him down this strange path? she wondered. Why did he and his sister persist in their fiction? And how could Sherry have fallen into such a trap? She herself had married Aubrey, but it had all seemed above reproach, and, she thought with a smile that was more of a grimace, at least above ground, as well.

The tunnel turned downward and the further down they went, the feeling of the place changed, the air becoming thicker and darker. It was like a grave and a womb. The quiet was so pervasive it was a deadened sort of sound; Eve's ears felt stuffed with felt. It was like being in the very belly of the earth, with the walls seeming to close in closer around them as they walked onward. And then Eve saw light ahead and quickened her pace. Since she now had to walk behind Aubrey, linked by his hand like a rope in a dark sea, he blocked her vision of the path ahead. When he suddenly stood upright, she discovered she could too.

The tunnel had widened and ended; she could feel a warm breeze and smell fresh fragrant flower-scented air. She came to Aubrey's side and looked out.

It was like being born into a new world.

The sky was shatteringly bright after the darkness they'd been in, but the luminosity of it was more than that. It glowed, the very air here scintillated. It was balmy. It was spring here, or summer, or glorious autumn, because it seemed to be all three at once.

There was a long rise of a meadow straight ahead; the grass thick and verdant, shorn as neatly as any flock of sheep could have made it, only there wasn't a sheep in sight. Eve looked around.

There were bushes of flowers, flowers embedded in the greensward, trees were heavy with blossoms, and flowers grew everywhere by the many fountains and streams, and beside blue pools of sparkling waters.

Peonies, lilacs, daisies, irises, sunflowers and roses, apple blossoms, chrysanthemums, meadowsweet and speedwell, all in full bloom, and all out of season, only not, because it seemed to be every season here. Full-blown fat purple grapes peeked out from where they twined among bright blue clematis, bittersweet berries glowed in the climbing laburnum, and ripe red berries grew beside trailing honeysuckle trumpets. Some trees bore only ripe fruit: peaches and cherries, apples and pears. Some bore fruit of silvery hues, cherries and chestnuts that chimed and rang like bells in the breeze. Golden plums and peaches glittered on other trees, all on the same branches.

Not only the eyes and ears were pleasured. The scents were wondrous—as were the people Eve suddenly began to see as they came dancing to greet her and Aubrey.

Just as the seasons were all one here, except for winter, the men and women Eve saw were all magnificently handsome, and none were old. They all had flawless faces, perfect graceful forms, and flowing, shining hair: silver as cobwebs and moonlight, black as a moonless night, yellow as daffodils, and gold as the heart of the sun itself. Their faces were bright and beautiful too. They were so light-footed they seemed to walk above the grass, and their laughter was sheer music. Eve watched, fascinated. Her heart felt lighter, even though the sight of all the beautiful people made her feel lesser, as a person. If this were all a charade, a masquerade, a deception, then she had never seen a finer one.

Aubrey watched her and not the scenery. He searched her expression as she took in every detail before her. She was smiling. But then, her smile faded. It didn't feel right to her. It only took a few minutes for Eve to feel uncomfortable. She realized it wasn't real, not in the way she knew life to be. And that unsettled her for many reasons, but mainly because she found, deep in her heart, that she wished it were real, after all.

Still now, the longer she watched, she more she noticed things that hadn't registered with her before. She couldn't help feeling something was askew. It wasn't just the precious fruits. She was a country girl and she knew that pear and apple blossoms shouldn't be falling, dappling the grass with showers of pink and white with every breeze, and then being replaced with more blossoms, rather than the little hard green knobs that would become fruit.

Larkspurs tinkled in the wind, and lilies chimed like church bells. It was a charming effect, but it couldn't be true. Peonies were her favorite flower, and here she saw some that were pink and white and rose red, and big as cabbages. But there were so many, and they were all so flawless that they lost their magnificence. Because there ought to have been buds as well as wrinkled petals, to show how they grew and changed, and then withered and died.

She didn't desire any silver pears, and her mouth didn't water for golden apples. And the chiming flowers were, after the first minutes, a bit too shrill, jarring to Eve's ears.

Her main objection to this glorious land was that it was all perfectly beautiful. Real perfection was rare, elusive, and always transitory. That made it more beautiful. This display was permanent, and so, to Eve, however beautiful, entirely artificial.

Even the beautiful people began to look too much alike for her tastes. They appeared less handsome because after the first moments of shock at seeing them, there was a certain sameness to them. There were no irregular features to be seen, no defects, no crooked teeth or bent noses, freckles or moles or lopsided smiles that gave a man or woman character, and appeal.

She looked at Aubrey. He was the most handsome of them all, perhaps because his chin was a jot too long and his face too triangular for perfection. He looked more human. That was what bothered Eve about all the others. Whomever they were, they were of different kind. They were interesting to see, but they didn't call to her, as he did.

But they certainly spoke to her.

"Welcome!" they cried in their musical voices. "Greetings, and joy to you, Eve!"

She ducked a nod of a bow. She tried to smile.

The happy throng of greeters stopped and looked at each other.

"This one, your wife," one of the men said to Aubrey, "she is different."

"She is other born," another said. "Mortal, but though she carries our seed, she carries other legacies as well."

"And other sensibilities," a golden-haired man muttered.

"Yes. Mortal," said a keenly green-eyed woman, wafting so close that Eve stepped back. "Of course. But I perceive there is more. She is not enchanted with us."

"She has lived with me for a time," Aubrey said.

"There are things she has become used to."

The others smiled again.

"But, no!" came a familiar voice. "Of course there is more. Fie, brother. Did you not prepare her for her visit?"

"I do not, have not, and will not try to mislead her," he said curtly. "She is my wife."

Arianna shook her head. She wore a sheer gown today. It slid over her perfect body like shadows, revealing even as it concealed. "What of it?" she asked Aubrey. "You ought to have done something to make her happier. She looks at us clear eyed"

"She sees what she sees," Aubrey said through tightened lips. "I don't coerce her. I vowed to never do that again."

"Indeed?" Arianna said. "And that's better? Her brother doesn't see so clearly, and he's very happy. Your wife seems perturbed."

"Sheridan?" Eve asked, grasping on word of her brother. "Sherry? Where is he? I've come looking for him."

"He is here, happy, with me," Arianna said. "Unlike you. Tell us, what *do* you see, little sister?" Arianna held her head up. Her corn silk hair floated out behind her like a trailing nimbus of streaming clouds. Her eyes were bright. Her gown was green, and she was barefoot.

"I see," Eve said slowly and deliberately, looking her up and down, "that your feet are dirty."

There was a gasp from the crowd around Arianna. And a stifled laugh from Aubrey.

But it was true. As Arianna drew up one perfect little foot, Eve saw that it was indeed grass-stained and her toes smudged with dirt. And that, though Arianna glowed, the glow wasn't as dazzling as the sunlight and became even less so as Eve concentrated on looking at her.

That was the trick of it, Eve realized. Aubrey's people didn't stand close, cold inspection. At least, not her close inspection. The harder she looked, the less breathtakingly beautiful they appeared, except for Aubrey himself. She found him more beautiful every day.

Eve turned to look at him in dismay. Had he enchanted her in some new, unknowable way? Arianna hadn't thought so. Unless, of course, Eve thought, this was all a plot, a sham of some sort, rehearsed and calculated. These were, if they were what they claimed, people who loved mischief. But they couldn't be what they claimed, or she'd see no imperfection in them.

"What is it, Eve?" Aubrey asked her, seeing her changing expressions.

"I want to go home now," Eve told him, looking into his eyes, trying to will him to see her sincerity and need. "And I want to take Sherry with me. This isn't real. Even if it is, then it can't be real for him, just as it isn't for me. Your land, your world, your whatever it is, is very fine. But it's not my world and can never be. Return Sherry to me."

Arianna smiled. "At least our world affects you in some fashion, little sister. You become a poet here. Still, I agree. There is something in you that resists us. But I do not think it is in Sheridan. He shall stay here with me, as he wishes to. He does. You'll see. Sherry!" she called, and clapped her hands. "Love! Come to me."

Eve startled as she saw her brother come walking down the long grassy slope. He was strolling, loose limbed, smiling at butterflies and grinning at the sky.

"He's foxed!" Eve cried. "Three sheets to the wind, and halfway amidships. He's drunk!"

"No, little sister," Arianna said with a smile as she walked to meet Sheridan and loop her arm in his. "He isn't. Tell her, Sherry, love."

"Eve!" Sherry exclaimed, focusing on his sister. "Isn't this the best place? The people are up to all the rigs. Such amusing companions! And the drink is fine, you can drink all night and you never get an aching head. And you should eat the food. Prinny's chef would *kill* for the recipes. There's such dancing and singing, you should

hear it. And though I'm not much of a singer, I
never go off key. There are games and sports and
such entertainments as I've never seen.

"I can't remember being happier. Of course,"
Sheridan added with a fond glance down at Arianna, putting his hand over hers where it lay on
his arm, "I've never been in such good company
before either. This is a wonderful place, Eve. Are
you staying here too? You and Aubrey, that is?
He's very well thought of hereabouts, you know."

He sounded sober. He was just happier than
Eve had ever seen him, even happier than when
he got his first pony, and more relaxed than when
he'd finally found out he'd been accepted into his
father's university. He might have groused about
the work there, but he seemed to have loved the
place. Yet now, he seemed almost childishly joyous. Sherry was young, and he was an easygoing
fellow, but he wasn't stupid. Now he didn't seem
like her brother anymore. He was simply too satisfied.

"Sherry," Eve said with care. "You do know that
none of this is real, don't you?"

"Real enough for me," he answered. "It's not
uncomfortable, if that's what you mean. Just look
around. It's wonderful. Even better than London.
There's no garbage. No horse dung, though there
are horses in plenty if you want to ride. Beautiful,

high-blooded creatures, sensitive to your every wish, and they don't even have to be shod! And the people! They know more than my professors did. And there are no poor people here, no one's starving, there's no war anywhere. Look around you! The flowers ring like bells, the fruit tastes like honey, the honey is—well, I'm no poet; I can't begin to describe it. And though these people aren't exactly people as we know them, or knew them, that is to say, Damme if they're not better, Evie. Because they are!"

Eve shook her head. "I don't see them like that, Sherry. I did at first. But not for long. They're different to me now, and none of it seems real. Aren't you ever coming home?"

"My home's with Arianna now," he said, and looked, for a moment, sad. Then he brightened. "But if you're not going to stay, you will keep coming to visit, won't you? And bring Father when you can. Because I don't think I ever want to go back. Not even for an hour."

"Don't worry," Arianna told Eve, as she patted Sherry's arm, smiling like a sated cat. "He can stay here for as long as he wants. Alas! He'll live no longer than he would if he stayed with you. I've already explained that to him."

"A pity," Sherry said lightly. "But I'm human."

"But he'll be happier," Arianna said. "And since

I can't live with him in your world without aging, and he loves me so very much as I am, that seems only fair for both of us, doesn't it?"

Eve stood still. "Does he know what you want of him?" she asked.

Aubrey turned his head and looked at Eve, frowning slightly.

"Yes, he knows," Arianna purred. "What do I want of you, Sherry, love? Day and night and always?"

Sheridan's fair face colored. "She's m'sister, Arrie," he whispered. "She ain't like your folk. I can't say."

"I can," Arianna said, staring at Eve. "I want his love, often. And he doesn't mind. In the end, I want his child, and that he certainly doesn't begrudge me."

"And if that child isn't like you?" Eve demanded. "But only like Sherry and me?"

"Why then, I want another," Arianna said.

"And the first one?" Eve persisted. "What of it then?"

"It can stay or go, as it wishes," Arianna said with a shrug. "It will probably love it here, unless it is like you. Really, Aubrey," she said to her brother, "I begin to wonder at your choice. She may be capable of what we want. That would indeed be a wonder and a thing to celebrate. It's why

I sought out her brother. Because hope is such a rare thing for us. But since your Eve doesn't care for us, will her offspring, do you think, brother?"

"Who can tell?" Aubrey said, stepping closer to Eve. "It is enough that I love my wife. You don't have to, although it would be more pleasant for Sheridan, and for me, if you did."

"Ah, very well," Arianna said with a shrug. "Good luck to you, brother. I could show you more, little sister," she told Eve, "but you'd like me less. You are welcome back to visit , or to stay, anytime you wish. I mean that, literally." She laughed, took Sherry's arm, and began to dance away with him.

Sherry looked back for a moment, to his sister, his eyes wide and confused. Then he whirled away with Arianna and her court of admirers.

"I want to go home," Eve said stonily, as she watched them dance out of sight. "You promised I could go if I asked. If you want to stay, I'll understand."

"I go with you," Aubrey said. "There's no happiness here for me without you."

They went back down the long tunnel in silence, and eventually emerged into the familiar wood and oncoming twilight. Eve wrapped her cloak around herself. Here it was cold; a breath away from winter.

"What was that?" she finally asked him as they walked home.

"The land I come from," he said.

"How much was real and how much illusion?"

"You had no trouble seeing that," he said, chuckling. "And doubtless, the longer you stayed the more you'd see. Even so, it's odd that you wanted to leave so quickly. Most people want to stay. I imagine you were overwhelmed. Don't worry. It gets easier."

"Does it? I wonder," she mused. "And so, if you had a child with me, you'd want him brought up there?"

"If he was like me, he'd want it," he said briefly. "It would be his wish as well as his heritage."

"Aubrey," she asked pensively. "Just what is it that your people do?"

He laughed. "What do your people do? We live, we enjoy life, we try to make it more beautiful."

"My people do all that," she said. "But we also create things, invent new things, try to better our world."

"Oh, yes," he said. "You create wars, invent weapons, and try to own the world and remake it to suit your whims."

There was nothing she could say to that. Eve walked on silently at his side. None of what she'd seen made sense to her now. She wondered if it had all been done by some kind of illusion, like a stage setting for a clutch of mad people, a coven of some sort.

In the last century there had been some famous titled gentlemen who had pretended to be monks at Black Masses that they held in the caves on the estate of one of their founders: Sir Francis Dashwood. They'd called themselves the "Hellfire Club" and had secret rites. They hired prostitutes to serve them in the caves, and pretended they were despoiling virgins. Wealthy, educated people playing at foolish, wicked games. Why couldn't there be well-bred people pretending pleasant things? Just as mad perhaps, but more benign?

Or had Aubrey somehow drugged or influenced her? Had those floral scents been opiates? But Eve had never heard of people under the influence of any drug all having the same dream. She'd heard of Franz Mesmer and his experiments in animal magnetism, and how he could control the minds of men too. She couldn't believe that of Aubrey.

He looked down at her and put an arm around her. "You're so pale, my love," he whispered. "So troubled. Don't be. You know I'd never hurt you. And Sherry won't be hurt. But you had to see."

She nodded. She wasn't a scientist or an expert on legends and myths. For all she knew such creatures as she'd seen did exist and their world was real. That would mean that her husband wasn't human. She didn't want to believe that of him. But she did think he believed it.

She hugged closer to the blessed solid real warmth of him as they went homeward, glad of the quiet. She had to think, now, while her experiences were fresh, while she still had the courage to see the truth.

One thing was absolute. Whatever she had seen, whatever Aubrey believed it to be, real or not, wasn't for her, and certainly not for her child. That became clearer with every step she took. Aubrey either labored under a delusion, or he might be something other than humankind. But if he was deluded, then so had she been. And she wasn't now.

That left only the impossibility of his being alien to her and her world. Which also meant he'd been drawn to her only because he'd believed she could provide him with the child that he and his people, whatever they were, yearned for.

Her brother had been seduced or stolen for that very reason too. So she was loved. But for the wrong reason. Her heart ached. Aubrey had never lied. She'd lied to herself because she'd been so astonished by him, his beauty, his mind, and his attentions. She'd always known he was too much for her, but she'd been glad to be carried away by his protests of love.

Eve had always been clear-headed. She'd lost that facility once, when she'd married Aubrey. She couldn't afford to again. Not now, not for a minute, not for any reason. Love required sacrifice. She knew then that she would have to sacrifice her true love for a new love. And so she'd have to leave Aubrey.

Chapter 20

"**I**'ll never run away from you again," Eve assured Aubrey the next morning. "But I must go to London to see my father. A letter would be a cold way to let him know about what happened to my brother. And in truth, I don't think I could write a convincing letter about something I myself don't understand."

"That's a great deal of to and fro-ing," Aubrey said quietly, looking up from his breakfast plate. "Are you sure you are up to it?"

"I wouldn't go were I not. This is a thing I must do."

"You would tell him what you saw?" Aubrey asked,

"I must," she declared. "Unless it is forbidden?"

"It's not. But I doubt he'll understand. He'll just think my sister is a fascinating older woman who has Sherry in her thrall," he said, setting to his breakfast again.

"Isn't she? Doesn't she?"

"And what will he think of me?"

She sighed. "I don't know. I'm not sure *I* know what to think. There's a great deal I didn't understand." She refused to say she hadn't believed him, because then she'd have to say she'd thought he was mad. She still didn't know and didn't want to just yet. "And how can you eat eggs and toast?" she whispered in exasperation, to divert her mind. "Aren't your people supposed to dine on nectar and whatnot?"

He laughed. "A little late in the day to ask that, isn't it? As for the nectar? At home, maybe. Or so we say. But certainly not in this world. We'd starve. Why are you so angry this morning? For the same reason you tossed and turned all night?"

"Yes," she admitted.

He lowered his voice, although no footman was in view. "For the same reason you told me you were too weary to make love?"

She nodded. She lifted her head and said, "I lied. I was too troubled. I couldn't sleep for thinking about my poor father. And my brother. I have to go to London, and today."

He looked up. "And me? If I want to come along with you? I know it's my husbandly right, but I want to know that you're in accord."

"Of course," she said. "I told you, I'm not running away." *Yet*, she thought.

He looked at her keenly, and then nodded. "I'll have the arrangements made. We'll leave before noon."

"There are a great many things I never bothered to ask you," Eve said as their carriage rolled toward London. She'd been mostly quiet, thinking, on the first leg of their journey. Aubrey had left her in peace. Now as they neared their destination, she spoke at last about more than the weather and traveling conditions with him. She'd nerved herself, and now had questions she felt she must ask.

Aubrey sat beside her, his long legs stretched out. "Ask away," he said, crossing his hands on his flat abdomen, as though it was commonplace for his wife to ask him things she should have before she ever became his bride.

"Can you fly?"

He sat bolt upright. "What?"

"Can you fly?" she asked doggedly. "It's something magical folk are supposed to be able to do."

"We're not ducks," he said, sitting back again with a suppressed smile on his lips. "We don't have wings. Where could we hide them? You've certainly seen every inch of me. We can move quickly and deceive the eye if we want to, but I'm afraid we can't fly."

"What else can you do? Does holy water scar you? How does iron hurt you? Tell me, please."

He sat up again, and turned to her. He took her hands in his. "Because you believe me now? Or because you want to know the depths of my madness? It doesn't matter. Once and for all, Eve, there are things I can do to deceive the mortal mind. Many things. Once upon a time we were arrogant because of that, we toyed with humankind and thought we ruled the world. But now our kind is dying out and we're not so proud anymore. I don't know why we fail to thrive now, not any more than I know why humankind prospers.

"I can withstand holy water," he went on. "I suppose the years made me immune to it. I'm not sure it was ever more than fear of its effects that harmed us. Fear can kill any living creature, you know. Iron still bites. It is antipathetical to our kind; it doesn't kill, but when I'm near it my bones feel like they're itching from the inside, and it's so freezing cold that it numbs my fingers. That isn't what accounts for our scarcity, though; I wish I knew what did. Because in many ways we are more suited for life on this earth than you are. We're stronger than your people, we can bend Nature to our will, and we live centuries longer than humankind. As to how we can affect you? The rest is simply bedazzlement, disguise, and mental confusion.

"I have already said I never had to use any spells or enchantments with you. I was lucky. You were attracted to me. I needed no help from any kind of magic. That would have cheapened what we have together. It's no pleasure to make love to an inferior. You've never been that."

"Is my brother? Does Arianna hold my brother in thrall with magic?"

He grew serious. "I think so. But I can't interfere."

"Or won't?" Eve asked.

"Both," he said. "Ah, don't worry. It won't hurt Sherry. Sorry to enlighten you but he's not a blushing virgin. A few months, and then she'll be bored with him and let him go. He'll be himself again. He's not being harmed in any way. All he feels is pleasure and a sense of his own attractiveness and value. When he looks back on his time with her it will seem to him like it was a pleasant dream of love."

"And if she conceives his child?"

"That's what she hopes."

"Do you think she will? Do you hope she will?"

He closed his eyes for a second. "What shall I

say? We speak of the future of a race. We cannot conceive with each other or with your people. But I have done. There is our hope. Whether she can, I can't say."

"Wouldn't that be cruel, to have his babe and keep it from him?"

"And how should he ever know? Would it be kinder to hand him a miraculous babe he can't hope to understand, and ask him to raise it? If such a thing happens, and Arianna keeps the child, it would be raised on silken cushions, fed sweet cream, educated and protected and entirely adored by all the folk."

Eve remained quiet, thinking. "Whatever happens, will she really let him go? Or keep him forever to find out if he can produce a child with her?"

"She won't keep him long. That, at least I can see to and promise you," he said, taking her hand to his lips.

Eve sat back. "I'm weary from being up all night. It's still a long way to London. If you don't mind, I think I'll close my eyes and try to sleep a little now."

"I don't mind," he said.

But when she closed her eyes, she didn't sleep. And his eyes remained open, studying her intently.

* * *

"This is terrible," Malcolm Faraday said, as he paced his study, his hands locked behind his back, his head down. "Terrible, terrible, terrible." He was muttering, distracted and very unhappy.

He looked up at his daughter. "Not just about Sheridan. Although that's bad enough, Lord knows. But I too think he'll outgrow this fascination with an older female. It happens. It's not the end of the world. But my poor girl! To have a husband who thinks he's magical or some sort of sprite or whatever? And you appear to be on the brink of believing it too? Ah, terrible, terrible.

"Aubrey's so clever and well bred, charming and kind. Who would have thought it? I was so happy for you! You were always beautiful to me, but you never caught . . . that is to say, no one ever caught your eye. And then along comes the masculine catch of the Season—of the decade—and wonder of wonders, he's in love with my little girl. And now this! What are we to do?"

"What am I to do?" Eve murmured. "I love him still."

"Well, I suppose he's harmless," her father said. "But deranged. Oh dear, oh dear. And the physician you saw last time you came to London said you should stay with him even so?"

"He said he doubted he was dangerous," Eve said.

"Well, so do I. He's kindly. But madness isn't a simple thing. It sometimes grows worse as the years go on. Not just madness, but any sort of idiosyncrasy. Your own dear mother was sweet and amiable, but with a terrible stubborn streak that just increased as the time went on. If the poor lady had lived longer, who knows what would have happened?"

"Mother?" Eve asked, recalling how much under her thumb she'd been told her father had been. If her mother had lived longer, she imagined her father would have been utterly squashed. "I remember people saying she was . . . forceful, but surely not mad."

"No, of course not. But she had certain ideas. She was as proud of her heritage as your Aubrey is of his. Mind, she never said she was an . . ." he shuddered, ". . . elf."

"One of the Old People," she corrected him.

"Whatever," he said waving a hand as if to shoo the terrible thought away. "I told you she bragged that her ancestors were here before anyone else came to England too. She couldn't prove it, of course, because no one could write back then, so who is to know? But you ought to have heard her go on about it. She said they were small and dark and quick, and very shy, but the true royalty of England. She spoke as though I were a peasant and she, a queen. Poor lady," he added quickly.

Eve stared. "She sounded like she was describing Brownies, or some such. Father!" she said, a sudden hope springing to her eyes, "did she ever claim she was of . . . fairy stock and mythical origin too."

"Of course not," he said. "She wasn't insane!"

Eve looked away.

"But now, what's to do about you?" he asked more gently.

"I wish I knew," Eve said.

"I think I do," Aubrey said, from the doorway.

They both looked up, like guilty things surprised.

"Eve," Aubrey said, ignoring his father-in-law as he came into the study. He carefully shut the door behind him. "I think I know what's best. But I won't do a thing unless you agree. I think your father would have been better off had he never heard a word of this. But if, in future, you decide I was wrong, you can tell him all over again should you wish."

"Damme, but I'm not a fool," Eve's father said in agitation. "I'm right here before you, if you didn't notice. What are you talking about?"

Eve looked up at her husband. His handsome face was grave, his eyes filled with regret. When he looked like this, it was hard to refuse him. And if he tried to do something to erase her father's memory, it would be a test to see if he possessed any of the powers he believed that he did, she thought. But she never wanted to jeopardize her father to her own doubts, or to her husband's possible violence. Because who knew what he'd do if she agreed that her father shouldn't have this memory? She couldn't see her own expression.

Aubrey could. Eve looked trapped. "I won't hurt him in any fashion," he said gently. "I won't so much as touch him. But I think he'd feel better if I did something to ease his distress. Forgetting all that has been said just now would do it. What good does such knowledge do him, after all? But I won't do a thing if you say not."

Eve hesitated. She looked at her father. He looked stricken. "He thinks he can cast a spell on me?" he asked her in horror.

Now she knew what had to be done. She doubted Aubrey would hurt anyone. Even so, this would be, she thought with sinking heart, the final test. She couldn't let Aubrey try and fail without admitting once and for all that it was all madness. If she saw him make a violent move toward her father, she'd leap at him, protect her father, and shout the house down. Whatever she decided she couldn't postpone the outcome now. She looked at Aubrey, and nodded. "Please," she said. "And quickly."

Aubrey nodded. He looked at Malcolm Faraday and raised a hand toward him negligently, as though he were brushing away cobwebs so as to see him better. Smiling, he opened his lips and murmured some musical, nonsensical syllables.

Eve's father looked at him in dismay.

Aubrey fell still, with a half-smile on his lips. There'd been no flash of light, no clap of thunder. Now there was just silence.

Eve's father still looked at him in dismay. Eve felt ill.

"I say," Malcolm Faraday said, passing a hand over his forehead. "What was I saying? The older I get, the more I forget. Ah well, if it's important, I'll doubtless remember it again soon. So, my children, it's good to see you again so soon. Tell me, have you come to tell me you've heard word of Sheridan? Do you have any idea of where he is?"

He noticed Eve's startled expression as she swung around and stared at her husband. "If he's in danger," Malcolm said quickly, "don't worry, I can deal with it. I may be old, but I'm not infirm."

"No, sir," Aubrey said. "There's no trouble, but there is a situation. We had word from him. It seems he was coming to visit us and met a certain lady in our vicinity who caught his attention. She's a fascinating female, a handsome older woman, and a wealthy one with a taste for younger men. He'd rather you didn't know about such doings, and so he begged us not to tell you more. We tried to dissuade him, urged him to go back to school, but he wouldn't be budged. I think the lady will weary of him soon, and he'll come home a great deal wiser. What would you have us do?"

"Oh, well," Malcolm said, his expression brightening. "Bit of dog, is he? Never would have guessed it. Well, well, well. She's handsome, you say? And rich? While I don't approve such things, certainly not! I don't think he can come to much harm in a few weeks or so, do you?"

"Only as much as he'd come to if he'd gone on the Grand Tour," Aubrey said, "and possibly less. This way, if he does go on a tour of the Continent when the war ends, there are many pitfalls he'll avoid. He'll no longer be an incautious, curious, randy young lad. Begging your pardon, Eve, my love, but that is the general state of schoolboys abroad for the first time, with a tutor or not. And many a young fellow has gotten more than he bargained for from hasty foreign affairs. You know what I mean, sir."

Malcolm rocked back and forth on his heels, trying to hide his smile. "I do, my boy, I certainly have heard of such, at least. I myself married when I was his age, and often wondered . . ." He coughed. "That's water over the bridge or under it, however they say it. You will keep an eye on the lad, though, won't you?"

"I've promised Eve that I would," Aubrey said. "And so I shall."

"Thank you," Malcolm said. "Well, not such a problem then, was it? You shouldn't have been leery of telling me, Eve. We're all grown up here now, aren't we? And thank you for relieving my mind. What a rascal the boy turned out to be, eh?" he chuckled to himself. "Now you two go get some rest, doubtless it was a hard journey. I'll see you at dinner, shall I? And if not, then at breakfast tomorrow. I know how travel can knock one around, which is why I dislike moving once I get somewhere."

"Indeed, it was a long journey, and thank you, sir," Aubrey said, taking Eve's arm.

She looked dazed as she left her father's study and went up the long stair to their guest room. When they got to the room, Eve dismissed her maid. She sank to the bed, and sat and stared, unseeing, into the air in front of her. She felt a large warm hand on the back of her neck.

"You didn't entirely believe me until just now?" Aubrey asked as he settled beside her.

She shook her head.

"And yet, you stayed with me. Or is that why you tried to run away?"

This time she nodded.

"And so now, what do you think?"

She turned to him. Her eyes were damp. She shrugged one shoulder. "You are what you said you were. It will take me a while to accept that. I don't know whether to be frightened or glad. At least you're not mad. But you're not precisely human."

"Does it matter that much to you? Have I ever done you harm? Do I mean you any harm? Do you think I'd ever do you any?"

Her eyes were large and dark as they searched his. "You've never wounded me in any way," she said seriously. "But if all of it is true: that you are centuries old, that you do magic; that you and your people think yourselves superior to us—then why do you love me? Or rather, how? As a man loves a good dog? As a man loves a child? Surely you can't think of me as on the same plane as yourself and your people."

He sighed. "The answer to that is that I don't know. I do love you. Not as a man loves a pet or a child, but rather I love you as a mortal man would, I think. My kind do not love other beings in that fashion, so I can't be sure."

"And when I grow old and finally die, and you

are still young, you will still remember me and mourn for me? Not long, I think. You'll go on and love again, and again."

"You think a mortal man would not?"

She shook her head. "True, true."

"As would you, if you outlived me," he said, placing a light kiss on her ear.

She turned and fixed him with a steady look. "You believe so? It's not a thing we can prove, at any rate." Her voice hardened. "I think, Aubrey, that if you care for me at all, it's because you believe I can end your sterility."

He sat back. "Oof! And how can I disprove that? By loving you even if you don't have a child? Again, that's not a thing we can prove now, is it?"

Her expression was still, her voice still curt. "You know better than that, Aubrey. I believe you've known my secret from the moment it began. Your sister did."

His eyes opened wider. "And so if I love you even more for what you'll give to me, where is the harm in that?"

She closed her lips on words she almost spoke. Instead, she cocked her head to the side and regarded him coolly. "What do you really look like, Aubrey? You're not so perfect as the folk I met in your land. I like that, but I begin to wonder if that's so."

"You rate me on a scale now," he murmured. "You see me without affection in your eyes."

"Do you want to bespell me to ensure it?"

His eyebrows rose. "That," he breathed. "That is what has always singled you out. I can't, or won't, bespell you."

"You enchanted me," she said, "however you did it. Can't you let me see what it is you really are?"

He rose from the bed in one swift movement. "I look much the same here or there," he said. "I think what you mean is how can I appear to be, should I choose to?"

"Yes," she said.

He stood still, and then he smiled down at her where she sat, waiting for him to change to something else. "Is it a snake you anticipate?" he asked. "A bear? A wolf? Here then, see."

The light around Aubrey blurred, and then began to scintillate. And then it glowed. Aubrey stood in the center of the nimbus of light. His jet hair was gone, replaced by brazen gold tresses that streamed behind him. His eyes were silvery gray. His face was exactly the same, as was his form, but he seemed almost godlike in his power and beauty.

"I was fair-haired when I pretended to be my father," he said. "So I had to be dark, when I became his son. Just as I was when I was being my grandfather. Mortals note the family resemblance; color always confuses them. A good hound wouldn't be fooled. But such a little thing makes me a new man every time in mortal minds. I'm grateful for it. And that's all. This is who and what I am, Eve."

She stared at him, and it seemed to her that the longer she looked, the less he glowed. Until, at last, she was looking only at her husband, but it seemed that he wore a golden wig. "I like dark men better," she said.

"That's not what you told me when we met," he said, smiling. He sat on the bed beside her. He was the man she had known again. He looked at her curiously. "I can't confuse you for long. I only hope I can still enchant you."

He waited a moment, and then he took her in his arms and kissed her. For a moment, she lay lax, in his arms. And then her mouth quivered against his, and her arms went around his neck, and she pressed herself close to him.

"This gown," he said, after a moment, "is certainly in the way."

"Not so much as your neckcloth and your shirt," she whispered.

They were out of their clothes in moments, and a moment after, they sank to the bed together.

"This," Aubrey said, his mouth against her breast, "is what we have, Eve. Mortal or not, of the Folk or the humans, there is no spell or magic that can do better."

She didn't speak. She only gave herself up to him. She held him close and when she lay back to let him love her, she stroked his back all the while. She ran her hands through his raven hair and over his hard body as though she were trying to memorize it to keep in her heart forever. When they joined at last, she clung to him, and when they reached ecstasy together, she wept. Because it was so powerful and beautiful, and because she knew she'd have to let him go, as soon as she could, and forever.

Instead of lying down with her as he usually did as their bodies cooled, he sat up and took her in his arms. He rocked her back and forth and stroked her back. They sat in the dark a long while in silence.

"You're going to leave me, aren't you?" he eventually asked.

"It will be easier from here. Are you going to let me?" she asked as answer.

"Why are you going?"

"I have to think a while, without you near. I have a life to think about, and not just my own."

"Ah," he said. "But you know I can always find you."

He felt her head nodding agreement.

"And you know I will always love you."

"No," she said softly. "Because you won't. I have to become used to that. I have to accept reality, many realities, even if they aren't realities I ever knew."

"I see," he said. "Then go. But know that you will come back to me."

"You promise you won't make me?" she asked.

"That you ask is an insult," he said. "You will be back."

They sat quietly together, until, exhausted, they lay down at last. They turned on their sides and slept, but not facing together, and not together in any way, not this night.

Chapter 21

They left her father's house together.

"No sense in upsetting him," Eve had said.

And they parted when they got around the corner.

They stood a moment, together. They made a pretty picture, and passerby smiled to see them. The tall, lean, dark-haired gentleman, his many-caped greatcoat adding to the impression he gave of height, power, and elegance, standing bent protectively toward a small, charming-looking young woman in a blue pelisse, a jaunty hat settled on her wind-rumpled curls. He held her gloved hand in his. They looked like a sentimental silhouette, the sort that lovers had cut and framed as keepsakes.

All Eve wanted to do was to fling herself into Aubrey's arms, and stay there forever. But she remembered that he was the only one who knew what forever was, or at least, he had a better idea than she did. He was more than a compelling gentleman. He was of another breed entirely, and his impression of superiority was well merited.

"I'll be safe, and I'll be comfortable," Eve told him. "My friend has a manor house in the countryside and is thrilled to know I'm coming to visit for a spell. Her husband is in the navy, and at sea. She's enceinte and can't go anywhere. Expectant ladies' lives are circumscribed. No one knows my condition yet, and won't for months, I hope, so I'm still free. I'm happy to see her again. We'll talk of old times, and I'll have time to think." But she didn't look at him as she said it. She hadn't really looked at him since that night they'd last made love. She'd looked in his vicinity, but never into his eyes.

"Have you enough money?" he asked. "You may always draw on your account if you need more."

"I do, but thank you. I won't need a great deal at first."

"Let us hope there is no more than an 'at first.'"

"You do understand?" she asked.

"I do. I lament it. But I do."

"You'll look out for Sheridan?"

"Of course."

They stood speechless for a moment.

"If you need me, you have just to call me," he said.

"Is that true? Your sister said I had just to wish."

"Both are so. I'll know," he said.

She nodded as she looked at the pavement. "I expect you will. That's what I must get used to, if I chose to. Aubrey," she said, raising her gaze and looking directly at him for the first time in a long time, "How many more years do you have?"

He checked. Then he tilted his head to the side. "If a pillar falls on my head in half an hour, then, half an hour. Barring accident? Another few hundred years, perhaps. I am at my middle years."

"I thought so. How can you say you love me when you have lived so long and known so much love? At least, be honest with me on that."

"At least?" His smile was crooked. "I won't lie to you, Eve. I feel differently toward you than toward any being I've ever known, in all my long years. That is true. Is that love? My kind doesn't love, not as you do, so how should I know? I don't want you to leave me. I don't want to be without you. I will suffer. But surely, love is more than that? Or else your people wouldn't carry on so about it; change your lives, sacrifice yourselves, even give your lives for the sake of love, would you? Your literature is based on love, your art is too, even your worship is. Love is what makes your short spans bearable, I think. But I cannot give you more than my idea of love, and my promise of total faithfulness and service to you for the rest of your life. I wish I could, but I cannot. I won't promise what I can't supply."

"I know," she said. "But tell me one more thing, please. How often must you return to your people and your land before the deleterious effects of my world begin to claim you?"

"Every year, at least," he said. "And that visit must be for months of your time. Think of it as half a year here, and half there. Like going to Spain for the winter, or to the Alps in the summer. Other mortals do that. You can come with me. I wish you would. But I must have that time there in order to keep my remaining years. And so may your son."

"Even you don't know that yet," she said.

"True," he said. "But I have my dreams."

"As do I," she said. "I know what you want most of all. But consider me. I'd hate to be the mayfly spending my only hours flitting around your long and happy lives. I don't know how long love can withstand such cruel envy. That's only one of the things I must find out." She slipped her hand from his. "Good-bye, Aubrey. You've given me much to think about."

"You've given me much," he said. "I'll wait for you."

He helped her up the stair to the carriage waiting for her. She settled inside, and looked out the window at him. Her smile trembled. "Adieu, Aubrey," she called. "I hope you understand."

He bowed. "I try," he said. "Safe journey, and safe return, my heart."

He stood watching her carriage roll away down the street, and frowned. "My heart"? Where had that come from? He'd never said that before. But so, he thought, as he walked in the opposite direction, so she was. And so she carried with her his heart, and the heart of his race: their future.

Aubrey walked a long time that evening. He paced down London's streets without seeing them. He walked through the parks until their gates closed without realizing where he was, until the wardens asked him to please leave. He didn't return to his father-in-law's house. He'd had his bags taken to his own town house. It was the one he'd used whenever he'd gone to London, through the years. Then he sat in a chair by his hearth until his servants had finished feeding the fire, and left him alone. Aubrey put his head back and closed his eyes.

He'd bought this town house when he'd first come of age. London had been a green place then, surrounded by fresh clean rivers and seas. Since then, he'd known generations of men, and women too, of course. He'd loved the pleasure he'd had with humankind. They amused him and puzzled him, and in time, they enchanted him. Some had great minds, some great skills: he'd always felt pity for them, having so much, having so little time.

His own people didn't think very much of humanity, except as sport. But as the humans kept coming and increasing in numbers, his folk slowly withdrew from the cities to their own lands again. They said it was because they were bored with humankind. Aubrey began in time to think it was because of something else.

The walls around London had been made of stone when he'd first come to it. There had been gates here and there, but a clever fellow could find his way through the city without ever touching iron. Now the city was falling in love with progress and human progress meant iron and steel being everywhere. It didn't kill. But it wasn't pleasant. His people loved pleasure.

And then there was envy. While short-lived,

humble, foolish humanity grew in numbers and wisdom, his people grew fewer every century. The women didn't produce children. Their men didn't either. When he saw that, he began to do more than toy with human women. He made love to many, and married some, and some, he liked very well. But it made no difference. The word that had made him wince when Eve had said it had been true, at least, until he'd met her. He'd been sterile. As were his people, with each other and with humankind. But now there was Eve.

He had no soul, it was said. He'd never missed it. He worshiped no gods. They'd never helped him. But he thought that he'd changed over the years, and he didn't know how. All he knew was that now he hurt. He missed Eve. If he missed her this badly now, how would he feel when she eventually died? He didn't want to think about it. She believed she'd go on, in some form, when she was gone from the earth. He didn't know about that. He'd never bothered to think about it. He did now.

She would bear his son. Whether the boy was of his kind, or hers, or a combination of both, he didn't yet know. But she would have the child, and he would take it from her. They both knew that. So he couldn't blame her for her brief try at freedom. She'd never be free of him. The problem was that now he wondered if he'd ever be free of her. Because he realized he'd be without her for a long, long time, even after she came back to him.

The next day Aubrey walked the city again. The next night he prowled the streets. He went to a play; he visited a gaming hall. He didn't sleep much, but his kind didn't need much sleep. He went to the menagerie at the Tower the next day, and communed with the animals, withstanding the bone-deep ache in the bars of their cages in order to step close and give them some comfort: dreams of green vistas, peace, and freedom. He did all the usual things he did when he was in Town.

But he didn't go near any females. He'd given his word. And it seemed he had really given his heart, as well as his desires. He wanted no woman but Eve. That didn't mean he didn't see them. Or they, him. But most of the time it was simply business as usual for the ladies of the night. They propositioned them, he refused, they moved on. He never bought a woman, never had to, and never would.

One night, as he wandered the streets deep in thought, a young woman approached him. Many had, as the hour grew later. But for some reason this one wasn't easily discouraged.

"Oh, c'mon, Guv, 'ave a treat," she cooed, winking one kohl-smeared eye. He looked more closely at her. She wore the usual uniform of a street-walker's tawdry splendor, but her face was fair, and her hair was the impossibly bright gold of his own people. It wasn't natural, of course, but it caught his eye, and made him remember. And for that memory, and because it was cold out, and she was, after all, young and fair under all her paint, he reached into his pocket.

He handed her coins, and dismissed her. "Go, be good to yourself tonight," he said.

She took the money, eyes wide. He didn't have to see the reflections in them to know what was happening. He heard her two heavy companions coming up behind him. Annoyed, and even so, glad of the distraction, Aubrey wheeled around. He raised a hand. As their hands tightened on their weapons and they raised them, he muttered a few words.

They dropped their cudgels and fell to their knees in terror, and groveled in the dirt at his feet. He stared down at them. "Go now," he said in an ominous tone, "to a church, confess all, and ask forgiveness."

They scrambled backward and then rose to their feet, turned and fled. Well, he thought, there were worse places he could have sent them. The girl stood, rooted to the spot, shaking.

"Mister," she said, "What d'ya want?"

"Nothing you can give me," he said. "Go now."

There was no one he wanted to make love to but Eve. There was no one he wanted to talk to but her. Not even his own people, not even if he could find any here.

There had been a time when his people had lived in the heaths near London, in the fields beyond it, on the grassy strands by the great river, in the very parklands. There were none now. He remembered them as though in a dream: his merry, beautiful folk as they danced in the moonlight and laughed through their days. Gone.

Even the other folk, not of his kind, but not of mankind: the shy and busy little brown nation who lived in holes in the earth; those creatures who had lived in the very river itself: the ugly and the lovely, they were all gone. From the smallest to the giants, even the tiny sparkling winged creatures who played at the foot of unsuspecting human's gardens were no longer there. He didn't regret the absence of those vicious, spiteful things. The only good they'd ever done him was the amusement he felt when Eve had asked if he had wings.

He didn't know where any of those folk had gone to, nor did he seek them. They had left; their day was over. The nights were emptier, except for the humans. And he didn't have anything to say to them right now. London depressed Aubrey more and more. But he stayed. She'd be back soon. He knew it.

He rode through the parks on his best horses. He sat by the banks of the Serpentine and watched the humans at play. Whenever he saw anyone who might know him, he became someone else. He was safe from criminals and well-wishers. He was in the largest city in Europe: invisible, alone, and deep in thought through each night, and all through the days. Waiting.

Eve sat in the sunny parlor and tried to read her book. Her friend was upstairs, napping. The household was quiet. Eve put down her book; she couldn't read. The sun poured through the window and glinted on the words on the page as it did on the snow on the ground outside, and it blinded her. Yet she couldn't bear to close the drapes to dim the room. It had been so gloomy for so long.

Days had turned to weeks; soon it would be months since she'd seen Aubrey. She began to realize that she wouldn't see him again, not until the baby was born in the spring, she supposed, and not even then if it was a mere mortal. Who knew where Aubrey had gone? Not her father, because there was no word of him in his letters. Her father believed they were still together. And she'd no word of Sheridan either.

If it weren't so cold and the roads so icy she might consider going to see her brother, and that way, maybe finding out where Aubrey was as well. Or so she thought until it thawed for a day and she realized she didn't want to travel now, and didn't want to chance seeing Aubrey again. Doubtless, he'd be with another female. Of what breed, she couldn't guess. But a man—a being— who'd lived so long and loved so often wouldn't go without lovemaking for very long.

She'd served her purpose. If she put a hand on the tight swelling in her newly forming belly she could sometimes feel the slightest fluttering now. She would have the babe; that was certain. The thing now was to stop grieving, and start planning. Because the longer she sat alone with this silent new life, the less willing she was to give it up.

It didn't matter what his father was. He'd said he was from another world, a different people. She hadn't believed it, now she did. What difference did it make? She was not a brood mare. She was a person. A human being, and that was not an inconsiderable thing. There was no saying that Aubrey and his sister were better because they were different kinds of beings. This was her world, and it would be her son's world in whole or in part. If it chanced that he wanted to go with his father when he grew older, so be it. But he would not be taken from her at birth. Women had very little choice in the matter of their children's upbringings in any world. But clever ones might.

Where could she go to find a safe harbor? Not his land. Not anywhere she knew in her own. She'd have to be resourceful. She had funds. She'd go to a new place, somewhere by the sea. She fancied living by the water. Perhaps she'd go to the east, to Rye or somewhere in Kent. Or maybe westward, toward Wales, or deep into Cornwall. Perhaps not Cornwall or Wales, she thought quickly, thinking of the magic and legends associated with both places: pixies and brownies, giants and all sorts of magical creatures.

Toward the east, then, Eve thought. She didn't dare cross the ocean, for fear of harming the babe. But if Aubrey broke his word and came to her instead of waiting for her, she would go there. He might have no power there.

In the meanwhile, she'd buy a cottage and call herself a respectable war widow. She'd have her baby in peace. She knew she'd never sleep in peace again, wondering if he'd ever come for her or her baby; wondering if she'd ever feel his long, strong body next to hers in the night, wondering if he'd ever really loved her.

She wasn't sure she could withstand him in either case. But if it were possible, by legal means and the force of her determination, she would. She bent her head over her book, and only raised it when she realized a good guest did not get a fine leather book stained with tears.

"Mrs. Ashford?" the butler said.

She looked up.

"You've a visitor, ma'am. Shall I show him in?"

She closed her eyes. Her father? Her brother? No, she knew who it had to be. Her pulses were already beating a tattoo, as though his very closeness had set her heart working too hard. She nodded, wiped her eyes, and sat up straight.

He wasn't just as handsome as she'd remembered. He looked even better, the shock of seeing him made him even more magnificent to her than she'd recalled. He wore simple, casual clothing but he glowed. His eyes were bright, and he smiled. She had to narrow her eyes as she had against the sunlight he dazzled her so.

"Eve," he said.

"You said you'd wait for me to come to you," she said, not daring to smile back at him. "You may go," she said.

Aubrey was taken aback. But she'd said it to the butler, who bowed and left them. When Aubrey realized whom she'd spoken to, he came into the room and to her side. "I said I'd wait," he said. "But I changed my mind"

She stiffened. "You lied? You went back on your word?"

"Yes," he said simply. "For two reasons. One is that I want you to know that there's a present waiting for you at home."

She waved her hand and looked away. "I don't care for jewels and such. Surely you know that?"

"Not care for your gem of a brother? How remiss of me not to know that."

She sat up. "Sherry? He's back?"

Aubrey smiled. "Yes, for a few weeks now. Ready to go back, remembering only having an affair of the heart with a heartbreaking older woman. It's done him no harm in any way. He left nothing behind him: no guilt, and no progeny."

"How did you get her to give him up?"

"He produced nothing but trouble, from me. We spoke and she agreed it seemed reasonable that your gift runs only through the female line. She has a short span of attention but a long memory, which gives her respect for my persistence."

He stared at Eve. "I did it because I promised to. But I also needed something to gain access to you. I had to see you, had to know how you've been. How are you?" Before she could answer, he went on, "I can see you flourish. But I've been wretched, and I'm not doing well at all. I need you, Eve."

"You need my son," she said after a moment.

He came and sat beside her in the window seat. "True," he said. "But I also need and want you. My son will come, and we'll decide what to do when he does. But I came here for you, never doubt it."

"No," she said, looking away. "We can't decide later. I won't have him raised in another land, and that's that. I don't belong in that place, even if he does. And I won't give him up to strangers."

"Am I a stranger then?"

Now she looked at him. "Oh, yes, Aubrey," she said sadly. "I've thought about it long and hard, and you are. Different blood, different worlds, different views of both worlds. If our child is like you I'll eventually let him go. I'll have to, as all mothers must do, in time. But I want the chance to rear him, to love him, to teach him about my world, my people, and the heritage I give him."

"I've thought long and hard too," he said, taking her hand. It was icy cold in his grasp. He ran his thumb over the back of it as though trying to restore warmth. "I come to think that all your people stem from the same roots. You are a repository of what came before. Nature is stingy. Nothing is thrown away. Those that were here and are gone, live on in your people. Who is to say what it was that your mother bragged about in her ancestry? You are the powerful ones, after all."

He looked at her seriously. "That's not to the point. The point is that the most astonishing thing has happened, Eve. You left, and you took the heart I never knew I had right out of me. And I believe that if I had one, you'd have taken my soul as well. I've lived a long time. I've lived for laughter and pleasure and amusements, and I've had more of those things than most creatures even dream of. But I've gained nothing. And I have nothing now."

"How much does any being have?" she asked. "You have more life than we do. We have this little time on earth, and must make the most of it."

"But at the end of life, if you've lived right, you have love," he said. "And memories of it. You also leave something behind you, apart from the echo of your laughter. You've contributed to your world. You have children, or you raise other people's children; you build for the future, you help preserve other creatures and the earth itself. We don't."

"Not all humans do that," she said.

"None of us do," he said. "We never have done. We can't. We use the world and other creatures. Maybe that's why we are become so diminished. The worlds, yours and mine, require something of us and if we can't contribute, it stops supporting us. I require you, Eve. I would stay here with you, and my son. If he's of my people I'll educate him and let him choose his own path. If he's yours, we'll do the same. And if he's a combination of our blood, he may do great things for both our worlds."

"But you can't stay with me that long," she said with a sad smile. "At least not for more than six months at a time."

"Why not?"

"Because you'll grow old. You'll lose your longevity. You said so. You have centuries left to live."

"Do you dislike me so much? Would you wish that for me?" he asked, gripping her hand tight. She stared at him.

"Do you know what it is like?" he asked her. "I didn't until just recently. It is centuries of nothing. It's an eternity of being with the same people who mean little to me, or finding myself constantly in new places among strangers who mean nothing to me. It is being without love in whichever world I inhabited. We don't love, Eve. My people lust, as you know. They're capable of liking, and they may even admire others, but they never love another creature. Now that I've found what love is I don't want to be without it.

"What is life without it? I can tell you. It's an endless road of mindless pleasure. It's hunger without appetite, and no matter how you fill yourself, never any satiation. Centuries go by in a blink, the world changes, but you never change or change it. That's never enough. You've changed me, though, Eve. I can feel it. I'm not mortal yet. But I may yet be, if only because I discovered my heart, and it is yours. Maybe I'll have a soul as well as a heart one day. I hope I can grow one. That's the strength of your people and the reason why you prosper. You have purpose. I want one too. And I want you."

"I suppose I can come with you for each six months," she said hesitantly.

"No. Haven't you been listening? I don't want that. I want life with you, and that means to live as you do, and die as you do too."

She bowed her head. "I can't take your heritage from you," she said in a whisper.

"No, you can't," he agreed. "I give it to you."

"You'll lose your powers."

"I don't think so. Not until I die, at any rate."

She picked her head up, trying to look deep into those splendid eyes. She knew what lay ahead even if he didn't, and so much as she wanted him, he had to know. "And will you feel that way when you find your first gray hairs?" she asked him.

"When you lose a tooth? When one hurts? When you see firm flesh wrinkling, turning softer, when you feel your strength diminishing and beauty fading?"

His eyes sparkled. "I'm shocked at you, Eve. Are you so superficial, to want to throw me over if I become less than beautiful in your eyes? Would you not want me if I lost a tooth? Which one?"

She laughed, but sobered quickly. "I was talking about your aging as well as mine. Aging isn't one of our virtues, Aubrey. It's just a certainty, if we're lucky to live long enough. It's not enchanting. Neither is death. Give up your life for me? It's too much of a sacrifice."

"There's no sacrifice if it's what is most urgently desired. I'm much wearier of living to no purpose than I am afraid of dying."

Her smile was wistful. "And what if I can't bear to see it happen to you?"

He didn't jest now. "You thought you would when we married," he said seriously.

She sighed. "Yes. True." She gazed at him with absolute sincerity. "But if we grow old and infirm, what if you grow to hate me for it? I couldn't bear that. Nor should you."

He smiled. "Hate you? I doubt it. But who knows? Maybe, at times, if I become human enough, I might dislike you at least once in a while. It sounds amusing. I want that choice. You people love, and argue, and make up, constantly. I've watched. I've seen it. You wrangle over the stupidest things, and fight to stay together after you fight. You're petty and foolish and gloriously alive. I've come to see that to live with the constant promise of approaching death is to come fully alive. Anyway, that's my choice. And I chose it. The only question is, do you? Will you have me as your husband, Eve?"

She touched his cheek. Her expression was grave.

He waited.

"I said yes once," she breathed, "before I knew what it meant with a husband such as you. Now that I've been married to you, I'll say it again. Yes. If you're sure."

He took her in his arms. She felt a great sigh move his chest. "I think I'm sure," he said. "How should I know?" He looked down into her face. "Isn't that astonishing? Isn't that miraculous? For the first time in my life, I don't know!" He looked as though he was going to laugh. But he kissed her instead.

Epilogue

Apple blossoms fell like fragrant snow onto the daisy-dappled grass. Lilacs bloomed, purpling the hedges surrounding the meadow and competing with the great cabbage-sized rhododendron flowers on the hedges that lined the paths. Daffodils shouted back the sunlight, wreaths of bright laburnum hung from every fence, and in the long meadows crimson poppies and anemones burned bright. It was warm, the sky cloudless blue, the breezes mild, and the golden-haired child lay cooing in his bower.

"This is better than being in the house today," Aubrey said, laying on the grass, his head in his wife's lap. "Come, Eve, why so silent. Don't you agree?"

"It's better than anything," she said, as she stroked his hair. She sat up, her back against a tree. She looked to the infant in his basket. "Do you think he's hungry?"

"Oh, we'd know it if he was," he said with a smile. "Believe it. But I meant that it's better because this is all transitory. In a month, it will all have changed. And," he added, slapping at a gnat that had been darting around his face, "it's especially fine because it's not perfect and, so, never boring. I can't remember being more content."

"Nor I," Eve said. "Aubrey? He's so good. He eats and plays, and smiles all day. What do you think? Does he have more of me, or of you, or of those others my mother spoke of, as well as any unknown others—who knows how many others, in my ancestry?"

"I think," he said, "that he's ours. And he's his own. And, in the end, it's better that we don't know any more than he does, and don't guess at what he will eventually show us. We have just to love him now, as we do each other."

"*That* much?" she asked.

They sat contented and silent then, listening to the birdsong, and the burst of sudden delighted laughter from their baby.

Next month, don't miss these exciting new love stories only from Avon Books

The Scottish Companion by Karen Ranney

An Avon Romantic Treasure

Gillian Cameron, companion to a spoiled bluestocking, has a plan to convince her charge to marry and produce an heir. What she couldn't plan for was her own attraction to the handsome Earl of Straithern. But when someone threatens the Earl, he and Gillian must learn to trust before it's too late.

Witch in the House by Jenna McKnight

An Avon Contemporary Romance

Jade Delarue refuses to be with a man because of a spell, but Mason Kincaid is difficult to ignore. Mason knows better than to fall for the stunning woman he's investigating, no matter how intrigued he is. But with magic involved, all the rules go out the window.

Seduction Is Forever by Jenna Petersen

An Avon Romance

Emily Redgrave hasn't been the same since the night she was shot. Determined to regain her confidence, she accepts a job tracking Grant Ashbury, not realizing he's also on assignment…to follow her! As they uncover a secret plot and a growing desire, the stakes will be raised to shocking—and scandalous—heights.

Sin and Scandal in England by Melody Thomas

An Avon Romance

Bethany Munro lives for excitement, and her new friends seem to deliver just that. But when a visit to the country reunites her with an old love—and uncovers a mysterious plot—Bethany may have found more excitement than she can handle.